NEGLECTED TRUTH

A DR. SAMANTHA JENKINS MYSTERY

STEPHANIE KREML

HIPE BOOKS PUBLISHING

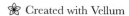

1

Dr. Samantha Jenkins rounded the corner and halted when she saw trouble brewing. On the opposite side of the clinic work area from her, at the entrance of a short hallway leading to the lobby, a man lurked. With a bear-like stature and a ruddy complexion, he stood under orange streamers and black spiders hanging from the ceiling, like moss over the entrance to a cave. He shifted his weight back and forth on his thick legs, as if ready to pounce.

A medical assistant named Cynthia passed by, and the man waved a stack of papers at her to grab her attention. Gray, fuzzy mouse ears—a minor concession for Halloween by the clinic management—bobbed on her head as she looked up and down between the documents and his fierce face. Then, in an instant, she seemed to take control of the situation, her feet in an authoritative stance despite her petite frame, and she spoke to him as she calmly pointed to the papers, occasionally glancing up as he towered over her to make sure he understood.

Sam crossed the space to her workstation, located on

the other side of a partition wall from them. She was ready to step in to help, even though it looked like Cynthia could handle it. Sam had a couple of things she needed to finish up before she could leave for the day, but as she approached the desk she shared with Jerry, the Physician Assistant who worked with her, he rolled his chair away from his computer, ready for conversation.

"So tonight's the big night?" he asked. He grinned, unaware of the drama just out of his view.

Sam made a slight smile as she nodded, her focus now split between Jerry and Cynthia's conversation on the other side of the wall. The man's low voice carried around the corner, laced with menacing overtones as he occasionally growled out a quick syllable.

It was just like Jerry Reid to be excited for Sam. He could have been her uncle, with his silvery gray hair and neatly trimmed goatee. However, despite having practiced medicine for almost as long as Sam had been alive, and despite having worked at the clinic for five years before she had come along, she was his supervising physician. She often relied on his decades of experience as a PA, garnering his advice on the best approaches for managing and treating the patients they saw, which were mostly workers' compensation cases with a couple of urgent care visits dotting the schedule each day.

He was right—tonight was a big night, but not *the* big night. While she had casually mentioned she would be introducing her current boyfriend to her father, Jerry didn't know Sam had been engaged previously. No need to go into that level of detail with a coworker.

"Yeah, Alex should be here to pick me up any minute," Sam said, but her awareness was still partially on the confrontation around the corner.

Jerry continued grinning. "I'm sure your dad will go

easy on him. Any father would be overjoyed to have their daughter dating a doctor."

"I hope so," Sam said. Never mind that she was also a doctor, she thought, but she let it pass.

Cynthia appeared from around the corner. "Dr. Jenkins," she said, motioning to the hallway, "there's a man who needs to speak with you."

"Who is it?"

"He's Miss Morales's supervisor."

Sam had seen Miss Morales for a newly sprained ankle less than an hour before. The case was pretty straightforward, so she couldn't imagine what he wanted to speak with her about. Perhaps he had a question about Miss Morales's restrictions.

As Sam approached, the man glared at her, and then she noticed Miss Morales cowering behind him, supported by her crutches, her left foot bound with the Ace wrap Sam had applied. She peered at Sam, then down at the floor, like a child who knew she was in trouble.

"What is this?" the man barked, thrusting the papers at Sam.

"I'm sorry?" She squinted at the documents. "I believe those are Miss Morales's discharge instructions."

He pointed to the top sheet. "Why the hell are you giving her a prescription for something she can get over the counter?"

"Miss Morales is in quite a bit of pain, so I gave her prescription-strength naproxen."

"That's the same stuff in Aleve. She can get that at the drugstore." He shook his head as he flipped through the pages. "And then you ordered physical therapy. And these restrictions." He slapped the sheaf against his leg. "She doesn't need any of this. It's just an ankle sprain. Happens all the time."

"Sir, not all sprained ankles are the same," Sam said as she held her arms out, palms up. "Given the amount of swelling and bruising over her foot, I'm concerned that she may have torn some of the fibers in one of her ligaments."

Sam had an X-ray performed on the ankle, and fortunately, it hadn't shown an avulsion fracture of the distal fibula, which Sam had been worried about based on how exquisitely tender Miss Morales's ankle had been. An X-ray didn't rule out ligament tears, though, and Miss Morales was in too much pain, with too much swelling, for Sam to do a thorough check for stability. She would perform a better exam when Miss Morales came back for her follow-up appointment. Plus, Bob, the physical therapist, would also assess for joint stability during his initial evaluation.

Sam continued her explanation. "Physical therapy will help Miss Morales recover faster, and the restrictions are—"

"I will make sure she's moved to a position where she can sit all day." The man lifted the papers, forcefully tapping his index finger on them. "There's no need for this."

"Sir, these restrictions are to ensure everyone's safety—for Miss Morales and for her coworkers."

"I make sure my workers are safe. I'll take care of her. No need for you to butt in."

Miss Morales inched backward with her crutches, the metal clanking as she moved. Heat rose in Sam's neck as the man's aggressiveness riled her desire to do everything she could to protect Miss Morales.

Narrowing her eyes, she said, "I'm sorry, sir, but I cannot do that. I need to ensure Miss Morales has time to heal and stays safe while she continues working with accommodations."

The man raised his voice, his nostrils flaring. "I told you, I'll take care of it."

"Are you telling me what to do?" Sam shoved her hands into her coat pockets. "Seems like you're practicing medicine without a license."

Raw anger flashed in the man's eyes, then he held up the papers in front of him, ripped them in half, and tossed them on the floor.

Sam sucked in a deep breath, furious that he dared treat her and her patient this way. The nerve of him. "What is your name, sir?" She was going to report him to his employer.

He stepped forward, his fists clenched by his sides, as if he was about to strike her. But suddenly, the tension in his face unwound just a touch, and he took a step back. She felt a presence behind her.

It was Jerry, looking as stern as Sam had ever seen him. "Do you need some help, Doctor?"

"This man is interfering with my patient's care," Sam answered.

Jerry put his hand on Sam's elbow. "Can I talk to you for a second?"

Sam stood her ground, keeping her attention on the medical interloper. "No. I need to make sure my patient receives the treatment she needs."

Jerry lowered his voice. "Please, Doctor. Let's just talk for a second."

"Fine," she said. She looked over her shoulder at the supervisor as she followed Jerry around the corner to their work nook.

"What is it?" she whispered fiercely.

"I know that man is being a jerk, but I've dealt with him before. Let me talk to him." He glanced at the clock on the wall above the whiteboard across from the nurses' desk, showing the status of the exam rooms. "You need to go anyway. The ladies in the front said Alex is waiting for you."

Sam tipped her head in the direction of the supervisor and Miss Morales. "Do you know if he'll do the right thing?"

"Like I said, I've dealt with him before—I've had a few patients who work with him, and they've always recovered without an issue. I don't know why he's acting this way. Usually he's quite reasonable." He nodded firmly. "You should go. I can take care of this for you."

She paused. He had been around the block a few more times than she had. Plus, she really didn't need to get worked up before seeing her father. She studied Jerry for a moment, then looked over at the supervisor. Finally, she nodded. "Okay."

Jerry walked over to the man, bent down to collect the torn papers on the floor, then stood up straight with his feet firmly planted. "Let's discuss how we'll handle Miss Morales's case."

The supervisor's jaw unclenched as he grunted in response.

Sam's phone buzzed. It was a message from Alex: *I'm waiting out front.*

"Are you sure you've got this, Jer?"

He turned to her, resolve in his eyes. "Yes, Doc. You should go."

2

S am was still reeling about the confrontation with Miss Morales's supervisor as Alex drove to the restaurant. *How dare that man challenge me?* At least he seemed somewhat intimidated by Jerry, but she was a little annoyed that it took Jerry's stepping in to diffuse the situation. She could have handled that guy on her own.

First thing tomorrow morning, she would look up Miss Morales's company and call the HR contact to let them know about the supervisor's conduct. Never mind that he refused to give his name to her. She would find out who he was, and he would not get away with his behavior.

Alex glanced over at her. "You're awfully quiet. How was your day?"

She sighed. "It was fine until right before I left." She wanted to vent, but that wouldn't be appropriate right now. "Let's not talk about it. Did you have anything exciting in your day?"

"No. Our census is pretty low, thank goodness. It's been pretty quiet now that the schools are back in session. But since it is Halloween, I'm sure we'll have a few revelers that end up in our ICU tonight. I'm just glad I get tonight off."

"I forgot how crazy the ERs get on Halloween." And as if on cue, as Alex turned down a street near the restaurant, Sam saw children in their costumes—superheroes and wizards—out to fill their pumpkin-shaped baskets with sweets and treats.

Her father had picked a swanky Japanese-fusion restaurant, only slightly more casual than its sister restaurant, which had made the chef-owner famous. Sam loved the food, but she'd always felt out of place eating there, with the other clientele wearing their trendiest garb. She figured her father had chosen the place because it was so close to the hospital where he performed many of his catheterization procedures, and his office was just a few blocks away.

After they dropped off the car with the valet, they walked into the restaurant and stood in line to speak with the hostess. They were behind a pair of young ladies making fish lips, posing for a selfie.

Sam rolled her eyes as she turned to Alex. "Are you ready?"

He put on a winning smile. "Ready as I'll ever be."

She thought he seemed rather calm. How many times had he done this before?

Her phone buzzed. "It's my dad—he and his girlfriend already have a table inside."

"Oh, I'm meeting his girlfriend too?"

"Don't worry—she seems pretty nice."

They squeezed past the fish-lip girls, past the crowded bar, and into the dining room, which was already full, even though it was fairly early for a weekday. Sam scanned the room and quickly spotted her father and his girlfriend at a four-top table.

The older couple stood as they approached.

Alex extended his hand. "Hello, Dr. Jenkins. I'm Alex Crawford."

The elder Dr. Jenkins gave Alex a firm handshake. "Please, call me Steven. And this is Millie."

Alex took her hand and kissed the back of it. He sure was putting on an extra layer of charm tonight.

"My, my," Millie said. "Such a gentleman. So nice to meet you." She gave Sam a hug. "How are you, darling?"

"I'm good. And yourself?" She took her seat next to Millie, putting Alex next to her father.

"Oh, the usual," Millie said with a smile. "Your father and his partners are always bossing us nurses around."

Steven looked over with a frown. "I do not. I'm just giving you orders because we have patients to take care of."

"Goodness, darling." Millie put her hand on his arm with a lopsided grin. "I'm just joking. I know efficiency is key during procedures. At least you're learning to relax a little more outside the hospital."

"So, Dr. Jenkins—I mean, Steven—Sam tells me you're a cardiologist. Have you had any interesting cases lately?"

As the men began to exchange war stories about patients with complex conditions, Millie turned to Sam. "How are your classes going? You're working on your MPH, right?"

She was surprised Millie remembered she had started taking courses toward a master's in public health. "Pretty good, actually. Now that the summer rush is over, and the clinic isn't quite so crazy, I have a little breathing room. Since I don't have to spend every evening charting, I now have time to study and do assignments."

"That's great, darling. What are you taking?"

"Biostatistics along with occupational and environmental health."

"Which is perfect since you'll need that for residency, right?"

"Right. Good memory." Sam smiled.

She had to admit, Millie was growing on her. When Millie and her father first started dating, she thought it was too soon after her mother had passed away, but Millie seemed very supportive of her. More supportive than her father ever was.

A series of waitstaff cycled by their table, first taking orders, then delivering drinks and edamame to start. The charred soybean pods had a lovely smoky scent. Sam bit on the end of a pod, popping a bean into her mouth, then took a sip of Riesling, melding all the flavors together.

After they enjoyed their entrees of delicate fresh fish paired with grilled brussels sprouts, glazed with a hot and tangy sauce, the waitstaff cleared the table.

Sam's father cleared his throat as he took Millie's hand. She looked at him adoringly, and he looked like he was as nervous as she'd expected Alex to have been earlier.

"Millie and I have something to tell you, Sam."

Sam looked back and forth between her father and Millie, then at Alex, who just shrugged.

"We hope this isn't too much of a shock for you," Millie said.

Sam opened her eyes wider, suspecting what was to come. All the goodwill Millie had built up over the last few months was on the line now. She had suspected, but now she knew.

"I've…" Her father cleared his throat again. "I've, uh…I've asked Millie to marry me."

Sam closed her eyes briefly, then willed herself to smile before opening them again.

"That's great," Alex said with a smile. "Congratulations!"

"Yes, how wonderful." Sam regulated her breathing, trying to keep it steady. "I'm so happy for you."

AFTER HER FATHER'S ANNOUNCEMENT, Sam stayed quiet. What could she say? Was she happy for her father? Of course. Clearly he had moved on from her mother's death. But Sam really wasn't ready for this. She was pretty ambivalent toward her father anyway, and she didn't think he had treated her mother very well. Until the end.

Once Sam's mom had been diagnosed with ovarian cancer, her father became the perfect gentleman, always there for her, never leaving her side, catering to her every need. Why hadn't he done that before? Why couldn't he have cared more when her mother was still healthy?

As they walked out of the restaurant, Millie asked Sam if she could stop by and drop off some things belonging to her mother. *Wow. The hits just keep coming, don't they?* So not only was her father getting married, but now Millie was clearing out her mother's things?

At that point, Sam felt numb, finding just enough energy to nod.

Millie slowed her pace, seeming to have picked up on it. The men, however, were oblivious, walking ahead, not paying attention to how Sam felt.

"Okay," Millie said cautiously. "I'll text you to find out a good time."

Millie held out her arms for an embrace. Sam took a small step toward her, but kept her arms close to her sides. Millie gave her a brief hug and then stepped back. "Why don't we do something together? Maybe a spa day, so we can get to know each other better?"

Sam stood there, nodding again, dumbly.

Alex and her father finally noticed the women weren't walking with them, and they turned around. Sam took a deep breath. *Snap out of it. Be happy for them.* She willed her lips into a smile.

"It was good seeing both of you," she said.

Alex shook her father's hand. "Very glad to meet you, sir. And congratulations."

"Likewise, Alex. I haven't had this much fun, discussing interesting cases over great food, since I went to that cardiology conference in Aspen."

"That was a nice time," Millie said.

Sam shook her head to get out of her stunned state. She stepped over to her father and gave him a hug. "Congratulations, Dad." To Millie she said, "Always good to see you, Millie. Let's figure out when we can do that spa day."

Millie relaxed in response and smiled.

"It's good to see the women in my life getting along," Steven said.

IN THE CAR on the way back to Sam's apartment—she had Ubered to the clinic that morning knowing Alex would be picking her up—he said, "I don't know what you were worried about. Your father's great. And so is Millie. They seem like a good couple."

Sam stared out the passenger window, watching the buildings pass by, catching glimpses of people in their Halloween costumes enjoying themselves. "Sure."

Alex glanced over at her, touching her hand. "Everything okay?"

Just be happy for them. She took a deep breath, then turned toward him as she squeezed his hand. "I'm fine."

3

Once Alex dropped Sam off at her apartment, she logged on to the virtual classroom for her environmental health class. She had invited him up but was secretly glad he had declined. He said he wanted to get a good night's rest before what he anticipated would be a long day and night on call. Perhaps he sensed she was not in the best mood after her father's announcement. It wasn't that she wanted to do school work, but she needed to focus on something else, to take her mind off the news she just learned.

Since Sam had left residency early, she was now in limbo. She had her medical license after passing all the steps of the USMLE—the United States Medical Licensing Exam—and completing two years of residency. In Texas, as it was with most states, passing the USMLE and completing one year of residency was the minimum requirement of the state medical board to qualify for a license.

But in order to become board certified in a specific area of medicine, and to obtain hospital privileges, she needed to complete residency training. She had chosen general surgery as her specialty and had begun a five-year program after graduating from medical school. It was to the dismay of her father, who thought surgeons were beneath the more intellectual internal medicine specialties. After her mother had passed away, she left the program. She had needed more time to grieve than the surgery department was willing to give her. Without her mom's support, she had lost some of the fire needed to push forward on her difficult career path.

That was the reason Sam was now taking courses in the evenings and on the weekends—to get her master's degree in public health so she could apply to a preventive medicine residency with a concentration in occupational medicine. It was a nontraditional path, recommended by her boss. It would allow her to keep practicing at the clinic where she worked, while still meeting the requirements of the residency program. If everything went well, she could finish in just one year once she was accepted.

When she logged into the virtual classroom, she found she had a new assignment that including reading sections of the Code of Federal Regulations outlining the standards pertaining to OSHA—the Occupational Safety and Health Administration.

Sam took a deep breath. Not now. She had a few days to do the assignment. She would figure out when she would fit it in to her schedule. Suddenly, she felt exhausted after the events of the day and dinner that evening. She went to bed and fell into a deep, dreamless sleep.

~

THE NEXT MORNING, Sam went through her normal routine and got to work ten minutes before the clinic doors officially opened.

The news of her father's engagement still stunned her. Sure, she was happy for him, but she had mixed feelings. And Millie... Well, she was certainly more encouraging of her decisions than her father, but having Millie move into her mother's home... Sam knew logically that her father needed this, but she wasn't ready for it. Maybe she would never be ready.

Ironically, when the night had started, she thought the big deal would be her father's meeting Alex. She needn't have worried though. They got along swimmingly, with the two men talking shop all throughout dinner. At least she didn't have to worry about that. She just didn't know how she felt about Millie becoming her new stepmom.

But Sam needed to concentrate on work. There were always patients to see, although things were a bit slower now that it was fall. Texas had the benefit of mild winters, so construction projects continued, but everything slowed down just a touch as the temperature cooled, perhaps because kids were back in school. She looked at the schedule. Only twenty-three patients on her schedule and nineteen patients on Jerry's. Very manageable.

She shoved thoughts about her father's engagement out of her mind—she didn't have time to deal with them now.

Since ObraCare, the company that owned and managed the clinic, had expanded their services to provide urgent care in addition to workers' comp treatment, the clinic had extended its hours in the evening. While most workers' comp patients needed care during normal business hours, most urgent care patients would want to be seen after work.

Jerry covered the evening, so he came in to the clinic

later in the morning, and Sam was on her own for the first couple of hours. She worked steadily seeing patients, and by the time Jerry came in, the whiteboard had filled up, so he jumped right in to see patients as well.

Sam finally had a chance to catch up with Jerry midafternoon, and by then, there was only one patient in the process of being roomed by Cynthia.

"How did everything go last night?" Jerry said as he stood, waiting for Cynthia to come out of the exam room and mark the board with the patient's information.

Sam paused typing and waved her hand. "It was fine."

"Did Alex and your father get along?"

"They got along just great. Like two peas in a pod." She cleared her throat, wanting to move on. "What happened with Miss Morales? Did you talk some sense into her supervisor?"

"Well, about that…I removed the restrictions you put in place."

"What?" She raised her eyebrows. "Why did you do that?"

"As I mentioned yesterday, I've dealt with that guy before," Jerry said. "He's not normally like that. He was very diligent with a patient I took care of a while back. The poor guy fell into a pit at work and ended up with an open tib-fib fracture. You might remember that case; it was around the time you started here."

"Goodness. It seems vaguely familiar. We took care of that here?" It surprised Sam that a case such as that had ended up in their clinic. They really weren't prepared to handle a limb injury so severe that both bones in the lower leg—the tibia and the fibula—broke, along with a break in the skin. It was something that would require emergent orthopedic care.

"No, not initially. The patient went to the ER and was

hospitalized for a week or so, but we took care of him afterward, for PT and follow-up care, along with the orthopedic surgeon. We had to keep him on antibiotics for a long time. Even so, his course was complicated by a soft tissue infection, but at least he didn't develop osteomyelitis. We followed him for months before we discharged him from care." Jerry shook his head at the memory.

"Oh, I think I remember that case now." She shook her head. "I'm still getting familiar with how this whole workers' comp system works."

"Yes, it's rather complicated," Jerry said with a sympathetic smile. "Anyway, even though that supervisor was a jerk yesterday, he came here quite a few times with that patient. I know he'll make sure Miss Morales recovers. He promised he would bring her back if she needed to be seen again."

"So you cancelled her follow-up appointment with me? And what about PT?" Her skin prickled on her face. "How could you let him treat her like that?"

He held up his hands. "I see you're upset. He said he's under a lot of pressure at work right now, and that their plant is expanding."

"But that's not our concern. Our concern should only be what's best for the patient."

He nodded. "I know. But sometimes——"

"Sometimes what? When is it ever okay to let the employer dictate how we care for a patient?"

"It isn't." He turned and leaned against the raised counter across from the board, resting his elbows on the surface, his head hanging slightly.

As soon as Cynthia came out and started writing the patient's chief complaint—the reason for the visit—Jerry walked over and put a magnet with his initials next to the room number, then proceeded around the corner to the exam room.

Sam turned to her computer. She was going to look up the employer for Miss Morales in the electronic medical record. The name of the supervisor should be listed, and if not, she could always call the point of contact to make a complaint about his behavior. Surely they would want to know about what had transpired the day before.

But before she could find what she needed on the computer, Cynthia pulled up Jerry's chair next to her and sat down.

"Dr. Jenkins, I have something I need to tell you."

"Sure, Cynthia. What is it? Is everything okay?"

"You know Elma Garza, one of your patients?"

Sam closed her eyes for a moment, trying to remember Mrs. Garza. She was much better at recalling faces, but the name was certainly familiar. "Is she the lady who injured her back after pushing a heavy dolly?"

"Yes, that's her."

"She was here last week with her son." Mrs. Garza had her adult son bring her to her appointment, and she had asked Sam to take a look at his eyes because they were red and watery. It had seemed to Sam that Mrs. Garza had used the ploy of needing a ride to the clinic to get her son checked out since he wouldn't go on his own. ObraCare's policy was that Sam should have had him checked in as a patient, but she briefly evaluated him during his mother's visit instead. After asking him a few questions, she figured he just had allergies since he had been outside the previous weekend, so she recommended he try some over-the-counter eye drops to start.

Of course, his eye irritation could have been from something else—marijuana use even—but she hadn't wanted to mention that possibility in front of his mother, who had been watching so earnestly. He had nodded when Sam talked about seasonal allergies and had promised to come back to the clinic if he still had symptoms.

"That's right," Cynthia said. She paused before she spoke again. "He died on Friday. I was at his funeral this morning; that's why I was late coming in."

Sam's heart jolted. "Oh, goodness. I'm so sorry to hear that. How is Mrs. Garza doing?"

"As well as can be expected," Cynthia replied. "You know, her husband passed away a few years ago, so it's just been Elma and her son. Now with Raul gone, she's devastated."

Sam was still in a bit of shock. Raul had been young—she estimated he was in his early twenties—and now she was second-guessing herself. Did she miss something when she saw him? "How did he die?"

"In a car crash."

The tension in Sam's shoulders dissipated slightly. It sounded like it was just an unfortunate accident.

"Do you know when I was supposed to see her again?"

"She was on the schedule for today, but she cancelled her appointment, of course. I learned about Raul's death because Elma lives a few houses down from me. I visited with her last night—you know, to bring her flowers and give her my condolences."

Sam nodded.

"She insists that his death was not an accident."

"Okay," Sam said, wondering where this was going.

"She wants to know if you can help."

Sam frowned. "I'll help in any way I can, but I'm not sure how."

"Could you at least stop by to see her? If nothing else, it would mean a lot to her."

"You know how many patients I see, Cynthia. As much as I'd like to, I can't visit everyone who has something bad happen in their family."

"I know, but…"

"But what?"

"Well, I may have told her how you solved that case several months ago."

"You what? Did you tell her this last night?"

"Not exactly." Cynthia plucked at the ends of her stethoscope hanging around her neck. "I may have mentioned it during one of our neighborhood get-togethers right after it happened. I mean, what you did was amazing. We all were talking about it."

"Who do you mean by 'we'?"

"You know, everyone here in the clinic."

Sam shook her head in amazement. How did everyone know about that? She supposed it was typical office gossip.

Cynthia went on. "So Elma brought it up again last night when I visited her. Since you helped solve the murder of your friend, she thought maybe you could look into what happened with her son."

Sam wouldn't really call the person who was murdered over the summer her friend, but she didn't correct Cynthia. She was at a loss for what she should do.

Then Cynthia gave Sam a pleading look. "Could you at least stop by to see her? All you have to do is just listen. It would mean so much to her."

Sam pursed her lips, unsure of what she should do.

"Please? If nothing else, could you do it as a personal favor for me?"

After Sam finished seeing patients for the day, she followed the directions Cynthia had given her to Mrs. Garza's house. The neighborhood had ranch houses in various states of upkeep, some with scattered candy wrappers and leftover Halloween decorations in their yards. Cars lined the street when she turned onto the Garzas' street, and she drove past the address because there was no parking. She found a spot a few houses down and pulled over.

Maybe she should just go home. She felt like she was crashing a private event. If she left now, she could tell Cynthia that she didn't make it over because she had too much work for her MPH classes, which was true—she did have an assignment due the next day.

But then Cynthia walked out of the house that Sam had just pulled in front of. She waved, so Sam put her car in park and killed the engine. She put a smile on her face as she got out of her car.

"Thank you so much for coming, Dr. Jenkins. Elma will be so glad to see you."

Sam took a deep breath as she leaned back into her car to pick up the small arrangement of flowers she had purchased on the way.

"Sure, anything I can do to help."

They walked past a house with a plastic swing hanging from an old oak and a couple of bicycles toppled on the driveway. Conversations, a family talking and laughing, drifted out of the house along with the smell of onions and garlic.

They turned to walk up the Garzas' sidewalk. A group of people, a mixture of young and old, had gathered on the front lawn. Cynthia proudly introduced Sam as the doctor from her clinic, and a young man in his early twenties, his temples shaved with longer hair on top, fixed his gaze on her for a moment before looking away. After some smiles and nods, Cynthia and Sam proceeded inside.

The front door opened into the living room, which was warm due to the crowd. There was soft music playing in the background and dim lights from lamps in the corners of the room. The floorboards creaked beneath their feet as they walked. The house smelled of flowers and freshly baked bread. As they parted their way through clusters of the other visitors, they found Mrs. Garza sitting on the couch, surrounded by women around her same age. Mrs. Garza dabbed at her eyes with an embroidered handkerchief as she clutched at a rosary and had a framed photo of her son on her lap.

Cynthia approached and said, "Elma, I found Dr. Jenkins outside. See, I told you she would be here."

Mrs. Garza looked up and extended her arms toward Sam. "Oh, thank you for coming, Doctor. Please, sit down." The lady next to her jumped to her feet so Sam could sit next to Mrs. Garza on the couch.

Sam obliged, and Mrs. Garza held up the picture

frame for Sam to see. It was of Raul and appeared to be his high school graduation photo.

"You remember Raul, Dr. Jenkins?"

"Yes, ma'am. I'm so sorry to hear about what happened. I remember he came with you to the clinic last week."

She handed the flowers to Mrs. Garza.

"Oh, how pretty. You are so thoughtful."

She turned to a young lady with purple highlights standing nearby, handed her the flowers, and said, "Please take care of these, Nina. Find a nice place for them."

Sam scanned the room. It resembled a florist shop, with bouquets topping every piece of furniture.

Mrs. Garza turned back to Sam. "I need your help, Doctor."

Sam's gut cinched up, anticipating Mrs. Garza's request. She knew she wouldn't be able to help, even though her nature would be to try.

"Help me find out what happened to Raul."

"I'm sorry, Mrs. Garza. I don't know if I can."

"Don't be so modest, Doctor. Cynthia told me you solved a murder when the police didn't even think a murder had happened."

Sam glanced over at Cynthia, who was standing by the doorway, returning Sam's look with one of encouragement.

"But that was a different situation, Mrs. Garza. I don't know anything about what happened to your son."

"Well, let me tell you. Then you can decide."

Sam took in a deep breath. What was the harm in listening? "Okay."

"Last Friday, Raul texted me to tell me he was leaving work early because he wasn't feeling well. He sometimes gives me a ride home from work, and since he was leaving early, I would need to find someone else to take me." She patted the hand of the woman sitting on the other side of her from Sam. "Fortunately, Betty drove me home that day, but when he wasn't here, I called his cell phone to see how he was doing. He didn't answer. He sometimes stays with his girlfriend, Nina—she's the one who took your flowers into the kitchen just now. So I called her, and she said she hadn't seen him either."

Mrs. Garza began sobbing. She dabbed her eyes and nose with a crumpled tissue, then she clutched the picture of Raul. Betty stroked her back, and Sam waited while Mrs. Garza regained her composure.

Cynthia moved closer to the couch and said in a quiet voice, "Later that evening, the police came to tell Mrs. Garza that he had died in a car crash."

"I'm so sorry," Sam said.

Mrs. Garza turned to her, took her hands, and squeezed as if the sheer will she had in her strong fingers would bring her son back to life. "Thank you. But I want you to know that there was something going on at his work. The day before he died, he told me he would start to feel bad as soon as he got there, and by the end of the day, he would have a headache and feel like throwing up. So I think that's what happened before he left, before he crashed his car."

"Where did he work?"

"At a solar panel company—CS Solar."

The name sounded familiar, but it really didn't mean anything to Sam. "I don't know what to tell you, Mrs. Garza. I don't know what I can do."

"But Cynthia told me you figured out what happened to your friend, how he died. Can you find out what happened to Raul?"

"I did discover what happened to my friend's brother,

but I don't think I could do that again. I'm a doctor, not an investigator."

"But that's not true. You helped figure out what was going on with my back. That's an investigation."

"Sure, but that's a different type of investigation." Sam shifted on the couch, turning to face Mrs. Garza directly. "Can I ask you, what did the police say about Raul's accident?"

"They said he ran into a pickup truck stopped at a light. And when the ambulance came to pull him out, they said he was in really bad shape. They worked on him, but he never..." Mrs. Garza began to sob again, and through short, staggered breaths, she finally finished her sentence. "He never woke up."

Sam sat quietly with her for a few moments and then said, "I don't know how I can help, but I may know someone who might be able to give you some answers."

Mrs. Garza squeezed Sam's hands again. "Thank you, Doctor. Whatever you can do."

Sam stood up and was about to leave when out of the kitchen walked the exact person Sam had been thinking about.

Dylan Myers, in his police uniform, stepped over to her. "Hi, Sam. What are you doing here?"

Seeing him again made her feel like the innocent teenager she had been when he had asked her out for the first time in high school. Their relationship had been short-lived, but she would never really get completely over her first romance.

Sam tipped her head toward the couch. "She's one of my patients."

Mrs. Garza, noticing them together, said, "Oh, you two know each other?" She looked at them with beseeching eyes. "Please, find out why my son died."

"I'll do what I can, Mrs. Garza," Dylan said. Then he turned to Sam. "Let's step outside."

Sam gave Mrs. Garza her condolences again, then followed Dylan out to the front yard. Fortunately, they found themselves alone, as the groups who had gathered there before had departed. The spark she had felt when he had entered the room minutes before diminished, and she calmed her mind, focusing on the issue at hand.

"How have you been, since, well…you know?" he asked, seeming as if he had been a bit flustered seeing her too.

The last time they had seen each other was a few months before, right after they had solved the murder of an old acquaintance from high school, the case Cynthia had told Mrs. Garza about. "I'm fine. Been busy with work, but thankfully, it has slowed down a touch this fall. How about you?"

"It's about the same. Growing city, growing crime rates."

Sam nodded. "How do you know Mrs. Garza?"

"She goes to my mom's church. And somehow Mama thought I could answer Mrs. Garza's questions about Raul's death."

"I happened to meet him last week," she said, "when she had him drive her to her appointment with me. I think it was just a ploy to get him to see a doctor though."

Dylan gave a faint smile. "I know about moms'—and aunts'—ploys. What was wrong with him?"

"Well, during her visit, she asked me to look at his eyes. He said they had been bothering him. They were pretty red and irritated, but it seemed like allergic conjunctivitis, like pollen was triggering inflammation." Sam waved at the surrounding trees, then lowered her voice. "Or it could have been that he was smoking marijuana, but I wasn't going to bring that up in front of his mom."

"Did he smell like it?"

"No, but you can't always tell."

Dylan grunted assent.

"Anyway," Sam continued, "I told him to try some over-the-counter eye drops and follow up for a full visit if he kept having symptoms."

"You must get stuff like that all the time, people asking you for free medical advice."

Sam shrugged. "Yeah, but I am happy to help. The clinic frowns on it though. They want everyone checked in so they can bill for it." She tipped her head toward the house. "What did Mrs. Garza ask you to do?"

"Same as you. Try to figure out what caused Raul's death, but Mrs. Garza has had a blind spot for Raul's activities in the past."

"What kind of activities?"

"He served a short sentence for drug possession. He was trying to impress the wrong people, trying to gain clout with a gang when he was busted. It did seem like he had turned things around, but you know how difficult it can be for young men to resist peer pressure." Dylan shook his head. "Anyway I told Mrs. Garza that she needs to wait for the medical examiner's report."

"So you're not going to ask your girlfriend to let you see the prelim?" Then she added, because she couldn't resist, "You're still seeing each other, right?"

"Yes, we are still dating, but I don't want to get into that situation again, not like last time." Dylan's girlfriend worked as an admin in the Medical Examiner's Office and had given him access to the preliminary autopsy report for their high school acquaintance. Then he had shared it with Sam.

Sam held up her hands. "No, I don't want to see the report. I really don't want to get involved. Sure, she's my patient, but I've only been treating her for the last month or so. And she has been getting better, so I'll probably release her from care soon." She paused. "As long as Raul's death doesn't set her recovery back."

"Well, don't worry about it. I'm sure the ME's report will provide some answers for Mrs. Garza."

Sam thought of all the different mechanisms for how someone could die in a car collision. "You said he ran into the back of a pickup truck, but his car had airbags, right?"

"It did. But the truck had a jacked-up suspension and was carrying a bundle of lumber in the bed with the tailgate down. When Raul slammed into the back of it, the front of his car plowed under it, and the lumber smashed through Raul's windshield and pummeled his head." He grimaced. "So the airbags didn't help at all, and this really seems like it was just an unfortunate accident."

Sam nodded. "Maybe so."

S am went home straight from Mrs. Garza's house and grabbed a quick bite to eat—a low-cal frozen dinner—then settled in to work on her homework for her MPH class, which was due the next day. The assignment required her to familiarize herself with OSHA regulations and write some long-form answers to a few questions based on what she had read. Fortunately, she was not required to read all the OSHA regs, just the sections most relevant to healthcare workers. Specifically, she had to read through 29 CFR 1904 and 29 CFR 1910, the sections of regulations for recording and reporting occupational injuries and illnesses and occupational safety and health standards.

The wording was mind-numbingly dull, but there was no doubt the creation of OSHA in the early 1970s had had a positive effect, decreasing the number of workers killed each year from fourteen thousand the year before OSHA was formed, to just over five thousand per year now, even though the US workforce had doubled in the fifty years since. But five thousand deaths still seemed like too many lives lost.

As she kept refocusing her attention on the dry regulations, her mind niggled at her, mulling over a few words she had heard the night before. "That was a nice time," Millie had said after her father had mentioned a cardiology conference in Aspen. Maybe Sam hadn't fully understood the entire context of the conversation, but as far as she knew, the only time he had gone to Aspen was for a conference a month or so before her mother had been diagnosed with cancer.

Was that why her father was getting married so soon? Had he and Millie already been seeing each other before her mother passed away?

Sam blinked a couple of times. Focus. She had lost her spot on the OSHA website. Where was she? Right. Section 1904.04: Recording Criteria.

As she read through the section, it dawned on Sam that Miss Morales's supervisor had not wanted to record her injury. The regulation stated that injured employees could be evaluated by a doctor or other healthcare professional immediately after their injury without making it a recordable event. But if the employee required any treatment beyond basic first aid or workplace restrictions, the injury would have to be recorded in something called the OSHA 300 log. By giving Miss Morales a prescription, ordering physical therapy, and putting her on restrictions, Sam had made her injury recordable. And if a workplace had a high rate of injuries, it could trigger an inspection by OSHA.

Is that the reason why the supervisor didn't want to record the injury?

She had completely forgotten to look up that supervisor —Cynthia had interrupted her and then Raul's death had distracted her. And Jerry—why would he change the restrictions for Miss Morales? Since Sam was his supervisor, if anything happened to Miss Morales, she would be responsible.

Just as she began reading through the regulations again to make sure she fully understood the implications so she could devise a plan to deal with the situation, there was a knock at the door.

She got up, stretched, and peeked through the peephole; it was her friend James Lewis, who lived one building over in the apartment complex. He had been spending even more time than usual visiting Sam in the evenings since he and his boyfriend, Kevin, had "decided to take some time off" from each other.

As soon as she opened the door, he said, "I got it!"

"You got the job?" Sam smiled. "Congratulations! When do you start?"

"Immediately. Since I was already doing freelance work for the paper anyway, they're just going to give me more assignments—plus a regular paycheck."

"That's great! And what about the wedding gigs?"

"I'll still do those on the side, when I can. Aunt Carol will keep me in the loop, but there are a lot of photographers around town, so there's tons of competition. This will let me have a steady income and not have to hustle for clients all the time." They sat on the couch. "So…how did dinner go last night?"

Sam filled James in on the details of the dinner, ending with her father and Millie telling her they were getting married.

"I'm still getting used to the idea," Sam said.

James arched his eyebrows. "Wow. How do you feel about it?"

She shrugged nonchalantly. "I really do like Millie, so I think this will be a good thing for him."

He gave her a skeptical look. "Are you sure you're okay with this?"

"What can I do? I can't tell my dad how to live his life."

"But you must have some feelings about this. You said before that you thought he started dating Millie too soon after your mother died."

Sam stared straight ahead. She didn't want to be dumping her feelings out on James, whom she could reliably say was probably her best friend right now.

He bumped her shoulder with his fist. "C'mon. Let it all out. That's what I'm here for. You certainly let me moan and groan when things weren't going well with Kevin."

She took a deep breath and closed her eyes, then nodded. "Yeah, I'm pretty miffed about it. How could he be getting married so soon? My mother hasn't been in the grave for two years yet, and now—"

"And now he's already moving on."

"The worst part of it is, I actually like Millie. She seems great. I just hope he isn't so distant with her like he was with my mom. She deserves someone who will watch out for her, who will be there for her." Sam let out a little laugh. "Although, she does tell it like it is and won't put up with my dad's BS. Maybe that's because she's been working with him for a while." She shrugged. "So yeah, I also feel guilty for being upset about this."

"You've every right to feel upset." He picked up a pillow and plucked at the corner. "Do you really think your dad will just ignore Millie, like he did with your mom—and you?"

"I guess it wasn't so much that he ignored us; it's that

he was just so obsessed with work all the time. His patients always came first."

"That's a better excuse than Kevin had for me. He's always at work, but there aren't people's lives at stake."

"But maybe that's what attracted you to him. That he's so driven."

"Yeah, I like driven people. Just like you." He cracked a grin. "So Alex and your dad got along?"

"They got along just fine. Like two colleagues who have been practicing together for a long time. Dad told Alex all about these interesting cases, stuff that he never tells me, even though I'm his daughter."

"And a doctor to boot," James said. "What did Alex think of the engagement?"

"He thought it was great. In fact, we kind of had an argument in the car afterward."

"What did he say?"

"Nothing really."

James smirked. "Oh, it was a silent argument."

"Okay, so we didn't really argue." She gave a half shrug. "It's just that he thought it was fine, and he didn't even realize that I was a bit shocked. Not like you."

"Well…he's a man."

"So are you!"

"But he's not as attuned to the nuances of emotions like I am." He grinned again; then the grin slipped off his face, as if he could read her thoughts. "There's something else bothering you though."

"I just…I just keep hanging up on something I thought I heard Millie say last night. She mentioned being in Aspen with my dad. Of course, it's not like I'm all over my dad's itinerary, but I think the only time he's been to Aspen was for a cardiology conference right before my mother died."

"So you're thinking…"

"I'm thinking that they might have been seeing each other before my mom died."

James's eyes widened. "Really?"

"Well, I know I don't have evidence of it, but it just seems that they know each other pretty intimately after only dating for a short time. And it would explain some things."

He nodded. "I can see that."

She tossed herself against the back of the couch and looked up at the ceiling. "Why am I so upset?"

He squeezed her shoulder. "Hey. It's okay."

"But I feel bad about it. And I might be imagining things, but what if they'd had an affair? Does that change anything?"

James turned toward Sam, pulling a leg up under him so he could face her fully. "No. It doesn't. And this isn't to invalidate your feelings at all, but frankly, we're all a mix of good and bad, right? Sometimes good people do bad things—and sometimes the opposite happens. People you don't expect actually do something good."

"So you're saying that if they did have an affair before my mother died, it's not that they're bad people? How could I ever forgive them if it's true?"

"Well, look at my parents. I still love them, but they just won't accept me for who I am. And I know they aren't really 'bad' people. No one really is." He looked away. "Thank goodness I have Aunt Carol."

"Yeah, she's great. At least she truly loves you unconditionally."

"She does." After a moment, James turned to her. "So what are you going to do?"

"I'm just not going to think about it too much." She glanced over at her computer. "I'm going to focus on work and school."

"Learning anything interesting?"

"Just a ton of government regulations."

He crossed his eyes and stuck out his tongue. "Fun."

"Oh, and I saw Dylan tonight."

"Really? Wait, what?" He blinked. "But you just…what about Alex? Does this mean—"

Sam shook her head vigorously. "No, no. I stopped by a patient's house tonight because her son passed away, and Dylan happened to be there."

"Wow! That's really nice of you. Do you go to all your patients' houses?"

"Goodness, no. One of the medical assistants who works with me is her neighbor and told me about her son's death. But apparently they were all talking about how I helped solve Brad's murder, and this patient thinks something may have happened to her son, so she wanted me to look into it."

"And Dylan was there?"

"Yeah. Turns out, his mom goes to the same church as my patient, so she asked Dylan to look into it too."

"What did he think?"

"He said Raul—that's my patient's son—just died in a car crash. Nothing really suspicious, just a tragic accident. But if there was anything that made it suspicious, Raul had a checkered history. He wasn't necessarily in a gang, but he hung around with a few of the members, and had been arrested for possession."

"Funny, what a small world. Well, now that I'll have access to some of the databases at the newspaper, I can dig around into some things too."

"Oh, you don't need to do that. Dylan told her to just wait for the medical examiner's report."

"You've heard that before. Is he still dating what's-her-name?"

"Sounds like it. Honestly, it doesn't matter to me." She wiped her hands across her face. "I really don't want to get involved. I'm just going to take care of Mrs. Garza so she can get back to her life."

"A life without her son," James said.

The next day, Sam dove right in to seeing patients as soon as she got to work. Sometimes she found that dealing with other people's problems—her patients' problems—allowed her to completely forget about her own. She really appreciated James's listening to her rant about her father's engagement along with her suspicions about his possible infidelities. And after she helped her first couple of patients—a baggage handler for a major airline who had strained his shoulder and a chef who had burned her forearm—she had almost cleared her mind of everything that had happened over the last couple of days.

As Sam came out of an exam room after seeing her fourth patient for the day, Cynthia stopped her. "Call for you on line two, Dr. Jenkins."

"Who is it?"

"It's Dr. Taylor."

Even though her boss usually had nothing but praise for her work, Sam still got a little nervous any time he called. Perhaps it was due to years of constantly being under the microscope, through high school, college, and medical school. It seemed like no matter what she did, it was never good enough. Sam picked up the phone and pushed the button to connect.

Dr. Taylor asked Sam a few questions about her MPH courses, how they were going, if she had come up with a plan for applying to residency programs the next year, and most importantly, if her coursework was interfering with her ability to see patients. She let him know that the decrease in the number of patients over the previous couple of months had allowed her to get all of her charts completed during work hours, which freed up her time in the evenings so she could work on her assignments.

"That's great," he said. Then he got to the point. "As you just mentioned, patient volumes have decreased, so we are actively working to address this. While there is some seasonality—it's fairly normal to have our business slow down in the fall—this year has been slightly worse than previous years. We believe some of this may be due to the strategic opening of CenTex clinics near our own."

Sam nodded even though Dr. Taylor couldn't see her. Over the summer, she saw as many as thirty-five patients on some days. Once school started and the summer construction projects slowed down, there were days when she would only see about fifteen patients during her shift. And she drove past the new CenTex location on the other side of the freeway from her clinic every day. CenTex focused on urgent care, but they also saw workers' comp patients. And they were in a better location, situated in the middle of a shopping center.

Dr. Taylor continued, "I also wanted to let you know that the marketing department has decided not to run the campaign with the photos you and some of our other staff posed for."

"Oh, really?" Sam was rather relieved. Even though

she had agreed to serve as a model for the company's promotional material for their urgent care services, she didn't really want her face to be all over town on brochures and billboards.

"Yes, we've realized that in order to sustain the urgent care business, we need to constantly advertise, and we just aren't seeing the returns on investment that we'd like. So there's been a deliberate decision to put our efforts into winning contracts with employers for pre-employment screenings to bring in more business." He cleared his throat. "If we aren't able to get those patient volumes up, I'm afraid we'll have to downsize. We may even need to cut staff."

As he said this, Cynthia bustled by, escorting a new patient to an exam room. She had been working at this clinic longer than anyone else, as far as Sam knew, but her job was probably one of the most expendable. Sam's job, on the other hand, was relatively safe—there's only a limited supply of physicians—but medical assistants only had to have a high school education or GED along with a certificate from a six-week training program. Sam knew that Cynthia had a husband at home who was on disability after a work injury, and she had to make ends meet for the household, including two teenagers.

Dr. Taylor went on. "Kyle has arranged an onsite visit with a client to convince them to renew their pre-employment screening contract with us. Normally we would only have sales take care of these deals, but having a doctor there to show how important we think this client is would greatly improve the chances of successfully extending this contract."

"What's the name of the client?"

"CS Solar."

Sam's mind raced. That was the company where Raul had worked.

Dr. Taylor continued, "I'd like you to go with him to the facility so you can answer any questions the client might have. Can I count on you?"

She wanted to stay on Dr. Taylor's good side since she didn't know what her career path held. And maybe she could learn more about Raul's work environment since Mrs. Garza was convinced it had contributed to his death. "Sure. I'll do whatever you need me to do."

"Great. I'll let Kyle fill you in on the details."

Sam was glad Dr. Taylor couldn't see the look on her face. She had not had the best experience dealing with Kyle before.

"We really need this win," he said. "CenTex is chomping at the bit to take some of our business away."

Sam assured him she would work with Kyle, then hung up the phone, got up from her workstation, and knocked on the door to Kyle's office. The door was open, and Kyle was on the phone. He held up his finger, indicating he'd be done in a moment.

Go figure, the doctor has to wait on the sales guy.

After a few moments, he hung up. "How can I help you?" He flashed a pearly white smile.

"Dr. Taylor said you need me for an onsite meeting?"

"Yes, CS Solar. They've got a facility with two hundred employees, and they're looking to expand that to fifteen hundred in the near term. And there's rumors they may grow even more in the future. Since they'll be hiring a lot of folks, and their existing employees need ongoing exams —you know the usual, including forklift certifications, audio testing, respirator fit testing—this will be a great opportunity for us."

Kyle's eyes sparkled as he spoke, as if he was anticipating his commission once this deal came to fruition.

"When is the meeting?" she asked.

"Monday. I'll forward the email with all the details to you."

"Have you let Jill know?" Sam asked. Jill was the office manager, and if Sam was going to be out, Jill would need to adjust the appointment schedule so that Jerry would not be overwhelmed.

"No. I thought you could tell her."

Of course he would expect her to manage everything. Before Sam walked up front to Jill's office, she checked the board. Only two patients listed, and Jerry had placed magnets with his initials next to both, indicating he was already seeing them, which left Sam with plenty of time to talk to Jill. But if the patient volume stayed this low, Jill probably wouldn't need to reschedule any patients while Sam was away at that meeting. She wished she had better insight into the financials of the clinic. Since she was "just a doctor," management didn't often share operations and business-related details with her. She wondered how bad the clinic was really doing financially. Would Jerry be at risk for losing his job too?

8

S am went to the front of the clinic, behind the reception desk, to Jill's office. Her door was open, but she was on the phone, and when she saw Sam, she put up a finger signaling that Sam should wait. As she stood by the door, she looked out at the lobby, where the staff had replaced Halloween decorations with Thanksgiving items—cornucopias and turkeys. She supposed it was more for their enjoyment than for the enjoyment of the working-class patients.

Several people were scattered about in the chairs, some watching a TV mounted on one wall, with others tapping away on their phones. Sam hadn't seen that many people on the schedule, so she assumed these people were here for drug screens, something that many employers sent new hires to ObraCare to perform.

Jill said goodbye to whomever she was speaking with, then called for Sam to enter. She sat in the chair in front of Jill's desk, putting her back to the window that looked out onto the waiting room. Jill had a blonde bob cut and was efficient in her management of the clinic, juggling vacation requests and schedules, and managing orders for vendors —from the clinical supplies Sam and Jerry needed to the paper supplies needed in the bathrooms—along with fielding complaints from patients and employers. And she had to do it all with a smile on her face as she watched the waiting room through her office window and made sure patients flowed through the clinic in a timely manner. Sam did not envy Jill's job at all.

"How can I help you?"

"Hi, Jill," Sam said as she stepped inside the office, pulling the door closed behind her. "I just talked to Dr. Taylor about the CS Solar account. Dr. Taylor would like for me to go with Kyle to CS Solar on Monday to help with his sales presentation."

"Oh, that would be great. I understand their contract is up for renewal?"

"Yes." Sam sat in the chair in front of Jill's desk, then leaned forward and lowered her voice. "Dr. Taylor said that our financials aren't great, and that there may be layoffs if CS Solar doesn't renew?"

Jill raised her eyebrows. "That's the first I've heard that, but I do know our patient volume has dropped significantly this fall. Paula told me that I may have to lay someone off." Paula was ObraCare's regional operations director and Jill's boss.

"Cynthia should be okay, though, right? I mean, she's been here longer than all of us."

Jill grimaced. "Well…it's not entirely up to me, but I heard from Russell, the operations director at the San Marcos clinic, that when he was told he had to lay off someone, Paula made him lay off their most senior medical assistant. Russell thinks it's because that MA had been at ObraCare so long that her pay was that of one and a half FTEs."

"What's an FTE?" Sam was used to tons of acronyms in medicine, but she was still getting up to speed on these business acronyms.

"Oh, sorry. It's a full-time equivalent."

"You wouldn't happen to know if Jerry's job is safe, would you?"

"Well…" Jill began again, "that would be in Dr. Taylor's domain since he's in charge of all the clinical personnel. But Russell did tell me that when they downsized, they did get rid of their PA since they only need one doctor to keep the clinic open."

"So how is that clinic doing?"

"It's been tough, but since Amazon has opened up a distribution center in San Marcos, they're seeing a lot more patients now."

"And did they hire more people to take care of those patients?"

"No," Jill said. "They just asked the doctor and the other staff to work extra hours. Russell said that he's had to run one of the drug-testing bays to free up some of the MAs to work in the back with the doctor. I suppose they think it's better to pay overtime than to hire someone back. And then he's been having to stay two hours past closing to get all of his regular work done."

"Goodness. Do you think that will happen here?"

"I certainly hope not." Jill shook her head. "Frankly, if they pull some of those antics on me, I'd quit. There are too many job openings in Austin right now, so I would not put up with that kind of treatment. I'm surprised Russell hasn't quit, but his family is all in San Marcos, and he doesn't want to have to commute up to Austin for work."

Sam wished she had those types of options. "Well, I'll do what I can to help Kyle renew this contract with CS Solar, which is the main reason why I came in here to talk to you. How does Monday morning's schedule look? Kyle said we're supposed to go to their plant at 11:00."

Jill pulled up the patient schedule on her computer, then frowned. "It doesn't look too bad, but it is a Monday morning, and you know how that goes."

Sam certainly did. Many people with minor urgent care issues would wait until Monday to be seen, because there weren't a lot of options for urgent care on the weekend—short of the ER—and who would want to spend their weekend in the ER? So patients often waited to call in sick to work on Monday morning and then show up at ObraCare to be seen.

"But if you need to go on this sales visit, then you need to go on this sales visit. We'll manage with Jerry."

Sam nodded. "Okay. I'll let Jerry know that he might get swamped once he comes in on Monday."

"Very well," Jill said. "Anything else I can help you with?"

"No, that's all."

So now Sam knew that she needed to be as prepared as possible for the sales visit to CS Solar on Monday. Good thing Alex had call over the weekend, because Sam would be working on her environmental health assignment and spending any extra time she had learning everything she could about the solar panel industry. She did not want to be the reason Cynthia and Jerry lost their jobs.

9

On Monday morning after arriving at the clinic, Sam saw patients until Jerry arrived. For the most part, Sam spent the weekend by herself, using the time to study for her occupational health test, finish a biostatistics assignment, and research as much as she could about the solar panel industry so she could be ready for the meeting with Kyle to convince CS Solar to renew their contract with ObraCare. She had only taken breaks to grab lunch with James on Saturday, and to have dinner with an old college friend on Sunday evening.

Once Jerry settled into his routine seeing patients—fortunately, without too many walk-ins to clog up the schedule—Sam left with Kyle to go to CS Solar. They sat in silence for the first few minutes of the drive; then Kyle glanced over at her. "Look, can we start over? I feel like we got off on the wrong foot."

We certainly did, Sam thought. Even though she had only been working at this particular ObraCare location for a few months when Kyle was hired as a sales rep, she thought it was a no-brainer that she should keep the only office in the clinic area, since she was the only doctor at the medical practice. But Kyle had insisted he needed the office because he was constantly on the phone making sales calls, so he needed the privacy.

But what about the privacy of her patients? She often had to discuss sensitive matters on the phone, not just with her patients but with other doctors and with insurance companies. Sam used her squatter's rights to keep the office as long as possible, but eventually Kyle got his boss to put pressure on Sam's boss, and Sam got the call from Dr. Taylor that she needed to move to the counter in the center of the open workspace.

"You need to maintain those NPS ratings. So keep an eye on the board, watch who's in the rooms, and make sure everything is flowing well," Dr. Taylor had said.

In the end, it didn't matter what she thought. Since healthcare was becoming a service industry, all management cared about was the NPS—the net promoter score. It boiled down to how patients answered the one marketing question proven to measure customer loyalty: On a scale of one to ten, how likely is it that you would recommend ObraCare to someone else?

Promoters were patients answering nine or ten, meaning they would likely return or tell others to seek care at the clinic. Scores of seven or eight signified a neutral sentiment, and scores of six and below indicated the person answering was a detractor and would probably speak poorly of ObraCare.

A marketing consulting firm had dug further into the opinions of ObraCare detractors and found the main contributor to their view of the clinic was perception of wait time. Not the *actual* wait time, just the perception that they had waited longer than they had expected. Didn't they care if they had received proper medical treatment?

No, they just wanted everything to be quick and convenient. So ObraCare promptly installed TVs into every exam room. What better way to pass the time than by watching TV?

Sales and net promoter scores. That's all anyone in business seemed to care about these days.

Kyle continued talking, nervously filling the dead air between them. Sam remained silent.

He finally got her attention again when he said, "I'm sorry about the office situation, but really, I do have to make tons of calls. They keep track of how many I make every day in our CRM."

"What's a CRM?" Sam asked. She was curious, but only slightly.

"It stands for customer relationship management software. I have to log every call, and if I don't meet my quota each quarter, big Kahuna Carl threatens to fire me. He says us sales reps are a dime a dozen."

She huffed. His attempts at gaining her sympathy weren't working.

"And if I don't make those calls, you won't have patients to see. There's lots of competition in this space. Patients only come to see you because I make these deals with their employers. I sell them drug screening and pre-employment packages at cost, and that puts us top of mind for sending their employees to us when they get injured. Then you take over, along with the physical therapists, and that's how we all keep our jobs."

Sam looked out the passenger window at the boxy buildings zooming by. They had left the strip mall where the clinic was located, and now they were driving through a series of industrial parks built on what used to be flat farmland. In the distance, she could see a neighborhood of tract homes under construction.

She had not known any of these business aspects by the time she graduated from medical school. She had spent all her energy on learning and remembering the volumes of conditions and diseases that affect the human body and the myriad of ways to treat them. Wasn't that enough? Finding patients and building a clinical business was a foreign world to her until she started working for ObraCare.

"So are we good?" Kyle asked.

Sam rolled her eyes and said, "Yeah, sure. Whatever."

She faced forward again and watched the white dashes zip by like a dribbling faucet, as the tires hummed on the blacktop. "What is the plan for this meeting? You said we're speaking with the site manager?"

"Yes, we're meeting with Henry Allen. We need to renew our existing contract with CS Solar, even though the original contract is technically with Tyson International. Tyson was a startup company that CS just bought, and CS —which is based in California—found a private equity investor to help them expand into Texas."

"Tyson International was a startup? Sounds like a pretty grand name."

"Yeah, these little startups like to make themselves seem bigger than they really are. Anyway, the existing contract only has a two-year term."

"Guess they wanted to keep their options open," Sam muttered under her breath. She turned to Kyle. "CS Solar. I've had a few patients who work for them. They make solar panels, right?" She knew this from her research, but it would help to learn what Kyle had to say about them.

"That's right. Their main headquarters is in California, but they're expanding into Texas since renewable energy is such a hot industry."

As she poked around online over the weekend, Sam had learned that despite the oil and gas industry's dominance in the state, Texas also had a significant renewable energy market. The massive wind farms in the western plains produced more wind energy than any other state, and the growth in the number of solar panel installations had increased the state's renewable energy generation as well.

"This site has around two hundred employees," Kyle said, "but my understanding is that they are building out a new manufacturing floor to increase their production capacity, so they'll be hiring a lot more soon."

He turned in to the parking lot in front of a two-story concrete industrial building. A chain-linked fence extended from either side of the building to surround the property behind it, where several smaller corrugated metal buildings sat along with a collection of large tanks and pipes running in between.

Kyle pulled into a spot out front labeled "visitor."

"Anyway, I've got my standard sales presentation for them, tailored with a few details specific for their business, of course. And don't worry." He smiled at her. "You don't need to say anything, but I'm sure they'll have some questions that only you can answer."

They both got out of the car and walked past the twin flagpoles out front, one with the United States flag, the other with the Texas flag, both flying at the same height. Sam had heard when she was growing up that since Texas was the only state that had been its own country, it was allowed to fly the state flag at the same height as the US flag. However, since then, she had learned any state could do the same, and Texas was not unique in this sense. Just another of the many things she had thought were true in childhood that were not.

Sam and Kyle checked in with the receptionist, a perky woman who introduced herself as Alvera. After giving them visitor badges, she escorted them to a conference room just off the lobby. An oval, glass-topped meeting table sat in the middle of the room surrounded by rolling office chairs.

While Kyle pulled out his laptop and hooked it up to the AV equipment at one end of the conference room, Sam opened her leather portfolio filled with papers. She had printed them out the night before in her preparation for this visit. They contained OSHA regulations that might apply to solar panel manufacturing, and she tried to anticipate any medically-related questions these clients might have. Even though she had really needed to study for her test, she didn't feel too bad about the time she spent doing this research—it overlapped somewhat with the test material, plus it gave her a chance to learn from a real-world application of dry OSHA regulations.

As she sorted through her papers, a man in gray slacks and a light blue button-down shirt entered. Kyle stood to greet him, shaking his hand. "Good to see you, Henry. Thanks for giving us the opportunity to speak with you."

"Of course," Henry said. He turned to Sam as she stood, and they also shook hands. "And you must be Dr. Jenkins, the one I've heard so much about."

"It's a pleasure to meet you," she said.

They all settled in their seats at the table, with Henry at the end, facing the screen on the opposite side of the conference room, and Kyle and Sam flanking him on either side.

"What do you have for me?" Henry asked.

Kyle ran through his presentation, showing the number of employers using ObraCare's services, how many drug tests and pre-employment exams they performed each year, along with details on their certification programs for safety-sensitive jobs, such as those required for forklift operators.

Then he moved on to ObraCare's stats on the injured employees they treated. He showed how ObraCare's average case length was shorter than most other clinics. He provided data on the financial benefits for treating employees early, and how ObraCare's main goal was getting patients back to work as soon as possible. For Sam, who had been pigeonholed in the clinic, concentrating only on the patients in front of her, this information was quite enlightening.

As Kyle continued through his presentation, he included specific numbers for CS Solar with projected cost savings from the services ObraCare provided. He closed his pitch with the advantages of using ObraCare versus some of the other competitors. "And you always have direct access to our treating physicians, like Dr. Jenkins," he said as he tipped his head toward Sam.

"This is good stuff," Henry said. "You've been a great partner for us, and I'd like to continue this relationship as we expand and hire on more talent to increase our production capacity."

"That sounds great," Kyle said. "What questions do you have?"

Sam sat there as they ran through costs associated with drug testing and pre-placement exams. She hadn't been privy to much of this information before, since it was all business-related and not in her domain of medicine, but the numbers they were talking about didn't make a lot of sense to her. From what she knew, it sounded like Obra-Care would be providing drug testing to new employees at a small loss, charging just a few dollars more than the testing assays cost, and the clinic would only charge thirty dollars for the pre-placement exams.

As Kyle and Henry finished hashing out details for the contract, there was a quick knock on the conference room door, and another man wearing khakis and a polo shirt entered.

Henry stood. "I'd like you to meet Anand Dhawan, our industrial hygienist. He can talk to you about our safety protocols for our employees."

They made another round of introductions, and when Anand spoke, Sam noted a pleasant lilt to his voice. She couldn't quite place his accent and wondered where he had grown up.

Then Henry said, "Anand's been quite busy working on the plans for our expansion, making sure we have the proper safety mechanisms in place. And since we've met all of our milestones, our investors are moving forward with the next tranche of funding so we can proceed with the buildout. If you have time, we'd love to take you on a brief tour. We can show you our existing operations, and then share our expansion plans with you."

"That would be fantastic," Kyle said without looking at Sam to make sure she was good with it.

She sighed. *I might as well enjoy this time away from clinic*, she thought. She gathered the papers she had needlessly brought along, quickly tucked them into her portfolio as she stood, then followed the men out the door.

10

The group walked down a short hallway and passed through double doors to enter a factory floor where workers bustled about, with most wearing lab coats and masks.

"Most of our assembly process takes place here," Henry said. "Right now it's quite manual, but we'll be implementing a more automated process with the expansion. We'll keep this area running, though, because this setup allows us to customize our panels more easily based on customer requirements."

"But only for a while, since it's not really optimized for safety or efficiency," Anand said.

A flash of annoyance crossed Henry's face; then he nodded. "Right. Only for a while. We'll retool everything once the expansion is online."

He led them between aisles of long workbenches and pointed out the various stations to Sam and Kyle, explaining how they received solar cells shipped from a fabrication facility in China. He said the workers first inspected and tested them, and then they soldered the cells together into strips. The group walked by several workers hunched over their benches using soldering irons to connect the dark squares, with curls of white smoke rising each time the red-hot tips touched the edges of the cells.

"Even though we're not required to," Anand said, "we have our employees wear goggles and respirator masks when they're soldering components together. We use lead-free solder, but the fumes can still be irritating."

"It doesn't smell that bad though," Kyle said. "It's actually kind of pleasant."

Sam had to agree. The air smelled a bit like incense.

Anand nodded. "That would be the rosin. It helps the solder flow to make a better connection."

The next area had workers standing on either end of newly assembled strips of solar cells. They grasped a tool with a long bar holding suction cups spaced over the cells to gently pick up each strip. As the workers squeezed the handles at the ends of the tool, the suction cups turned on, allowing the workers to move a strip and place it on a table, alongside other strips to form a grid. Then the workers laid a piece of tape along the edge and used soldering irons to connect all the solar strips together.

"In our expansion, we'll have robotics assist with these soldering steps and the lamination process that you see over here in this conveyer oven," Henry said as they followed the workers who had assembled a grid of solar cells to a large, flat table on the end of a stainless steel box with a conveyor belt. Another pair of workers stretched out a sheet of plastic before the first pair placed the grid on top of it and went back to their station. The workers at the oven then stretched another piece of plastic over it before feeding it onto the conveyer belt. As the solar grid fed into the machine, a man with a clipboard in his hand came around from behind it.

As the group moved on to continue the tour, Henry said to Sam, "You have an interest in robotics, isn't that right, Dr. Jenkins?"

Sam raised her eyebrows, surprised that he knew this about her. It was true, when she was in medical school and applying to surgical residency programs, she had done some research with an attending studying the utility of robotic surgery on gallbladder disease.

"I saw it in your profile on the ObraCare website," Henry explained.

She nodded. "Oh, that's right. I forgot that was on there."

"Well, you'll just have to come back for another tour once the new machines and equipment are in place," he said. Then he looked behind her, motioning for someone to come over.

"This is Dale Cooper, whom you may already know," Henry said as Sam and the others turned to see Dale approach them.

Sam zeroed in on the man's face, his jaw clenching briefly when he looked at her with recognition. Her skin prickled. It was the supervisor who had confronted her last week, the one who ripped up her patient's papers.

Henry continued, not noticing the brief exchange. "Dale is one of our supervisors, so he'll be your point of contact for functional requirements when our employees are hired on or need to get back to work." Denim-clad Dale merely grunted. He did not seem happy to see Sam.

Henry looked at his watch. "I apologize, but I have another meeting in a few minutes, so I need to get back to my office. Anand will continue your tour."

Kyle thanked Henry and invited him to tour the clinic.

Once Henry was out of earshot, Sam said to Dale, "And how is Miss Morales doing?"

He retorted with a smug look. "She's doing just fine."

Anand, who had continued walking ahead of them, stopped and looked back. "What's this about?"

"Isabel Morales. She just twisted her ankle, and she's fine," Dale said.

"Oh, right." Anand nodded. "She's the one you told me about, the one who had been requesting a move to intake."

"And now she got what she wanted," Dale muttered.

"She needs—" Sam began.

Kyle elbowed her and gave her a pleading look, as if to say, "Don't screw this up."

Sam stewed for a moment. She knew what she had seen when Miss Morales first presented with her injury. It didn't matter if Miss Morales had wanted to be transferred to another location or not; she had a significant injury and needed time to recover. And for Kyle to cut her off—it made her mad just thinking about it. But she swallowed her anger and moved with the group.

They passed a restroom with caution tape across the entrance and walked to the back of the factory floor, where two wells sank into the floor. They were like the type you'd see in an auto shop, only instead of cars over them, scaffolding supporting solar panels stretched across the wells. When Sam stopped to figure out what these pits were for, someone bumped into her from behind, knocking her portfolio out of her hand and scattering her papers on the floor.

She turned, and a young man with dark hair shaved on the sides said, "I'm sorry, miss." As he knelt to pick up the papers, she thought he looked familiar. He stood and handed her the portfolio. "Please excuse me."

"No problem; it was an accident. Thanks for picking these up," she said. She focused on him a moment, trying to place him, but then she thought she must have seen him at the clinic at some point. He nodded, then walked to one of the pits and climbed down into it.

She looked around to find the group. They had already moved on. She caught up to them right before Anand pushed through another set of double doors.

"What are those stations for?" Sam asked, pointing to the pair of pits.

Anand was about to speak, but Dale answered. "They're inspection stations, to ensure there are no defects in the construction of the panels."

"Those pits seem odd, though, like it's a car shop," Kyle said.

Dale nodded. "They were for vehicle maintenance way back when, but we found another use. It makes it easier to get under the panels and take a good look at them."

"Unfortunately, we only have one station working right now." Anand sighed. "The other one has been shut down because...because we're down a person right now."

He pushed open the door behind him, and they followed, entering an expansive space the size of an indoor arena.

Anand passed out construction hats to everyone as Sam took in the rows of large pallets along the walls, some topped with massive boxes, others holding equipment wrapped in gauzy plastic. Brightly striped yellow tape outlined lanes on the floor as several forklifts zipped about, emitting loud beeps every time one backed up.

"And this is why we really need your help," he said, raising his voice to be heard. "I'm sure Henry went over the numbers with you, but we'll be hiring and onboarding hundreds of new employees in the coming months. Our investors are keen to get production going since renewable energy has a lot of upside in the market."

As they walked between the rows of pallets, Anand told them how they were converting old warehouse space into a modern manufacturing floor, describing the various pieces of equipment and machinery still crated up around them. A lot of what he said went over Sam's head, but she did understand bits and pieces from her robotic surgery research. Kyle nodded enthusiastically throughout Anand's explanations, and Dale looked somewhat bored.

They stopped at a drafting table midway down a row next to a column, and Anand pulled a set of blueprints from a canister next to the table. He unrolled them, spreading them out on the surface, securing them with metal bars on the top and bottom. He pointed to various markings on the plans and described some of the same things they had seen on the other factory floor, but Anand told them that on this side most of the work would be automated by machines and robotics, integrating many of the steps currently completed by hand. He said the new equipment would ultimately make the place safer to work, improve the overall quality, and increase their production capacity tenfold.

Sam stepped back and surveyed the space around her to take in everything. She felt so small in this environment, but there must be so many factories like this sprouting up. Every day, the local news outlets crowed about the number of companies bringing operations like this to Austin, fueling the economy with more jobs. As she tried to imagine what the factory would look like once all the equipment was installed, she hadn't noticed how far she had wandered, until someone pulled her backward by her elbow.

She turned to find Dale had stopped her. He pointed behind her and then at the ground. She had stepped over one of the yellow caution lines, and when she looked back, she saw a huge yellow hook hanging on chains from a hoist mounted on rafters above them. The hook swung back and forth from a sudden stop, right at the level of her head, and apparently had been moving her direction. If Dale hadn't pulled her back, she would have stepped into its path.

"You've got to be careful where you walk," he said, then nodded to a man holding the black controller box hanging from the hoist once Sam was safely out of harm's way. The man with the controller nodded back, pressed a button, and the hook continued on its journey.

ANAND LED Sam and Kyle back the way they had come in, leaving Dale on the old factory floor. They made one last stop in a bright white room where workers unpacked boxes of the solar cells. One wall had windows that looked out onto the lobby, something that Sam hadn't noticed when they had first arrived.

"This is where we inspect and test the individual cells before they go out to the production line."

Several workers peered into large, lighted magnifying glasses on gooseneck stands to scrutinize the iridescent squares, while others sat at stations with computer monitors.

Miss Morales sat at one of these stations, her set of crutches leaning against the wall beside it. She picked up a solar cell, slid it into a bracket next to a monitor, and pressed a button. After a flash of light, a tracing appeared on the screen followed by the word "PASS" in green letters.

"And that's it," Anand said. "Now you've seen everything."

Kyle had a huge grin on his face. "This is great."

Sam followed the men into the hallway and noticed a set of restrooms opposite the room they had just exited. Anand led them back into the lobby.

"I'll follow up with Henry on that contract," Kyle said. "I just need to get my laptop. Where's the conference room?"

"It's right over here." Anand started toward the other side of the lobby.

"I need to use the restroom," Sam said, and the men nodded in response.

She made her way back down the hallway, but instead of turning in to the restroom, she entered the inspection area again and hurried over to Miss Morales.

"How are you doing, ma'am?" Sam whispered.

Miss Morales looked up, surprised. "I'm okay."

"Is your ankle getting better?"

"Yes, yes. And everything is good. It is much better in here than on the floor."

Sam tipped her head toward the crutches. "Can you walk without those?"

"A little. Each day is a little better."

"I'm glad." Sam slipped her a business card. "Please come back and see me if you have any problems."

Miss Morales took the card and nodded.

Sam looked up, and through the window into the lobby she saw Kyle and Anand coming out of the conference room. She rushed back out to the lobby to join them.

"It was a pleasure meeting you," Anand said to both of them; then he turned to Sam. "And if you have some time, I'd appreciate your clinical opinion for some of the protocols we have. Do you think you could come back so we can discuss them?"

"Of course," Sam said. "I'd be happy to."

11

The afternoon passed quickly after Sam returned with Kyle to the clinic. She had felt like she wasn't really needed on the visit to CS Solar until the very end, when Anand asked her to go over protocols with him. Unfortunately, since Sam's primary role was to just see patients in the clinic, she didn't have the ability to block off time for meetings. So she scheduled a time to meet with Anand during her lunch break the following week.

Right as Sam got home, she got a text message from Millie asking if it was still okay for her to come over. She had forgotten that Millie was going to bring her some of her mother's things that evening. She didn't know if she was up for it, but she figured there was no point in avoiding the inevitable, so she texted back that it was fine.

She sat at her desk and checked on her computer to see what she needed to do for her classes. At least all of her research on OSHA regulations and potential occupational exposures in the solar panel manufacturing industry wouldn't go completely to waste. Some of the material might be on her upcoming test, plus, her instructor had just assigned a term paper with several topics to choose from. Perhaps she could work with some of this material for the assignment.

Before the trip to CS Solar, she had thought there would be a lot of different chemicals and protocols to review, but she hadn't realized that the actual fabrication of the solar cells occurred overseas. That part of the manufacturing process was very similar to semiconductor manufacturing—the process of making computer chips—and required the use of clean rooms with air scrubbers and water purifiers to ensure environmental standards were maintained. What was going on, at least at the plant in Austin, was the final assembly of the solar panels, which, fortunately, had minimal risk for toxic exposures as far as she could tell, but she could verify that when she met with Anand again.

She opened up her portfolio. The papers were all jumbled since she had dropped them on the floor earlier in the day, so she began sifting and sorting, thinking about questions she could ask Anand and what she might use for her term paper, when she found a slip of paper that wasn't hers. It was from a notepad with the CS Solar letterhead on it, and scrawled in pencil were the words: Raul didn't have to die.

What is this? She was flummoxed. What did this even mean? And how did this get into her portfolio?

Sam thought through the visit to the plant. How did that get in her portfolio? And then she remembered the young man with dark hair, shaved on the sides, who had bumped into her. She had recognized him, and at the time, she could not remember where she had seen him before. And then it hit her—he was at the Garzas' house the night Mrs. Garza asked her to look into Raul's death. The young man had been standing in the front yard when Sam had walked up to the house with Cynthia.

What did this mean?

A rap at the door signaled Millie's arrival, and Sam quickly pushed the papers back into her portfolio.

When Sam answered, Millie stood at the door, her arms full with a banker's box. Sam took the box from her and invited her in.

"Thanks so much for bringing this," Sam said, although part of her wondered why Millie couldn't have just left her mother's things at her father's house. In Sam's mind, it would always be her mother's house too.

"You're quite welcome, darling." Millie hugged Sam after she placed the box on the floor next to her desk. "How have you been?"

"Busy. You know, seeing lots of patients. But I did get to tour a solar panel factory today."

"That's interesting. What brought that about?"

"Well, as I'm learning in the world of workers' comp, our clinic has a sales force that sells drug screening packages to employers, with the hope that they'll send their employees to us if they get injured."

"Huh, I never really thought about that before," Millie said as she sat on the couch. Sam was hoping she would just drop off the box and leave, but obviously that was not her plan. Millie patted the spot next to her, beckoning Sam to sit.

The door was still ajar, since she hadn't expected Millie to stay, so Sam rushed over to secure it closed before joining Millie, but she sat in the chair next to her, instead of on the couch.

"Now," Millie said, clasping her hands together in her lap, "I know this thing between your father and me must be a bit…awkward for you. I want you to know that in no way do I want to try to replace your mother."

Then why did you remove my mother's things from her home? Sam thought. Instead, she slowly nodded once.

"And I want you to know that despite your father's… attitude toward your career, I honestly believe you are an amazing young woman, and you should be proud of everything you've already accomplished."

"Thanks." Sam smirked. "If you're trying to win me over, it just might be working," she said, even though she thought these were empty platitudes.

The older woman took Sam's hand, her face completely serious. "I know how hard it must be for you. Medicine has changed enormously over the last few decades." Her eyes took on a distant look. "My late husband, Chuck, was a general practitioner. He was a bit older than me, so he had started practicing back before all these specialty boards gained so much power. After he graduated from medical school, he served in the Air Force and became a flight surgeon. You only needed one year of postgraduate training back then, and frankly, they counted all the work he did while serving in the military as on-the-job training. We married and settled down near Marble Falls, back before it became a big retirement area, and he treated the whole town. He did everything—delivering babies, performing minor surgeries—he was a true country doctor."

Sam was astonished at how much Millie was opening up to her. She truly didn't know what to say.

"So my point is," Millie went on, "despite how hard your father has been on you—and believe me, I've heard it all from him, and I'm trying to temper his views on this— I'm really proud of you. And I'm so glad you've picked yourself up and found a path forward, even if it isn't the 'ideal' path or one that everyone expects."

Wow. How can this woman, who hardly knows me, be proud of me?

"I know your father has been tough on you. He's a... let's just say he's a difficult man sometimes. But he means well."

Sam regarded Millie, her curiosity pushing her to ask, "Then why do you love him? How could you love him?"

"There's more to him than you know." The distant look returned to Millie's eyes. "I love him because he was there for me when Chuck died. And I was there for him—"

Another knock at the door. Sam wanted to ask Millie what she meant. And when had her husband died? Had she really known her father that long? "When you say—"

The knock came again. Sam raised her eyebrows and got up from the couch. The moment had passed, and Millie stood now too, gathering up her purse, not ready to reveal any more.

Sam opened the door. It was James.

Well, it was probably best that she didn't dig too deeply into what had happened between Millie and her father. At least not with Millie. Sam couldn't tell if she was just trying to flatter her or if she was truly being supportive. She seemed to be. But if Sam wanted to dive further into the past, she should probably ask her father, not Millie.

"Sorry to interrupt," James said when he saw Millie.

"No, darling, that's okay. I was just about to leave. You must be James."

Sam and James both looked at Millie, surprised she knew who he was.

Millie leaned toward Sam, placing her hand on her shoulder. "Your father is more observant than you think, and he does talk about you incessantly." To James, she extended her hand and said with a smile, "I'm Millie."

James shook her hand. "Soon to be Sam's stepmom, I presume?"

"That would be correct," Millie said, then glanced at Sam. "If Sam will have me."

"I…I…" Sam stammered. "Of course?"

"Oh, darling." Millie flapped her hand at Sam. "I'm just teasing you. Let's schedule that spa day soon."

After Millie left, James said, "That was…interesting."

"I think she's trying to butter me up." Sam scrunched her nose. "However, she really does act like she thinks my father is too hard on me."

"That is definitely true."

"She opened up a little about her late husband. He only had an intern year before practicing for his full career as a general practitioner in Marble Falls." Sam wiped her hands over her face. "I don't know. I'm so mixed up right now. She says she doesn't want to replace Mom, but then she brings some of Mom's things over. It's like she's removing some of Mom from the house. And then she admits my dad can be…well, you know." She sighed. "So I asked her why she even loves him, and she said he was there for her when her husband passed away. I don't know how long ago that was, but it surely was before Mom died. So there's something else going on. I'm even more sure now that they had an affair." She waved her hand. "But enough about that situation. What's up? Why'd you come over?"

Excitement popped on James's face. "The paper wants me to do a profile of one of the companies expanding here in Austin!"

"That's great, James! So they want you to write as well as be a photographer?"

"Well, this gives me more options, and now I can make use of my English degree. They'd prefer it if I had a journalism degree, and maybe they're taking advantage of me. A profile is a bit of a puff piece, but it's a start. They gave me a list of companies and told me to choose one. I suppose it will also depend on which companies are willing to let me do an interview and all that, but who would want to pass up free publicity?"

"That's true. A write-up in the paper sounds like something many companies would pay for."

He gave her a conspiratorial look. "Honestly, a lot of companies hire PR firms to do just that."

"Do you have the list with you?"

James dug into his pocket and pulled out a folded sheet of paper. After he smoothed it out, Sam peered over his shoulder and scanned the list. She didn't recognize most of the names, but CS Solar was there, in the middle of the list.

"Hey, that's the company I visited today," she said, pointing to the name.

"I was considering that one, especially since solar and renewables are a huge area of interest right now." He frowned. "But why were you there? I thought you usually spend your day at the clinic."

Sam went on to explain the situation to James, that ObraCare needed to close the contracts for employee drug testing so there would be a somewhat guaranteed stream of patients. "It's kind of a double-edged sword, I suppose. I don't really want anyone getting hurt at work, but if they do, I'm there to take care of them."

"So if there's a sales guy, why did they need you there?"

She shrugged. "Honestly, I don't know. My boss called

me last week and instructed me to go. But I just felt like a sales prop."

"Huh. That doesn't seem like a good use of your time."

"I agree, but I gotta do what my boss tells me." And then Sam had an idea. "You know how I told you about how a patient wanted me to look into her son's death?"

"Yeah," James said, with a sly smile. "And you ran into Dylan at her house."

"Of course you have to bring up Dylan," Sam said, rolling her eyes. She went over to her desk, pulled out the mysterious note from her portfolio, and showed it to James. "I found this just before you came over."

He scanned the note, then looked up at her. "Where did you find it?"

"It was tucked in with my other papers. During the factory tour today, a man bumped into me, and I dropped my portfolio. He helped me pick everything up, and I think he might have slipped it in with the other papers."

"Who was he?"

"I don't know. While I was at the factory, I thought he looked familiar, and I just assumed he was a patient at the clinic. But when I found this, I remembered I had seen him at Mrs. Garza's house after Raul died."

"So you think he knew Raul?"

"It looks that way. Why else would this man have given me this note?"

"That settles it then. I'm doing a profile on CS Solar. Then I'll have an excuse to snoop around and ask questions."

"And while you're at it, see what you can find out about a man named Dale Cooper. He was a total ass to me in the clinic the other day and wouldn't let me take proper care of my patient. He actually ripped up her paperwork in front of me!"

James's mouth dropped open. "How could he do that?"

"He's her supervisor, and I think he didn't want to record her injury." She told him what she had learned about the OSHA 300 log and recordable injuries, then that she saw Dale again at the factory during her visit. "So I'm not sure what happened to Raul, but there's definitely something hinky going on. If nothing else, even if management is saying they want to put employee safety first, Dale is one person who isn't making it a priority."

12

B ack in clinic the next day, Sam saw Mrs. Garza's name on the schedule. She thought the appointment must have been booked before Raul had died and that Mrs. Garza had forgotten to cancel it. But then she saw Cynthia leading her through the clinic work area into an exam room. Sam pulled Cynthia aside after she had left the room.

"I'm surprised to see Mrs. Garza is here. Shouldn't she be home?"

"I agree," Cynthia said. "But Elma says she needs to work—to pay for Raul's funeral."

Sam felt awful that Mrs. Garza was in this situation. She entered the room and found her patient slumped in the chair next to the exam table. She slid the stool over and sat next to Mrs. Garza. "How are you doing…you know, with everything?"

"Not so good, Doctor. I just ache all over. And sometimes I feel so tired, but when I lie down in bed, I don't sleep." Mrs. Garza began to weep. "I just…he's gone. I can't believe he's gone."

Sam grabbed a tissue from the box next to the sink and handed it to Mrs. Garza. "I'm so sorry. You need to go home, to be with your family."

"But I have to work." The older lady dabbed her eyes, then blew her nose. "I need the money."

A pit formed in Sam's stomach. Even more stress for this poor woman in her time of grief.

"There's bound to be a way to help you with the cost."

"Oh, my church has been so supportive, and everyone is pitching in to help, but we are not a rich community. It's getting me most of the way there, but I don't have much, and with all of my other bills, and now Raul isn't around…" Another eye dab. "He helped pay for things too."

Sam didn't know what else to say.

"Please, Doctor. I just need to get back to work. Let me go back so I can make the money I need for everything. If you remove the restrictions, not only will it allow me to return to full duty, but my company will let me work overtime."

"Are you sure? It's perfectly natural to need some time to grieve."

Mrs. Garza nodded. "I know. When Raul's father passed—God rest his soul—I was devastated. Back then, I could stay home. But I can't do that now." She sat up, straightened her clothes, then looked at Sam with determination. "Besides, when I started working again, it helped me heal."

Sam knew that could be the case. Sometimes keeping yourself busy, distracting yourself with work, could help ease the pain and allow healing to continue. Although in Sam's case with her mother's death, while she could perform some basic tasks, she just couldn't deal with the intensity of residency.

She looked at Mrs. Garza, conflicted with what was the best course of action.

"Okay," Sam finally said. "Let's take a look at you and then decide."

But as Sam performed her exam, it was clear that Mrs. Garza was still in pain from her sprained back. Sam palpated her lower back muscles, feeling tightness and knots, the muscles spasming under her fingers. Her range of motion was limited, and when Sam touched Mrs. Garza's arm, she pulled away, as if Sam's hand had shocked her. In fact, all throughout the exam, Mrs. Garza seemed to be a bit hypersensitive, reacting in anticipation a split second before Sam would touch her.

"I'm sorry, Mrs. Garza, but you are still recovering from your injury. I honestly cannot let you go back to regular duty."

Mrs. Garza shook her head in small arcs. "No, no. I have to go back. They won't let me work overtime if I still have restrictions." Her eyes pleaded. "Please, Doctor."

Against Sam's better judgment, she said, "If I do remove the restrictions, do you think you can perform your job functions without any issues?"

"Oh, Doctor, I don't really need those restrictions."

"Are you sure?"

"Yes, Doctor. Before…before Raul died, I was doing everything I normally do at work, even with your restrictions in place."

Sam thought for a moment. She could remove them, and from what she understood, Mrs. Garza stood for several hours each day working on a production line, occasionally having to lift a box of supplies or push a loaded dolly, which is how she hurt her back in the first place. "If I do remove these restrictions, do you think you can avoid lifting or pushing anything heavy?"

Mrs. Garza nodded fervently. "Yes, Doctor. I can always ask Hector—who is much stronger than me—I can always ask Hector if I need anything; I usually do. It's just that the day I hurt my back, he was out."

"And what if he is out again?"

"I'll find someone else. It was stupid of me to think I could have moved that dolly by myself."

"Okay." Sam sighed. "I'll remove the restrictions, but if you have any problems at all, you come right back here and let me know."

"Can I keep going to physical therapy? It really does help."

"I believe so, but that really depends on your company. Some companies let employees keep going to PT after they're back at full duty, but others assume that once an employee is off restrictions, they no longer need PT."

"I will try to keep going then."

"But Mrs. Garza, it seems like this isn't going to solve everything for you. Is there something else I can do?"

Mrs. Garza grabbed Sam's hands. "Please, Doctor, something happened to Raul. I just know it. Can't you do something to find out?"

Sam lowered her voice. "I talked to Dylan Myers a little more, after I saw him at your home last week."

"Yes, yes. His mother is such a good woman. Raised her sons right."

"Dylan looked at the reports he has access to," Sam said, "but there doesn't seem to be anything unusual."

"But Raul sent me a text message. He wasn't feeling well. He said he had a headache and he was going home." Mrs. Garza dabbed at her eyes. "That place where he worked—he said they were always pushing too hard, and it wasn't always safe."

"And you said he worked at CS Solar?"

"Yes."

"That's interesting, because I was just there. They really seem like they want to do more to improve the safety of their work environment, to do more to help their employees." Then she thought about Dale. "At least, that's what the manager said."

"Of course they would make it seem that way. Raul told me the bosses would say all the right words, but when it came to fixing things, they would drag their feet. Plus, Raul would never admit it, but you know how boys are—how men are." Mrs. Garza picked at the wadded tissue in her hands. "They've always got to show their machismo. And if Raul said he wasn't feeling well, then it must really have been bad. What if he crashed his car because he passed out from something he breathed in at work?"

Sam thought for a moment. It was something to consider. Although, from what she had read during her preparation for the sales visit, an exposure would be more likely if the plant fabricated the individual solar cells. There were a variety of toxic chemicals used in that process. The plant in Austin only did final assembly of solar panels, and it didn't seem like there were very many substances that could cause that level of harm. But she was too new at this to be sure. It was something she could ask Anand about when she met with him.

Then she remembered the note. "Do you know the name of a young man about Raul's age? His hair is shaved on the sides, and he has a Texans tattoo. I saw him at your house."

Mrs. Garza thought for a moment. "That's probably Ernesto. He went to school with Raul. Why do you ask?"

"I saw him at the plant—literally bumped into him, actually—and I dropped my papers. When I got home, I found a note that I think he put in my portfolio. It said Raul didn't have to die."

Mrs. Garza's eyes widened. "See! I told you."

Sam regretted telling her about the note as soon as she saw hope spark in the woman's eyes. "Okay, Mrs. Garza. I believe you. But I don't know what to do about it. It doesn't sound like there's much to go on." She patted Mrs. Garza's hand, but this time she didn't react like Sam's touch caused pain.

Mrs. Garza tugged at her ear, then said, "Maybe you should talk to Ernesto. Since he worked with Raul, he would know more about how things were at the plant."

"Uh, sure, I suppose I could do that." Sam really didn't want to go down this rabbit hole, but the more she thought about it, the more she realized that Mrs. Garza's health depended on it. If she couldn't gain closure from her son's death—which Sam still believed was probably just a terrible, tragic accident—then it would hold her back from fully recovering from her injury.

13

El Morado was located in a strip mall near a cluster of industrial parks on the north side of Austin. Sam and James entered the crowded bar, nodding at the linebacker-sized man by the front door as they walked past. Tejano music, with plenty of accordion, blared from the band on a small stage at one end of the room.

Sam was glad James had agreed to come with her as several men ogled her. *Why does it always have to be like this?* she thought. She had not dressed in an alluring way; in fact, she was still wearing her work clothes: comfortable slacks and a conservative blouse. Many of the women were wearing skimpy clothes to show off their curves, with heavily applied makeup, like peacocks on display to find their mates. Except in the bird world, it's the males who have to put on the display to draw attention. Of course there were plenty of men doing the same, just not with garish colors. Instead, they wore tight jeans, snakeskin boots, and black Stetson hats.

Definitely not Sam's type of place, but she needed to talk to Ernesto.

They made their way to the bar. James squeezed between two men with embroidered cowboy shirts who could have been twins. He scooted closer to one of the men, who seemed happy to have a reason to move in on his female companion. Sam slipped into the small space James had created. She looked down the bar, cluttered with longnecks and small wooden bowls of salty snacks.

"Is that him?" James asked, tipping his head toward someone behind Sam.

Sam shifted her position so she could see. Ernesto stood at the other end of the bar filling drink orders. "Yeah, that's him." She opened her purse to pull out the note while James raised his hand to signal Ernesto.

As Ernesto approached, he squinted; then recognition came across his face when he saw Sam. "I was wondering why a couple of *gringos* were here, but you're the doc that was at Raul's house."

"And we ran into each other at CS Solar." Sam slid the note across the bar. "Did you give me this note?"

Ernesto shook his head, but his eyes betrayed his denial.

Someone down the bar called for him. He glanced over and held up a finger. "Look. I'll talk to you about Raul, but I'm kinda busy right now." He checked his watch. "It should slow down soon, in probably a half hour or so. If you stick around, I can talk to you then."

"We'll do that," Sam said.

She and James found a cluster of booths away from the stage, but all were full, so they hovered nearby until a group left one of the tables to head to the dance floor.

They slid into the booth, the purple vinyl seats still warm from the previous occupants, the table sticky with puddles of spilt beer and brown glass longneck bottles, scattered like the oversized pieces of a board game.

"Do you want anything to drink?" James asked.

"No," Sam said, looking around at the bodies writhing on the dance floor, bathed in purple lights flashing to the beat. "I'll pass, but you can get something if you want."

"I can't. I'm on call in case any big news stories happen tonight." He smirked. "Makes me feel like a doctor."

"It can be exciting at first," Sam said. "I hope it stays that way for you."

James used the back of his forearm to slide the empty beer bottles to the edge of the table and started to put his elbows down as he leaned forward, but seemed to think better of it. Instead, he planted his arms on either side of him, anchoring his hands on the seat as he leaned forward and said, "So I did some digging on that fellow you mentioned—Dale Cooper."

"Oh, you did?" Sam said, raising her eyebrows. "What did you find?"

"Not much, but there were a few articles where he was mentioned—assuming it's the same Dale Cooper." He leaned to one side to pull his phone out of his jeans pocket, then straightened up and tapped his phone a few times. He showed Sam a picture. "Is this him?"

"Yep, that's him," Sam said. In the photo, Dale stood with a group of demonstrators on the lawn of the Capitol. "So what did you find?"

"Well, the first article I found was about a hit-and-run accident," James said as he put his phone in his lap.

"He hit someone with his car?"

"No, his daughter was hit and killed by a drunk driver."

Sam sat back, bringing her hand to her chest. "Oh, no. How long ago was this?"

"About two years ago. She was on Sixth Street, out with some friends on a Friday night, and this car ran into her as she was crossing the street. She was taken to Brackenridge, but she died later that night."

"That's awful." Sam shook her head. "Did they ever find out who did it?"

"Fortunately, her friends got the license plate, and the cops tracked the car down to the owner. But he told the police he had lent the car to his cousin who turned out to be an undocumented immigrant."

"How old was she?"

"She was twenty-two."

Sam shook her head again as she started to see Dale in a new light. What a terrible thing to experience—the death of a child.

"But here's the thing," James continued. "His name shows up again in some articles from later that year when the legislature was considering the bill to allow police officers to ask about immigration status. There are a few articles including quotes from Dale where he talks about his daughter's death as a reason he supports the bill."

"Why? Would it have made a difference?"

"Apparently, the guy who killed his daughter had been stopped the week before she died for a traffic violation, and Dale said that if the bill had been a law at that time, his daughter would still be alive."

Buzzing came from James's side of the booth, and he picked his phone up out of his lap. His eyes grew as he looked at it. "I need to take this," he said. "It's the paper."

"Of course."

He answered, then after a series of "yeses," he said, "I can be there in ten minutes."

After he hung up, Sam asked, "What was that about?"

"There's an apartment fire, and they need me to shoot some pictures for the morning edition." He hesitated.

"Then you should go. It's your job, right?"

"Yeah." James hesitated again, scanning the room. It was still fairly packed, but some groups were starting to thin out, heading home for the night. "You going to be okay here?"

Sam waved her hand. "I'll be fine." She saw Ernesto was still busy at the bar, but instead of the crowd being shoulder room only, there were now just a few couples scattered about. "I'm sure he'll be done in a bit. I'll grab an Uber after I talk to him."

James slid out of the booth, glancing around the room once more as he stood. "You're sure about this?"

"Yes. This is a big opportunity for you, to show the paper they can count on you." Sam flipped her hand in a shooing motion. "Go."

He nodded once, then bustled his way to the front exit.

Within seconds, Sam regretted telling James to go. As soon as he disappeared through the door, a couple of young men standing at a nearby high top table, one with a cowboy hat, leered at her.

14

___

Sam looked toward the bar. *What is taking so long?* There were only a few people left lingering around, but Ernesto was deep in conversation with a blushing young woman. The band packed up as music with a slower beat played overhead.

Sam started to slide out of the booth; she would sit at the bar as she waited for Ernesto to finish up.

But the duo who had been eying her slinked closer. The one with the cowboy hat tipped it, as if he were being courteous, even though his swagger and smug smile said otherwise.

"What's a pretty little lady like you doing here all alone?" Cowboy Hat said. He eased into the booth beside her, blocking her way out.

His accomplice said nothing as he slid onto the opposite bench. He tugged on the ends of his bolo tie nervously. The other booths around them were now empty, with the remaining patrons gathering near the bar and the exit.

Would Ernesto—or anyone else—notice this encroachment? The only way she could get a clear view of the room would be to lean into the presumptuous man next to her. She rested her hand on her purse on the seat alongside her leg.

Cowboy Hat put his hand on her thigh as he leaned closer, the sour stench of cigarettes on his breath. "Why don't you come with us? We'll show you a good time."

A frown flashed on Bolo Tie's face, but when Cowboy Hat glanced at him, it disappeared.

Sam fumbled blindly with the zipper on her purse, keeping her eye on Cowboy Hat. His foul breath made her nauseous.

"Or we could have some fun right now," he said as he grabbed her chest and squeezed her breast.

Sam raised her hand and pressed the trigger on the pepper spray she pulled from her purse. She hit her target square in the eyes.

Both men scrambled out of the booth, with Cowboy Hat falling on the floor, his hands covering his eyes. "You bitch!"

She aimed the pepper spray at Bolo Tie, his eyes now wide with fear. He held up his hands and backed away.

Ernesto was now next to them, along with one of the bouncers from the front door. They pulled the man up off the floor, his face red, his eyes tearing. "What happened?" Ernesto asked.

"That bitch sprayed me in the face," Cowboy Hat snarled.

"Take him over to the bar and tell Amanda to get some milk from the store on the corner," Ernesto told the bouncer. "She needs to soak a wash cloth to put on his eyes."

The bouncer nodded, then dragged Cowboy Hat away. Bolo Tie trailed behind.

By then, Sam had escaped the booth and was ready to leave. It had been a mistake coming here.

"You don't fuck around, do you?" Ernesto said.

"No, I don't. They trapped me, and that man grabbed me."

"Amanda has called the police. They should be here any minute." He looked around. "You really cleared out the place. What happened to the guy who was with you?"

"He got called away, but I decided to stay so I could talk to you." Sam narrowed her eyes. Might as well find out what she could, before the cops arrived. "Did you slip me that note?"

Ernesto flattened his lips, then nodded.

"What did you mean that Raul didn't have to die?"

"The day he died, he left work early because he wasn't feeling well."

Sam nodded. "That's what his mom said."

"Raul was feeling bad that day...I mean *really* bad," he said with a grimace. "He threw up a few times, so our boss told him to go home. Raul worked next to that bathroom —you know, the one that's being repaired? Did you see it?"

Sam thought back to the tour, and she remembered there was caution tape blocking the entrance to the restroom on the factory floor. "Next to the pits, right?"

"That's right. We'd been telling our boss for weeks there was something wrong. It stank something awful, like rotten eggs. But he did nothing." He shook his head in frustration. "Then right after Raul dies, they finally decide to take care of it."

"What was wrong?" she asked.

"There was a sewage backup."

"So you think Raul got exposed to something?"

"Maybe." He shook his head again as he wrinkled his

nose. "Man, that bathroom reeked. Sometimes when I used it, I'd get dizzy."

A woman came over and tapped Ernesto on the shoulder. "The police are here."

At the front of the building, two officers stood by the door speaking to the bouncer. One looked like he had just left the military, his hair cropped with a buzz cut. The other had darker hair that was a little longer. Something about his gestures as he spoke seemed familiar.

After a few moments, the bouncer looked up at Sam and pointed in her direction. When the cops turned to follow his gaze, she realized the dark-haired cop was Dylan.

When he saw Sam, he lowered his head with a slight shake. He leaned over to his partner, said something, then walked toward her and Ernesto while his partner went to the bar.

Once he was closer, he said, "Sam. What's going on here?"

"That man attacked me," Sam said.

"I'm sure they weren't going to hurt you," Ernesto said.

She frowned at him. "You didn't have his hands pawing you. I had to defend myself."

"Where did he touch you?" Dylan asked.

"He put his hand on my leg, then he grabbed my breast."

Dylan nodded. "That's assault. Do you want to file a report?"

"You mean press charges?" Sam asked.

"No." He smiled slightly. "That's what they say in movies and TV shows. Only the DA's office can decide to press charges."

As Dylan gave the explanation, his partner had come

over to join them. A silver tag on his chest bore the name Walsh in all caps.

"Mr. Ramirez says he wants to file a complaint," Walsh reported.

Dylan shook his head. "Dr. Jenkins was defending herself." He looked up at a camera mounted near the ceiling with a perfect view of the booth. To Ernesto, he said, "Does that camera work?"

"Yes," Ernesto answered.

"How long do you keep the recordings?"

"A month."

"So it wouldn't be a problem accessing it?"

"No."

"Then I don't think that man's argument will hold up."

Walsh nodded. "Got it." Then he walked off.

Dylan turned to Sam. "So the question is, do you want to file a report?" He tipped his head toward the camera. "With the video recording, the prosecutor would have a decent case."

Sam looked over at the bar. Cowboy Hat—Mr. Ramirez—glared at her as best he could with his eyes still watery and red. She sighed. What was she thinking even coming to this place? "No, I don't want to file a report."

Dylan nodded. "I'll be right back."

He headed over to the bar, then spent the next few minutes scolding Mr. Ramirez, waving his finger a few times, and pointing at the camera in the corner by the booth. But the Ramirez fellow remained defiant, a smirk on his face with his chest puffed up.

As she watched the drama play out, Sam took the opportunity to ask Ernesto a few more questions.

"So you told Dale about the bathroom? When was this?"

"Yeah. We started complaining a few weeks ago. At

first, it just smelled really bad, but then after a while, I'd get a headache almost every time I went in there."

Sam thought about Miss Morales. She said she had just used the restroom and felt light-headed right before she tripped and twisted her ankle. Sam would have to ask her if it was that particular restroom she had used.

"But nothing was done about it until after Raul died?"

"That's right."

"How do you think this is related to Raul's death?"

"I'm not sure…but it had to be something at work. He said he'd be fine in the morning, but by the afternoon, he'd feel like crap." He shrugged. "Plus, he got sick."

Sam pressed her lips together as she thought. There may have been something going on, but what could she do? And what Ernesto told her was rather vague.

"You don't believe me," Ernesto said.

"It's not that I don't believe you, but how can it be shown that Raul's death was a direct result of something that happened at work?"

Ernesto hesitated and glanced in Dylan's direction. Then he said, "I can prove it."

Sam raised her eyebrows. "Okay. I'm supposed to go back to CS Solar next week. Can we talk then?"

Ernesto nodded as Dylan approached again with his partner.

"Everything's all cleared up," Dylan said.

Across the room behind him, Ramirez and his friend slinked out the door past the bouncer.

"I've got to close up the bar," Ernesto said. "Do you still need me?"

The two police officers exchanged a quick glance. Then Walsh said, "No. You can go about your business."

Ernesto hurried off, like a rabbit scampering away from foxes.

Dylan scowled at Sam and said, "What the hell are you doing here?"

"I needed to talk to Ernesto."

"Why?"

Sam pulled out the note from her purse and handed it to Dylan. "He gave this to me, and I wanted to find out what it meant."

Walsh looked over Dylan's shoulder as he read the note. "Who's Raul?"

"It's a long story," Dylan said. "He died in a car accident, and his mother—who happens to know my mom from church—thinks something nefarious happened. But there was nothing unusual on autopsy. He probably just got distracted." He flicked the piece of paper in his hand. "Stuff like this doesn't help the situation." He looked up at Sam. "When did you get this?"

Sam explained how she'd gone to CS Solar and how she'd bumped into Ernesto and dropped her papers. "I recognized him and thought he was one of my patients at first, but then I realized I'd seen him at Mrs. Garza's house. When she came for her appointment yesterday, I asked who he was. She told me he has to work two jobs to make ends meet, and this is where I could find him in the evenings."

Dylan rolled his eyes. "So Mrs. Garza knows about this note? This will just give her another reason to bug me." He sighed. "What did he say?"

"That Raul kept feeling bad at work and that he threw up right before he left the day he died," she said. "I know that's pretty vague, but it might be why Mrs. Garza tricked him into bringing her to my clinic so I could take a look at him." Then she had a horrible thought. "But if there really was something making him sick, I must have missed the diagnosis."

"Hang on," Dylan said. "You told me his eyes were red, like he'd been smoking weed."

"Yeah, or that he just had bad allergies. It was only a brief interaction with him, but if I missed something big…" Sam closed her eyes and took in a deep breath. "I just feel awful that I didn't talk to him more, that I didn't ask him more questions." She shook her head. "I don't know if the stuff at work had anything to do with his death, but what if he had a condition that caused him to crash his car? What if I could have prevented his death?"

Dylan's features softened. "Hey, it's not your fault." He glanced over his shoulder at Ernesto clearing empty bottles and wiping down the bar. "And don't be fooled by Ernesto. He's…let's just say he's not one to be trusted."

The radios clipped to the officers' shoulders squawked simultaneously. Walsh tapped Dylan's elbow with the back of his hand. "We need to go."

Walsh took a step toward the exit, but Dylan held up his hand and stayed with Sam. "We'll walk you out to your car."

Sam pulled out her phone and started tapping. "Actually, I need to call an Uber."

"How did you get here?" Dylan said with his brows furrowed.

"James came with me." She made an ironic smile. "To keep guys like them away from me. But then he got a call to take photos of an apartment fire for the paper."

Walsh nodded. "We heard the call over the air." The radios squawked again. "Let's roll."

"We can wait until the Uber driver gets here," Dylan said, "just in case those bozos are out there waiting, getting ideas."

Sam glanced at her phone. "The driver is pulling up now."

Once Sam was safely in the Uber car, the cops drove off. And Dylan had been right: as the driver pulled out of the mostly empty parking lot, Sam caught a glimpse of two figures leaning up against the building, the streetlight barely illuminating them, one with, and one without, a cowboy hat.

15

As the car turned out of the parking lot, Nico ran his fingers down the strings of his bolo tie. "Man, why'd you have to go after her? I thought we were supposed to be low-key, just keep an eye on Ernesto. But then you had to go after her, and then the cops show up."

Ramirez turned to Nico and pointed his finger. "You don't have anything to worry about. Hey, she was a sweet piece of ass and all alone. I was just trying to have some fun." He put his arm around Nico and lightly punched him in his ribs. "Don't tell me you haven't gone after *chichi* like that before?"

Nico blushed as he looked away. No, he hadn't been quite as aggressive as Ramirez had been, but he wasn't a saint either.

"Look, the *jefe* says we just need to keep doing what he asks for a couple more weeks. Then we'll get our payout."

Nico had no idea who this guy was that gave Ramirez the job. He hoped it wasn't someone in the Syndicate, since Ramirez and Ernesto had been involved with them.

He'd tried to stay clear of any illegal activity, but he didn't have a lot of options since he lost his job. Sure, he was picking up extra shifts when he could at Comida Rapida, but he was only making minimum wage dishing out tacos to grumpy customers.

Ramirez said he would pay Nico enough to cover his rent for the rest of the year, and maybe he'd have enough left over to make it a nice Christmas.

"And all he wants us to do is tail Ernesto?"

"That's it. Nothing more."

16

After the incident at El Morado, Sam chastised herself for going there in the first place. *What was I thinking?* She had plenty of other things to keep her busy, and she didn't need to put herself unnecessarily in danger.

She got through the rest of the week in clinic without any difficult cases. She could see why many of the doctors working for ObraCare were semiretired—the vast majority of the workers' comp cases were low acuity and proceeded along an expected path with good results. The complicated cases were few and far between, and the catastrophic cases usually went to the emergency room.

Since she had an occupational health exam she had to take before Monday, she spent most of the weekend rewatching the lectures and working through extra assignments. The hours of studying left her confident enough to complete the test Sunday afternoon, a full day before the deadline.

The only break she had from studying was Saturday evening, when she and Alex went to his friend's house to watch *Avengers: Infinity War*. His friend had just installed a new sound system, so he wanted to show it off to Alex, who was duly impressed. Figures. Men were still boys, just with more expensive toys.

Sam wasn't really into comic books and superheroes, but she had to admit the movie wasn't bad. And that villain was quite unnerving—he thought *he* was the unappreciated hero. But how could you be the good guy if you eliminate half the universe?

By the time Sam got to work on Monday, her concerns about Raul's death had faded. But then she saw the appointment with Anand on her calendar.

Before she left, she checked with Jerry to make sure he was okay covering patients in case she ran a little late coming back from her lunch break. "The industrial hygienist wants me to go over some of the health and safety protocols with him," she explained.

"Sure, Doc," Jerry said. "No problem. It seems like you're really getting into this occupational medicine stuff. You should become a consultant yourself." He raised an eyebrow. "Or at least you should charge for your time."

"Yeah, maybe I should. Or maybe," she said with a smirk, "I could get a cut of the commission Kyle gets from this deal, since I'm helping him sell it."

"That'll be the day," he said, shaking his head. "A sales guy sharing his commission."

When Sam arrived at CS Solar, Alvera was on the phone, but she put the caller on hold as Sam approached the desk. "Are you here to see Mr. Allen?"

"No, I'm here to see Anand Dhawan."

"Just one moment." Alvera picked up the phone and punched in an extension number. After a few moments, she pressed the switch hook to disconnect as she rested the handset on her shoulder. "It appears he's not at his desk.

Let me check on the floor." She punched a couple more buttons, and Sam could hear a tone, followed by Alvera's voice amplified on the PA system, muffled through the wall behind the desk. "Anand Dhawan, come to the lobby for a visitor."

"Please have a seat," Alvera said, motioning toward the chairs behind Sam. "He should be here shortly."

No sooner had Sam sat down on an elegant, if not very comfortable chair, one that seemed more like it belonged in a contemporary art museum than a business, Sam heard someone say, "Dr. Jenkins."

She looked up, expecting Anand, but found Henry instead. She stood to shake his hand, a little awkwardly since the chair was low with no arms to help herself up.

"To what do we owe the pleasure of your presence today?" he said.

"I'm meeting with Anand to go over some of your health and safety protocols."

"Fantastic. I love how you're proactive." He gave her an appraising look. "You know, many companies need help developing these protocols. You might have a future if you ever wanted to leave medicine."

Sam nodded. Perhaps Jerry was right; there could be consulting opportunities for her. "I just want to make sure we're keeping everyone healthy. Plus, if I know more about the work environment of my patients, I'll be better prepared when I treat them for any possible injuries."

Henry grinned. "That's great. We can scale safely if you work closely with Anand. And I think your clinical insight will help us anticipate any issues we might have, so we can prevent injuries before they happen."

"That would be even better than treating them after the fact."

"I'm glad we can count on you and ObraCare." He

glanced at his watch. "I'd love to keep chatting, but I've got my next meeting in a few minutes. Please let me know if there is anything you need."

As Henry rushed off, Anand appeared in the hallway next to Alvera's desk.

"Thanks so much for coming back," he said.

"It's not a problem." Sam gave a half shrug. "It gives me a break from the monotony of the clinic."

Anand motioned toward the conference room just off the lobby, where Kyle had given his sales presentation the week before. "Let's have a seat in here, and we can go over some of these protocols," he said as he raised the thick binder in his arms.

"I'll try to help as best I can. Frankly, I'm sure you know much more about OSHA's requirements than I do," Sam said as she followed him. She had hoped they would go further into the building so she could have a chance to look for Ernesto, but this would have to do for now.

"But you understand the clinical implications better than me," Anand said. "You can provide perspective on the consequences of safety violations." He smiled. "And that will give me the arguments I need if I get any push-back when I ask for budget increases."

They went over several of the protocols, which Sam was somewhat familiar with from studying the dry pages of the US federal code for OSHA. For each, Anand would explain what the company was doing to mitigate the risk of injury, and then he would ask Sam to explain the clinical conditions mentioned in the regulations.

"You're too modest," Anand said at one point. "You know these OSHA regs pretty well."

"That's because I had an assignment to read them last week," Sam said.

He furrowed his brow. "An assignment? Are you taking classes?"

"Yeah, I'm working on my master's in public health."

His face brightened. "Oh, that's great! I've been thinking about enrolling in a program." He grimaced as he motioned toward the back of the building. "But I've been a little busy here, and it doesn't seem like it's going to let up anytime soon."

"Just curious, but why are you interested in getting an MPH?"

"Well," he said, looking a little bashful, "I might pursue public office someday." He flicked a page edge in the binder. "I figured if I learned more about policymaking in an area close to what I do here, it'd be easier for me to understand how the legislative process works."

"What a noble thing to do, to go into public service," Sam said. "I'd be happy to answer any questions you might have about the program I'm in."

"Thanks, I might take you up on that offer."

She finally felt comfortable enough with Anand to probe a little, to satisfy her curiosity. "I hope you don't mind my asking, but your accent—it almost sounds Irish, but not quite."

Anand smiled, his white teeth complementing his light sienna skin. "You've got a good ear. I was born in Dublin —my parents had moved there from India—but we came to the US when I was a kid." He shrugged. "My accent has faded, but it still rears its head, especially when I say certain words, like tornado." The word rolled with soft vowels as he spoke.

"That's a pretty important word here in Texas," Sam said, and they both laughed.

They continued to review a few more protocols, and as they finished Sam said, "It seems like you're following some of the guidance for the semiconductor industry, but not all."

His eyebrows jumped. "You really *do* know a lot of the OSHA regs."

"When I was preparing for the visit last week," she said with a shrug, "I thought you were making solar cells here."

"No, we're just assembling panels. If we had a fab, we would need a whole team to manage safety, and we'd probably have a clinic onsite too." Anand waved his arm toward the factory floor. "There's no way we could fab those cells here in this old building. We'd need a billion-dollar clean room with very stringent criteria to keep particle counts down. But you're right, we do follow some of the semiconductor industry guidelines, mainly those that apply to nonfabrication processing."

"That makes sense," she said. "From what I've read, there are some nasty chemicals used in fabrication, but you don't seem to be using anything too concerning here." As they'd been going over the protocols, she'd been watching for anything that might have caused Raul's symptoms, just to give Mrs. Garza and Ernesto the benefit of the doubt.

"Yes. While we do have some substances with hazardous potential, most of them are much less caustic."

"And I assume you have some kind of training for everyone?"

"Excellent question," he said as he leaned back in his chair. "All new hires have to go through basic safety training, but because of this acquisition, we had everyone repeat it." He frowned. "But it appears that not everyone received training when the company was still Tyson International. In fact, some hired through a work reentry program seemed to have been skipped over."

"What kind of program?"

"The previous owners wanted to take advantage of the tax breaks for hiring convicted felons out on parole."

"Sounds like a good opportunity for them to get a fresh start," Sam said.

"It is a great program, and it's another reason why I'm interested in public policy. But even though we've gained a lot of hardworking talent, and the state provides fidelity bond coverage, our new parent company is concerned about the risk." Anand sighed. "We've had issues with a couple of individuals, so we're no longer participating in it."

"That's too bad," Sam said as she checked the time on her phone. If she left now, she would get back to the clinic right at the end of her lunch break, but she needed to find Ernesto.

"If you have a few minutes, could we walk around on the floor again?" she asked. "There are a couple of things I'd like to check out."

He narrowed his eyes. "Like what, in particular?"

She scrambled to think of something that would sound legitimate. "For instance, I'd like to see how the eye wash stations are positioned relative to the workers who may need them." She gave him a small smile. "You know, things along those lines."

Anand crossed his arms and put on a poker face. "Sure, we can do that. But I assure you, everything is located where it should be."

Sam held her hands up. "I'm sure it is." She paused, trying to find a way to convince him to take her out to the floor. "But sometimes, when a patient comes to the clinic, it helps to visualize where they work—you know, what their environment is like—so I can understand the mechanism of injury."

He didn't respond immediately, so Sam pushed on.

"Plus, I'm just curious, and..." She faltered for a moment, then said in a quieter voice, "And honestly, I was a bit overwhelmed last week, seeing it all for the first time. You know, sometimes it helps to see things again."

Anand nodded. "Very well then. Follow me."

They walked out to the manufacturing floor, and Sam tried to absorb it all. She'd been telling the truth about being overwhelmed—since it wasn't as unfamiliar as it'd been before, she could see the reasoning for the placement of different pieces of equipment now. She also scanned around the area for Ernesto. She was hoping they could find some way to talk.

"We have an eye wash station over here," Anand said as he pointed to the middle of a wall. "So it's easy to access from either end of the line, and it's conveniently located near the work locations where employees are at highest risk for exposure."

Sam nodded, maybe a little too enthusiastically.

"And of course," he said, giving her a strange look, "we require workers to wear goggles in those positions."

As Anand showed her more of the safety features in the plant, Sam tried to listen in earnest, because what she had said before was true, that she did want to know more. But she also continued to look around for Ernesto. She finally spotted him heading toward the back of the building. She drifted closer to him even as Anand tried to lead her in the opposite direction.

Anand motioned toward a hallway. "Let's go this way so I can show you where we keep our PPE."

"Just a moment," she said, raising a finger. "I see an old patient of mine, and I just want to check on him."

She walked closer to Ernesto and spoke in a lower voice. "You said you had proof that Raul's death was related to something going on here. What do you have?"

Fortunately, Anand had bought the patient spiel and kept his distance.

Ernesto subtly pointed his finger toward the back wall of the building. "You need to see where he worked—in the pit between me and the bathroom."

"And what did he do there?"

"Same as me. He inspected solar panels to make sure there were no defects, right before final test." Ernesto guided Sam closer to the pits in front of two oversized garage doors.

Sam looked back and saw Anand trailing behind them.

They stopped at the edge of the pit next to the restroom, which was still cordoned off with yellow caution tape. Ernesto put his hand on the railing and discreetly tipped his head. "Down there. There's cracks in the concrete."

The pit was not in the best condition, and the cracks, while not huge, traversed the length of the pit wall closest to the restroom. There was a small amount of concrete floor between the edge of the pit and the wall of the restroom, about five feet wide. "Okay, so what does that mean?"

"I don't know." Ernesto shrugged. "But that bathroom is backed up. Maybe that had something to do with it."

Could this have been the source of Raul's symptoms? Possibly. But headaches and nausea are nonspecific. Anything could have caused them. She'd need to do some research.

By then, Anand was lurking closer.

"Okay, thanks." Sam put her hand on Ernesto's shoulder; then she said in a slightly louder voice, "I'm so glad you're doing better."

"I'll get you more proof," Ernesto whispered, then walked to his station, a matching pit next to the one they had been inspecting.

"You're pretty dedicated to your patients," Anand said as he joined Sam at the railing. Then he frowned. "But I don't remember Ernesto having an injury. I'm notified of all cases since I'm the safety officer."

"He wasn't a workers' comp patient," she said. "We also see urgent care patients in the clinic." She tilted her head. "But I really shouldn't have told you he was a patient at all."

He nodded in understanding.

"Anyway, it's always great when I can see someone after they've been back to their normal lives. With urgent care," she lamented, "I don't have the continuity that a primary care doctor has, and I wonder how patients are doing sometimes."

Anand looked down at the pit. "You know, there was a workers' comp case we had earlier this year, just before I was assigned to this site. One of our workers fell into this pit and broke his leg. It was Dale's brother-in-law, now that I think about it. He's still on disability." He tapped his hand on the railing, causing the metal to ring. "So we had to install these to make it safe."

"Ah, that's why these are here," Sam said. "I thought it was strange that the railings blocked the garage doors."

"Yeah, it is, but we never needed to use these pits for vehicle maintenance. When the startup company formed, they got this old building at a steeply discounted rate, and they decided to repurpose these automotive service pits for solar panel inspection. Seemed like a good idea, but most industries avoid using pits like this now." He shook his head. "They're a safety hazard—essentially a confined space with the potential to accumulate hazardous fumes, especially when they're used for automotive maintenance. It's not really an issue with what we do here, but once the technology improved to make lifts safer and less expensive, most auto shops switched over to using those instead of pits."

Sam thought about that for a moment. "You know, now that I think about it, I remember all the service stations having pits when I was growing up. But you don't really see them so much anymore."

"Yep. Lots of regs came down requiring shops to retrofit their pits with safety railings and ventilation systems. And there's a lot of discussion about whether these are technically confined spaces, because then anyone using them would need additional certifications." He looked toward the doors leading to the new manufacturing floor. "Once we get everything set up with the expansion, we can put these pits out of commission for good." Then he shook his head and laughed. "But you probably didn't want to know all this minutiae."

"No, that's okay," Sam said. "I find it interesting to learn why things are the way they are."

They continued walking around, and now that Sam had spoken with Ernesto, she could pay more attention to what Anand was saying. She hadn't really thought too much about what was required to keep a manufacturing facility safe before, but she was glad someone was on top of it.

After they finished, Anand took Sam back to the front lobby. Henry was in the conference room now, pacing back and forth while he spoke to someone on the phone. He looked up and spotted Sam watching him, so he smiled and gave a small wave.

Anand thanked Sam for meeting with him, adding that she was welcome to come back anytime, that he would be happy to answer any questions she might have. She left the building, and as she walked toward her car, she heard her name and turned around. It was James, more dressy than usual in a button-down shirt and slacks along with his camera bag.

"What are you doing here?" Sam said. "Oh, wait, are you working on that profile?"

"Yeah," James said. "I have an interview with Henry Allen."

"He seems like a good guy," she said. "I was meeting with their safety officer. And I got to talk to Ernesto a little bit. He didn't have any hard proof that Raul's death was related to something here at work. Just some speculation about the bathroom next to Raul's workstation. But it has given me some ideas for things to research."

"You'll have to fill me in later," James said as he peered at his watch. "I need to get inside for that interview. Any prying you want me to do?"

"Yeah. There's a new owner and new investors for this company. Anand Dhawan is the safety officer, and he hasn't been here very long. And Henry is pretty new too. Maybe you could find out more about them."

"Will do," James said. He turned and entered the building.

17

Although Ernesto had acted like he had evidence concerning Raul's death, Sam was underwhelmed by what she had seen. At least Anand agreed to let her come back to the plant if she had more questions, so maybe she could snoop around if she needed to. Could it really be an issue with the bathroom that had made Raul feel sick? And even if it had, was that related to his death?

When Sam got home after an uneventful afternoon in the clinic, she logged on to the virtual classroom to see what she needed to work on for her environmental health course.

Damn. The term paper. She had forgotten about it and had missed the due date to let her instructor know which topic she had chosen to write about.

She should drop this foolishness.

But the lingering possibility that she didn't take care of Raul the way she should have, although he wasn't really her responsibility, kept surfacing in her mind. If she had spent more time with Raul when he was in the clinic, if she had done a more thorough history and physical without his mom in the room, she might have discovered something to prevent his death.

Or perhaps not. Like Dylan had said, it appeared Raul's car accident was just that: an accident. Maybe he'd just been distracted. That—combined with the tragic coincidence that he slammed into a truck with lumber hanging over the edge of the tailgate, smashing into his head—was why he died.

Sam blinked a few times to get back to the task at hand. Pick a topic for her term paper. She scanned the options and then decided; she would write about fatal inhalations in the workplace. That way, she could learn more to see if there was something that had affected Raul, as Ernesto and Mrs. Garza seemed to believe, and she could get her work done for her assignment at the same time.

She sent an email to her instructor informing him of her decision, then ventured on to various websites, orienting herself with the available information. Fortunately, the federal government had amassed a lot of data, and although the overall numbers were not large—around thirty to fifty deaths each year—as she read through some of the case reports, she found almost all of these deaths were preventable tragedies.

After an hour of researching, she stretched her arms over her head, then pushed her chair back from the desk and kicked the box of her mother's things that Millie had brought over. She really should go through this stuff. But did she have the energy to deal with those memories?

Since Millie had mentioned going to that conference with her dad, the one at that fancy ski resort in Colorado, Sam couldn't let go of the thought they may have had an affair.

And why had her father suddenly changed from the distant spouse to the attentive and doting husband? What was that about? Did Sam really want to know?

But maybe…maybe there were answers in this box. She sat on the floor next to her desk and pulled out the banker's box from the footwell, plain and white with red stripes along the side. This cardboard container, so nondescript, held pieces of her mother's past. Who she was.

Sam stared at the box, like it was a foe mocking her, for a good five minutes. She either needed to go through it or put it somewhere else so it wasn't a constant reminder to her. But she had to deal with this at some point. Was she really ready to dig into her parents' past? Did she really want to know these details? Or should she just let it go? Sam wanted to hold on to her mother the way she remembered her.

She finally pulled the cardboard lid off the box and sifted through some of the items—a mix of trinkets and papers. There were lots of things she had given her mother: artwork from school, little notecards with loving phrases, a necklace she had bought for her mother's birthday while she was still in high school. She remembered saving up her babysitting earnings for months to buy that necklace. It wasn't anything fancy, just a simple silver hummingbird on a delicate chain. Her mother had worn that necklace all through her chemo and radiation therapy, until the day she died. And here it was, on top of these papers in a plain cardboard box.

Sam held the necklace in her hand, squeezing it, the hummingbird's beak poking her palm. *I miss you so much.* Grief welled up inside of her, as the tight package of pain she had entombed deep within her cracked open, finally releasing in a rush of tears.

At that moment, Sam hated Millie, hated her for

bringing over her mother's things in such a nonchalant way. Hated her for moving in to her mother's final home. Hated her for gaining her father's affections.

She cried until she seemed to run out of tears, her grief spent for now, her mind empty of thought, and her body empty of feeling as she sat on the floor next to the box like a child. She gently unlatched the chain and strung it around her neck, centering the hummingbird just below the notch at the base of her throat.

Suddenly like a switch, she felt guilty. Millie had seemed like she could sense Sam's discomfort with the situation, and it wasn't Millie's fault that her mother had died. But was it Millie's fault that her father was so distant before her mother got sick?

Then Sam looked in the box again, and the next item on the stack of papers was a legal document. *Jenkins vs. Jenkins*. Her mother had filed for divorce. One month before her cancer diagnosis.

18

Sam washed off her face, the cool water calming her. What should she do, if anything, about the divorce papers? She was staring at her image in the bathroom mirror, noting the features, the angle of her jaw, the structure of her cheekbones, how she could see pieces of her mother in her own face, when there was a knock on the door.

"Hey," James said, once she opened it. "I need your help."

"Sure. What's up?"

"Ana's birthday is Saturday, and I need to get her a gift."

She opened the door wider. "Come on in. I'm sure we can find something online."

James lingered by the entrance. "Well, actually, I was hoping you'd come with me to go shopping. I could get something off Amazon, or wherever, but that's kind of impersonal. Plus, I always wonder who is actually selling some of the stuff online, and whether it's counterfeit or stolen. I'd rather get something from a local place."

"Yeah, I won't argue with you there." She looked over her shoulder to her desk, at the divorce papers, but also at her research notes for the term paper. After her discovery, she really didn't feel like doing her assignment.

"Do you have time to go with me?" James said, seeming to read her mind.

"Uh…" *Why not?* Sam needed to take her mind off things. And her paper could wait for a little while. She grabbed her purse off the table next to the door. "Yeah. Let's go. What did you have in mind?"

"How about Toy Joy on Second Street? I know I'll find something there."

James and his sister, Ana, had a tradition of giving each other anime gifts for each other's birthdays. Ana was only a year older than James and had moved to Chicago after she graduated from college to work for an ad agency. It seemed that she had wanted to get away from their parents as much as James had, but her chosen profession— and her degree in graphic design—had made it much easier for her than it had been for James.

Sam considered his suggestion, then agreed. Going to Second Street would work out well. It wasn't far away, and James should be able to find something at Toy Joy, no problem. A brief break, then she could get back to working on her paper.

"You eat dinner, yet?" James asked over the hood of his car as he dug in his pocket for his keys. "We could grab something while we're down there."

Sam hesitated before she got in the car. She did need to eat, but she was already behind on her assignment.

"We can just go to Jo's. It'll be quick."

"Okay." She got in the car. Jo's was a coffee shop that served sandwiches and the like. They'd probably be gone no more than an hour or so, and then she could get back to work and make some progress.

James started his car, wound his way between the buildings of their apartment complex, then out onto the road.

"How did your interview go?" Sam asked.

"Oh, it was great." The engine revved as James squeezed between a couple of cars and merged onto Mo-Pac. It was dusk, rush hour continued, and they were surrounded by a sea of red taillights going with them, with bright headlights shining in their eyes from the opposite direction. "Henry filled me in on the whole history of the company—the Austin site, anyway. It was originally a startup company called Tyson International."

"Tyson International was a startup? Anand had mentioned it when I talked to him today, and I thought it was a big company."

"Yeah, the cofounders thought if they used a big-sounding name, they might get more business. And they did okay, but it seems like they had some cash flow issues for a while, and then CS Solar acquired them a couple of years ago."

This type of talk was foreign to Sam. The world of business seemed so superficial to her, and she preferred sticking with medicine. She found comfort in the predictability, the repeatability of science.

She looked out the passenger window, taking in the view over Zilker Park, where she could see the giant Christmas tree of lights being strung up on the moontower, then out over Lady Bird Lake to the forest of construction cranes and skyscrapers downtown, with lights twinkling in the darkening sky.

James followed the exit ramp off Mo-Pac onto Cesar Chavez to take them into the middle of the mess, fueled by the tech boom.

"When I talked to Anand today, he mentioned they just got more funding. He called it a trench, I think? What's that?" she asked.

"I think you mean a tranche. When an investor funds a company, they often split up the money into smaller amounts, and those are called tranches. So when CS Solar —which originally stood for CalStar Solar, but they shortened to CS Solar when they started to expand into other states. Anyway, when CS Solar acquired Tyson International along with a few other small solar panel companies in Arizona and Nevada, they got a private equity group to help finance the acquisitions." He drove just past Austin City Hall, turned onto Lavaca, and then immediately turned again into the garage entrance, where a line of cars had formed to descend and park below the building.

"Huh, I wasn't expecting it to be busy," Sam said, "but I guess it's always busy now."

"Maybe there's a taping going on."

"Oh, of course."

The Moody Theater sat one block north of City Hall and was the new location of the *Austin City Limits* music television show. The garage at City Hall was the closest parking and quite convenient for concertgoers. Plus, the workers had left for the day, allowing nighttime visitors to use the spaces that would be empty otherwise.

She looked over at James. "Have you ever had a chance to shoot anything for ACL?"

"Are you kidding? That would be awesome, but I haven't had any luck landing gigs that big. Plus, the show has had the same photographer since the very first taping over forty years ago. He's got an awesome portfolio with images of all of the greats in music." He smiled as he shook his head. "I'm sure he has some amazing stories."

He pulled up to the gate attendant and started to lean over to pull his wallet out, but Sam already had a ten-dollar bill in her hand.

"I was hoping I could just get the ticket validated, but I guess they don't do that when there's a show," James said. "I'll pay you back."

"It's no big deal. Don't worry about it."

"But I dragged you out, and now you're paying for it."

After he pulled past the gate, Sam asked, "What else did you learn?"

"So apparently, for this CS Solar site here in Austin, once the management could show that they had met certain milestones, the private equity group gave CS Solar another tranche of funding."

"You're starting to sound like some financial genius."

"Ha. I just learned all this stuff myself over the last couple of days, plus I asked Kevin about it, since he's more in tune with the startup world."

Sam swung her head to look at James. "You talked to Kevin?"

"It's not like we're completely broken up and have stopped talking to each other," James said with a smile. "Like I told you, we're just taking some time off. Anyway, the transactions for these deals are completely private. Kevin asked around, and it seems like Henry and Anand got nice bonuses for getting this site to reach its milestones at the end of this fiscal year, which was the last day of October."

"So the fiscal year ends on Halloween?"

"Right."

"Why don't companies just use the regular calendar?" Sam asked.

"From what I've read, it seems like many companies don't want to close out the books in December since a lot of people take vacation for the holidays. Another reason is a lot of companies want their fourth quarter to be the strongest in their reporting, and for many companies, this happens right after the summer months."

"I guess that makes sense."

"Henry really touted the site's safety record," James said. "He told me that it helped them stay under budget during this last fiscal year because they had no downtime and no unexpected expenses. And now they're going to finish purchasing and installing equipment on the new manufacturing floor that they've added on to their original building."

He finally found a parking spot three levels down and pulled into it.

"Elevator or stairs?" he asked after they exited the car.

"Stairs."

They climbed the open stairs, next to a wall of limestone, water trickling over the rough surface. The architect had designed this as a water feature using only condensation from the air-conditioning units on the roof that also allowed natural light into the parking garage during the daytime.

They emerged in front of City Hall, facing Cesar Chavez Boulevard, across from Lady Bird Lake. They walked around an amphitheater built into one side of the building, with stone tiers that served both as seating and part of the architecture, a tribute to the live music cherished in this city. Once they were on the backside of the building, the could see the crowds lined up for the concert at the Moody Theater, and a bronze statue of Willy Nelson frozen as he played his guitar greeting visitors.

"I forgot—Toy Joy is on the other side of City Hall," James said.

"No problem," Sam replied. "I like watching all these people. I wonder who's playing?"

They stuck to the City Hall side of the street, avoiding the crowd, and crossed in front of Lambert's, a barbecue restaurant in an old brick storefront, a pillar of smoke rising from its roof.

Toy Joy sat just on the other side of an alley stacked with logs of wood, separating Lamberts from its modern neighbor, with the corner cut out like a missing piece of cake to accommodate the historic structure.

Sam and James went through the front door of the store, into a blind entrance, which guided them down a ramp to a tightly packed space filled with colorful aisles of knickknacks, gadgets, and, of course, toys.

They perused the offerings from all over the world, with playsets from Europe and anime figurines from Japan, every square inch containing something interesting to look at. After half an hour, James had gathered a collection of trinkets for his sister and checked out, then they headed a few blocks down to Jo's.

This location was not quite as funky as the one on South Congress, which was housed in a green cube with the "i love you so much" mural on one side that tourists used as an Instagram backdrop. But it had some of the same vibes along with a giant red ball above the door. They ordered and decided to sit outside along the sidewalk so they could people watch.

After they got their food and had a few bites, James said, "Here's something else that may interest you: Henry said there were a lot of issues after the birth of his son."

"Really? What happened?"

"He was born prematurely and had to stay in the hospital for a long time. When they could finally bring him home, they were so glad he was not in the hospital anymore that they didn't really think much about how the bills would be paid because they both had good insurance."

"That must have been a rough experience for them." Sam remembered the rotation she had in the NICU—the neonatal intensive care unit—during medical school. It was filled with tiny preemies, some weighing no more than a soda can, struggling to stay alive. There were rocking chairs for parents and nurses to sit with the minuscule babies, their skin delicate and translucent. They were so helpless, and their parents so distraught, but they kept fighting to live each day. With the help of incubators and the amazing nurses tracking every gram each baby ate, along with the weight of every tiny, soiled diaper, almost all these pocket-sized people plumped up and grew, eventually leaving the NICU to go home. "But I suppose there was a problem?" Sam asked.

"They used his wife's insurance when they went to the hospital for the baby's birth, but then they switched the baby's coverage to Henry's insurance because he had the more comprehensive plan. But when *his* insurance found out about *her* insurance, they used an obscure rule to get out of providing coverage. And then the amount they had to pay out of pocket went into the six figures."

"What? How could they do that?"

James shrugged. "I don't know. Henry said they complained about it, but nothing happened, and since they didn't have enough money to pay off their debt, the collectors started calling. It was only after a national health news website wrote a story about their situation that the health insurance companies and the hospital all came together and settled the issue. But really settling only meant that they decreased what Henry and his wife owed by a small amount. They still had to take out loans and do a GoFundMe campaign to pay for most of it."

"That's just tragic." Sam shook her head. "How is his son doing?"

"Henry says his son is now a happy, normal toddler."

---

couple of days later, Alex came over to Sam's apartment to hang out with her after work. This was becoming a frequent thing. She loved having him over even though it meant that she would have to stay up late to work on her class assignments after he left. Of course, it was nothing like the long call nights Alex sometimes had. He was on call this evening, and while most call nights were not too difficult for him, some resulted in his working all night in the hospital, catching only a few minutes of sleep in the call room if he was lucky, then working a regular full day afterward.

The last few weeks, they had been watching *Breaking Bad*, usually just limiting themselves to a couple of episodes each night. Sam leaned up against Alex, feeling comfortable in his warmth, his arm draped around her. This felt right.

In the show, when Skylar revealed to Walter that she was having an affair, Alex said, "That's just like a woman."

Sam sat up, pulling herself away from him. "What is that supposed to mean?"

"Well, she knows that's the only way to hurt him."

"She feels trapped."

"I know. But she should have just gone through with the divorce."

Sam rolled the remote in her hands. "You know, I think Millie and my father were seeing each other before my mom died."

"What makes you say that?"

"The night we all went to dinner, Millie mentioned a conference in Aspen she and my dad were at together. That conference was only a couple of months before my mother was diagnosed. I remember it because my mom had wanted to go, but she hadn't been feeling well—probably because of the cancer. But now I wonder…"

"I'm sure it wasn't anything."

"How can you be sure?"

Alex shrugged. "It makes sense that Steven and Millie were both there. I mean, they work together." He scratched his chin. "In fact, I'll have to look into conferences in Aspen. It would be great if I could go there and expense it."

Sam stood up and began pacing back and forth in front of the TV. "It just seems off to me. I can't believe my father would do that. And Millie…"

"I thought you liked Millie."

"I do. More than I thought I would. In fact, she seems much more supportive of my efforts to finish residency than my father. She's very encouraging and…and she reminds me of my mother at times."

"So what's the problem? It's all in the past."

"The problem is that my father may have cheated on my mother. And now he's going to marry the person he cheated on my mother with."

Alex just sat there, staring straight ahead at the blank TV screen.

Sam put her hands on her hips, scrutinizing him. "Aren't you going to say anything?"

He looked up at her. "What is there to say?"

"That you understand."

"Well…" He squirmed in his seat. "Not really."

"What do you mean 'not really'?"

He leaned forward, clasping his hands together, and looked up at her. "So what if they had an affair? That's all in the past. Why does it matter now?"

Sam felt the heat rising in her chest, her face pinched in frustration. She had been pretty tired before, but now she was fully alert. How could he say that? How could she just accept Millie, knowing that she was the other woman in her father's life when her mom was still alive?

How can Alex not see this?

Of course, he didn't have any of this kind of tension in his home growing up. His father was an internist, and his mother stayed at home taking care of Alex and his two brothers. They were the epitome of Americana.

Suddenly, Sam wished Alex was gone and James was there with her instead. He would understand. He wouldn't just sit there and take her father's side or say it was no big deal, that it didn't matter. He would be there for her.

Alex's pocket buzzed. He looked a little relieved as he pulled out his phone, then swiped and tapped it. "It's the ICU. A patient I admitted this morning is declining. O_2 sats are trending down. The respiratory tech reports diminished breath sounds over the right middle lobe." He stood up. "I gotta go in."

"Probably needs a bronch," Sam said.

"I concur," Alex said with a grin. He called in to the

hospital and gave orders to set up a bronchoscopy tray so everything would be ready when he got there.

Sam watched him, taking in his confident but gentle tone as he spoke to the nurse, how his concern for his patient came across during the discussion. It just made him more attractive, and now she felt bad.

Is Alex right? Am I making a big deal out of something that I can't do anything about anyway?

After he hung up, she opened the door for him. He pecked her on the lips, almost absentmindedly, before he stepped out onto the landing at the top of the stairs.

"It looks like the weather's going to be great this weekend. Want to go out to Fredericksburg on Saturday?" Sam asked. Maybe a trip out to Texas's burgeoning wine country would do some good for their relationship.

"Oh, I forgot to tell you," Alex said, turning toward her, "Steven and I are going to hit the links on Saturday."

Sam blinked. "Okay." Her father and Alex had hit it off better than she had expected.

"I'll call you when our round is over and you can join us for lunch."

"Uh, sure." Sam didn't know if she really wanted to see her dad again so soon. Once a month was enough for her.

"Great. See you la—" Alex turned, but stopped abruptly.

Sam followed his gaze. Dylan stood at the bottom of the stairs.

20

―――――――

"I know you," Alex said. "You're that police officer I met a few months ago...when Sam's friend was in the hospital, right?"

Dylan scrambled up the stairs and shook Alex's hand. "That's right. Dylan Myers."

"Alex Crawford." He looked at Sam, then back at Dylan. "What's going on?"

"Something has come up with...an acquaintance of ours, and I want to discuss it with Sam."

Alex's face showed a glimmer of skepticism. "I see." He looked at Sam again. "Anyone I would know?"

Sam hadn't the foggiest idea of what Dylan was talking about, so she just shrugged.

"It has to do with that individual you spoke with the other night," Dylan said. "At El Morado."

"A Tejano bar?" Alex furrowed his brow. "What were you doing there?"

"It's a long story," Sam said. "I went there with James to talk to someone, to find out more information about the son of one of my pa—"

Alex's phone buzzed. He glanced at it, then said, "I've gotta go. You'll have to fill me in later. Bye." He ran down the stairs.

"Okay, see you later…" Sam's voice trailed off as she realized Alex wasn't even paying attention. She looked at Dylan, took a deep breath, and extended her arm toward her apartment. "Come on in."

Dylan entered but remained standing, hooking his thumbs on his utility belt. "Ernesto is dead."

"What?" Sam blinked. "When?"

"Early this morning, just after midnight. Someone shot him. Looks like it might have been related to a drug deal. There's some suspicion that El Morado is a front to launder money for one of the local branches of the Texas Syndicate." He cleared his throat. "And, uh, one of those two yahoos harassing you the other night is suspected to be an enforcer for the gang."

Sam's eyes widened. "Enforcer? You mean like…"

"Yes, I mean like he may have been involved with a few assaults and, uh, possibly some unresolved homicides."

"Unresolved homicides?" Her scalp prickled, her pulse picking up. "Am I in danger?"

"You shouldn't be." He rocked back and forth on his heels. "There's an ongoing operation with the Texas Rangers, so I can't tell you much, but—"

Sam frowned. "What do you mean I shouldn't be in danger? You just told me that a couple of suspected killers cornered me—one of them had his hands on me!" Her heart knocked in her chest. "And I shot him with pepper spray! He thinks I assaulted him. What if he comes after me?"

Dylan held up his hands. "Now, let's not get too excited here. They don't know who you are. I think they just saw a beautiful woman by herself, and they saw you as an easy target, but you proved them wrong."

She almost reacted when Dylan called her beautiful, but she was too freaked out that she may have been stalked by hit men.

"Then why are you here? Why are you telling me this?"

"Well…I just wanted to let you know about Ernesto before you heard about his death somewhere else and got the wrong idea."

She narrowed her eyes. "But you still think there's a possibility these men could come after me, don't you?"

Dylan hesitated a moment, then said, "Look, just be careful. And give me a call if you see anything suspicious. If you haven't already, you should drop looking into what happened to Raul. I told you before that he had served time for possession, and so had Ernesto. They may have still been involved in some illegal activity, and based on what happened to Ernesto…" He shook his head. "I shouldn't speculate."

"Do you think Raul's accident wasn't really an accident?"

Dylan closed his eyes and shook his head again. "I shouldn't have said anything." He glanced at his watch. "I've gotta go. But, seriously, I don't think you're in danger. However…on the off chance you see something, give me a call."

He went out the door and trotted down the stairs.

Sam was confused. Dylan's logic seemed inconsistent. The men who had attacked her were dangerous, but she shouldn't be concerned about it?

She would worry anyway, because by coming to her apartment, Dylan must also be worried.

21

T he man in the tailored shirt with silver cuff links spoke to Nico like he was three years old. He wanted guacamole on the chicken taco, not the beef taco. Was that too much for Nico to understand?

God, Nico hated this job. He was almost done with his double shift, and there always had to be one asshole who came in right before closing.

Nico took the man's tray and said, "I'm sorry, sir. We'll fix this and get it out to you as soon as possible."

"You better, or I'm never coming here again!"

"Fine with me," Nico muttered as he picked up the tray and placed it in the pass-through window to the kitchen. "We need to redo this order. The guac's on the wrong taco."

"I'm on it," Kristen said. She was always so perky, but she kept making mistakes. Mistakes that he always got blamed for since he was working the counter and she was shielded in the kitchen.

How could she be so cheerful?

Oh, that's right, because she has only been here for four hours, not since the crack of dawn like I've been. She worked part time after school, so she could take this job or leave it. Not like Nico. Now this was his only job, besides whatever it was that was going on with Ramirez.

Nico hunched over to peer through the pass-through window so he could see the clock on the back wall of the kitchen as Kristen worked on the tacos, her ponytail bouncing. Just a few more minutes, and then he could leave since it was Kristen's turn to close.

He needed to talk to Ramirez and find out what had happened to Ernesto. He had seen cops set up in front of one of the buildings of his sister's apartment complex when he dropped off his kid with her that morning, but he didn't know what it was about until his sister texted him that Ernesto had died. She didn't know much about what had happened, but she thought Ernesto had been shot during a drug deal. At least that's what she had heard through the rumor mill in the complex.

When Nico's shift ended, he clocked out and drove to the dive bar where Ramirez usually hung around. Sure enough, Ramirez sat at one end of the bar, nursing a bottle of Modelo.

Ramirez laughed when he saw Nico. "You look like a *marica*."

Nico looked down at his clothes, somewhat embarrassed. Maybe he should have changed before he came here. He was still wearing his uniform from work, a polo with Comida Rapido embroidered on the front and his chinos.

"And why the fuck did they name that restaurant 'fast food'? Stupid *gringos* just see Spanish and think that makes the food authentic."

Nico laughed. Ramirez had a point. Then he got to

why he was there. "What happened to Ernesto? I thought we were just supposed to follow him."

"We were, and we did."

"Did you have anything to do with it?"

"With what?"

"His death."

"Nah."

Ramirez didn't even act surprised. Why didn't he ask Nico what had happened? It was like he already knew about it.

"What happened to Ernesto?" Nico asked.

"His past just caught up with him."

"But you're part of his past," Nico said. "You knew him before you were in the clink."

"I know what you're thinking. I'm not tight with the *Sindicato* anymore." Ramirez rubbed his forearm, over the Texans tattoo he used to show off all the time.

"So we're done then? Have you heard from *el jefe*?"

"No," Ramirez said. "There's still more he wants from us, to get our *dinero*." He jutted his jaw. "Trust me."

Nico stared at Ramirez. *Did he kill Ernesto? And if he did, why?*

Ramirez took a swig of beer, set the bottle down, and licked his lips. He glowered at Nico. "So you with me?"

Nico breathed in slowly, then nodded. He really needed the cash, but as soon as this job was done, he'd figure out how to part ways with Ramirez. He had to handle this carefully though. The last time he pushed back when he was concerned about something, it only cost him his job. Not his life.

22

The next morning in clinic Sam found it hard to keep her mind on her patients; she still could not believe Ernesto was dead. How could two people who were friends and who worked together both die within a couple of weeks of each other? It seemed like it was more than a coincidence, but maybe Dylan was right—maybe something from the past caught up with these two young men. She certainly didn't know everything about them, especially since Anand had mentioned the previous company had hired parolees. *Were Raul and Ernesto hired through this program?* Dylan was definitely in a better position to know what was going on, and as far as Mrs. Garza was concerned...well, denial could be a strong coping mechanism.

As Sam came out of an exam room after seeing a patient, she found Jill giving Henry a tour of the clinic. Jill led Henry over to Sam, and said, "And this is our wonderful physician, Dr. Jenkins."

Sam smiled, and Henry said, "We've had the pleasure of meeting already."

"Oh, right," Jill said. "I forgot Dr. Jenkins went to your factory with Kyle."

As Jill went on to explain the typical patient flow through the clinic to Henry, Sam glanced over at the last patient she'd seen, waiting at the check-out desk. He needed the paperwork Sam held in her hands before he could leave, so Sam was about to politely excuse herself. But Cynthia approached them and said, "I'm sorry to interrupt, Jill, but there's a patient who needs to speak with you. He has a question about his bill."

"Could you take a message? I can call him back in a few minutes."

"He's waiting at the front counter," Cynthia said, then lowered her voice. "He's being very pushy and demanding. Could you speak with him right now?"

"I'm sorry," Jill said to Henry, "but it sounds like I need to address this issue,"

He smiled. "I used to work in a customer-facing role, so I completely understand."

"Would you mind continuing the tour?" Jill asked Sam. "I was just beginning to show him the clinic area."

Sam glanced at the board. It seemed manageable for now, so she nodded. "Of course, but I need you to take this up front." She opened the chart and scribbled on the paperwork inside, then handed it to Jill.

After they left, Sam showed Henry one of the empty exam rooms. There was really nothing special about it, except for the TV mounted near the ceiling, in the corner above the sink. It was on with the volume low, displaying a talk show, the hosts bantering and the audience laughing. He pointed to it and said, "So this is what my employees do when they come to clinic—sit around and watch TV?"

Sam shrugged. "Apparently it helps prevent complaints about long wait times if patients are distracted." She picked up the remote and turned off the TV, something she'd had to do many times when patients were also too distracted by it to answer her questions.

"I see—I was just joking by the way. I know that anyone who comes here really needs your help, and that hospitals and clinics sometimes care too much about the wrong things."

Sam laughed as she guided him to the X-ray suite. They were now on the far end of the clinic from the lobby with the exam rooms and clinic work area sandwiched in between. "We have two radiology techs to perform our imaging. It's all digital, so I can see the results immediately; then we send the images to Central Texas Imaging for a final read by one of their radiologists."

"What happens if you need something more?"

"You mean like a CT or an MRI?"

"Exactly."

"We can send an order to Central Texas Imaging, or another imaging center if they aren't in network for insurance. Of course, for workers' comp cases, we usually have to get pre-authorization before the patient can get the study."

"Does our workers' comp insurance do that?"

"I don't remember, but probably."

Henry shook his head. "Damn insurance companies."

Sam agreed with Henry's sentiment, but she didn't say so. She'd certainly spent her fair share of time haggling with various people at insurance companies trying to get approval for tests, referrals, and treatments—anything her patients needed. In fact, Sam had recently spent several hours over a few days playing phone tag with adjusters and peer reviewers to get an MRI for one of her patients. It really dragged her down to play these games where nonmedical insurance employees second-guessed her clinical judgment.

She took a deep breath, reset her mind, and led Henry around the corner, past a couple more exam rooms, to a large opening connecting the clinic area to a gym-like space. "And here is where our patients can receive physical therapy."

She introduced Henry to Bob, the head physical therapist, who gave Henry a brief tour of the PT room. It was large and spacious, running alongside the clinic area between the exam rooms and the parking lot. There were several pieces of exercise equipment lined up along the window looking out to the parking lot and several padded exam tables on the opposite wall. The far wall was covered in mirrors, allowing patients to make sure they used proper form while completing their exercises, and the end that shared a wall with the lobby had a reception desk next to a door that led directly to the parking lot. This was so patients wouldn't have to enter through the clinic if they only had an appointment with PT.

Henry thanked Bob when they finished, and Sam led him back to the clinic side. "So that's it. I believe you've seen everything."

"This is fantastic. What a great setup you have. Thanks so much for showing me around, Dr. Jenkins." He glanced at his watch. "Kyle was supposed to meet with me to go over some of the terms of the contract."

Sam looked around. Kyle's office door was ajar, but the room was dark. "I don't know where he is right now, but you're welcome to wait for him in here."

She flipped on the fluorescent lights and showed him into the room. Henry took the visitor's seat in front of the desk.

"I'll see if I can find out where Kyle is," she said. "Would you care for anything to drink?"

"Coffee would be great."

"I'll let Jill know."

Sam cut through the short hallway next to Kyle's office to the front lobby, the hallway where Dale had torn up Miss Morales's papers a couple of weeks before. Maybe she should tell Henry about that incident. But then she remembered Dr. Taylor's warning about downsizing. Henry seemed to trust Dale, and she didn't want to do anything to jeopardize the contract or her coworkers' jobs.

Her entrance to the lobby drew the attention of several waiting patients. They looked at her expectantly. She immediately regretted coming this way, even though it was shorter.

Jill was deep in conversation with a patient at the front counter, presumably the one who'd had a question about his bill.

Cynthia opened the door next to the counter and called a patient's name. Sam rushed over and got to Cynthia before the patient. She asked where Kyle was, and Cynthia just shrugged, then turned to greet the patient before leading him to the drug-testing area.

"Guess I'll just have to get the coffee myself," Sam muttered.

She made a cup with the single-serve coffeemaker in the waiting room. She stared at the machine as it churned, avoiding the eyes of those who seemed to wonder why a doctor was getting coffee instead of seeing patients. When she brought Henry the steaming cup, he said, "Please, sit. Take a break with me. You could probably use one."

Sam leaned out of the room and glanced at the board. Only one patient had been added since she last checked. Sure, she could use a small break.

As she sat in Kyle's chair behind the desk, Henry said, "I admire doctors like you, constantly sacrificing yourselves to take care of others. I never fully realized how totally dedicated doctors and nurses are to their patients until my wife and I spent so much time in the NICU."

"Oh, what happened?" Sam feigned ignorance, not wanting to reveal that she had learned some of his personal details from James's digging into CS Solar.

"We have a beautiful boy, but he was born prematurely with gastroschisis. You know what that is, right?"

Sam nodded. She knew from her pediatric surgery rotation that gastroschisis was a congenital anomaly where a newborn baby's intestines protrude through a hole in the abdominal wall near the belly button. But she often got gastroschisis confused with omphalocele, a similar condition. One was more common, but the other could be associated with heart defects and chromosomal abnormalities. She would look up which was which later, even though the information had no practical use for her in treating workers' comp patients, just because she would want to know. She could never fully turn off her curiosity.

"How long was he in the NICU?" she asked.

"A few months. The hole in his belly was pretty large, so they had to use one of those plastic cones for a while before they could do the first surgery."

He must have meant a silo. Surgeons used them to let gravity help the intestines gently descend back into the baby's belly. At the same time, the abdominal wall would grow large enough to hold all the baby's internal organs, eventually allowing surgeons to close the defect. "How many surgeries did he need?"

"He needed only two, but we were worried he would need another for a while. We were finally able to take him home when he was three months old."

"How old is he now?"

Henry smiled as he pulled out his phone. "He's three. And running around like a normal little boy." He swiped through several photos, showing Sam a beaming toddler playing with his toys, splashing about in a sprinkler, smearing chocolate frosting on his face.

"I'm so glad he's doing well."

"I felt so helpless," Henry said as he put away his phone. "I would have done anything for him. But the doctors and surgeons came through, doing everything they could. When we brought him home, we thought everything was fine, that we could continue on our new lives with our precious little boy." A sudden flash of anger darkened his face. "Then the hospital, along with those damn insurance companies, started hounding us. We somehow got trapped in a loophole—my wife and I did. Even though we both had good health insurance through our jobs, each one did everything they could to avoid paying." He paused with a small shake of his head. "Sorry for the outburst. I'm sure you don't want to hear all of this."

"That's okay," Sam said. She really wanted to know more about what had happened, especially when so many patients took their resentment out on doctors, the main face of medicine. But healthcare is a complex system that even most doctors didn't truly understand. At least Henry seemed to get that the roots of his frustrations grew from all the other parties involved, not the physicians. "What happened to all those bills? What was the loophole you fell into?"

Kyle appeared in the doorway just then. "So sorry I'm late."

Henry stood to shake his hand, a bright smile replacing the shroud of frustration. "Not a problem. Dr. Jenkins showed me around the clinic—gave me the grand tour. Nice facilities you have here."

"Thank you," Sam and Kyle said at the same time.

She stood and squeezed past Kyle so he could take her place behind the desk, then she extended her hand to Henry. "I'll let you two get to talking business. Good to see you again, Henry."

He shook her hand. "Always a pleasure to see you too, Dr. Jenkins."

23

S am rushed around from patient to patient for another hour after giving Henry the clinic tour. As lunchtime approached, she passed by the opening to the physical therapy area. Several patients were exercising with machines, stationary bikes, and free weights. Bob was working with a patient lifting a kettlebell as a tech checked in a patient at the desk.

Sam spotted Mrs. Garza at the far end of the room by herself. She crossed the open space, nodding to a couple of patients as she passed by, with weights clanking and flywheels whirring around her. Bob whooped loudly all of a sudden, causing her to jump.

The patient he was with had just completed all of his reps, and even though she knew Bob liked to cheer on his patients, often with raucous exclamations, she hadn't gotten used to it yet.

Mrs. Garza lay with her back on an exam table, looking up at the ceiling as she held one bent knee to her chest. She extended her leg, set it down on the table, then brought her other knee up to her chest. She didn't notice Sam until she was right next to the table.

"Oh hello, Doctor." Mrs. Garza put her bent leg down.

Sam helped her sit up and said, "I see you were able to keep coming to PT even though you're back on full duty. How does your back feel?"

"Much better. I could barely do this exercise last week, and now it's no problem."

"You're doing okay at work?"

"Yes, everything is fine. I do the stretches Bob showed me whenever I have a break, which has helped a lot."

"That's great, ma'am." Sam leaned closer to Mrs. Garza and lowered her voice. "Have you heard about Ernesto?"

"No, what happened?"

"He was killed early yesterday morning."

The color drained from Mrs. Garza's face. "How? In a car accident? Like my Raul?"

"I don't think so. My understanding is he was stabbed."

"Stabbed! Who stabbed him?"

Sam hesitated. "Dylan told me it might have been drug related."

Mrs. Garza flipped her hand in a dismissive gesture. "Dylan thinks everything is related to gangs and drugs. He's a cop; that's what he's supposed to think."

"But he told me—and I don't want you to get upset—but he told me that Raul might have been involved with—"

"Gangs? Yes, Raul made some bad decisions when he was younger. He served his time. And he swore Ernesto is…wasn't doing those bad things anymore." The older woman hung her head for a moment. "Ernesto was…he was a good boy, like Raul. They just got pulled into the wrong things." She looked up at Sam. "Did you talk to him before he died?"

Sam was surprised Mrs. Garza so readily admitted Raul's past with bad actors, but maybe she was in denial about how much the men had been involved before their deaths. "I went to El Morado the other night, and I was only able to speak with Ernesto briefly. He admitted to giving me that note, and he confirmed what you said—that Raul would get headaches a lot at work."

Mrs. Garza's eyes widened. "See, this has nothing to do with drugs. There was something going on at his job. You have to find out."

"Well, that's the thing—I went to CS Solar earlier this week, and Ernesto didn't really have anything solid to show me. Just some cracks in the wall of the pit where Raul did inspections. Since there was a sewage backup in the bathroom next to the workstation, he thought that it may have caused Raul's symptoms. But I'm not sure."

"Swamp gas," Mrs. Garza said.

"I'm sorry?"

"Swamp gas. My sister told me that a man at my nephew's company died from swamp gas when he was working on a sewer line."

"Really? When was this?"

"Last year."

"Where does he work?"

"For a utility company in Richardson." Mrs. Garza put her hand on Sam's arm. "You should talk to Raul's girl-friend, Nina—she was at my house the night you came over. Like I told you before, these boys don't talk about what's bothering them, especially with their mothers. I think Raul didn't want me to worry about it, but some-thing was wrong, so maybe he told Nina. He was spending a lot more time with her, before he…he…" She stopped talking and looked down at her hands in her lap, her lower lip quivering.

"I'm so sorry." Sam placed her hand on Mrs. Garza's shoulder. "Are you going to be all right?" She grabbed a tissue from the cart next to her and offered it to the older woman.

"Yes," Mrs. Garza said as she dabbed her eyes. "I'll be okay. Most of the time I can handle it, but every once in a while…I just feel so sad. But I'm okay." She looked up, focusing directly on Sam with imploring eyes. "Please, could you talk to Nina?"

Sam took a deep breath. So many thoughts swirled in her mind. Henry had just been there visiting the clinic, and he, along with Anand, really seemed to be committed to ensuring things were safe at CS Solar.

But then there was Dale, who had blocked her from taking care of Miss Morales appropriately. Ernesto had told her that he and his coworkers had complained about the smell in the restroom to Dale, but nothing was done until after Raul died. Maybe Nina could help Sam understand what it was like for Raul to work with Dale.

She blew out her breath, and said, "Yes, I'll talk to Nina."

24

W hen Sam got home from work, she called the number Mrs. Garza had given her for Nina. It went directly to voice mail, so she left a brief message, then she sat down at her computer to work on her assignments. Fortunately, biostatistics was pretty straightforward, with a set of problems that didn't take Sam very long to work through.

With that out of the way, she turned her attention to her term paper. She would need to summarize the regulations regarding occupational inhalation of harmful substances, along with the measures companies could use to prevent exposures and deaths. The ultimate question posed by the assignment was: do OSHA regulations prevent morbidity and mortality? So she would need to find data to determine if this was the case.

Mrs. Garza had mentioned that her nephew's coworker had died while working on a sewer line—exactly the type of situation these regulations were put in place to prevent. Sam wanted to learn more about the incident. Maybe the details would help her understand if there was even a remote possibility of Raul having been exposed to a toxic substance, leading to his death.

Sam did a Google search for utility company deaths in Richardson, Texas. There were several results about other crimes involving fatalities in the town just outside Dallas, but there were no news articles about the death. Then she found what she was looking for. A page on the OSHA website had details of an inspection after the incident. It didn't include a lot of information, just that the employee was overcome by hydrogen sulfide and methane in the trench he was working in and died.

How many other workers died like this? She picked up her notepad off a stack of papers and placed it in front of her to jot down the details. She could include this in her paper. The company had been fined over $270,000 for one serious and two willful violations of OSHA standards. She wrote down the standard numbers listed on the web page, but they didn't really make sense to her. She would have to look them up.

After spending a few minutes trying to answer her questions with more Google searches, Sam's stomach grumbled. Time to grab something to eat.

She stood, and then noticed the divorce papers on top of the stack on her desk.

What was going on between her parents back then? Why had her mother filed for divorce?

Then Sam thought about the previous night, about the argument she and Alex had right before Dylan showed up. How could Alex not understand how upsetting it was to her? For her father to be marrying the person he was unfaithful with? While her mother was still alive? Men could be so...so mind-boggling. If he had that attitude toward infidelity, how would he be if their relationship progressed? And what if they got married?

She had to remind herself that Alex had a reputation for being a player when they were in residency together. *Do men change?* Someone had once told Sam that women look for the right guy, while men tend to wait until they are ready to settle down, and then they choose the best candidate at that point in time. Was Alex getting to that point?

But maybe she was making a big deal out of nothing. Sam only had her suspicions about Millie and her father. Perhaps it was time to find out if her suspicions were correct.

Sam drove over to her father's house. She would make this a quick visit, and she would tell her father that she needed to work on her term paper as an excuse to leave after she got her answers from him. Millie's car wasn't there, so she was relieved she wouldn't have to deal with her right now.

Sam parked and walked to the front door. Even though she had a key, she always felt awkward just walking into the house. Her parents had downsized to a smaller bungalow after Sam went to college, so she never really felt like this was her home.

When her father answered the door, a broad smile spread across his face, his eyes looking kind, something she rarely saw when she was growing up. He truly was happy. Maybe stirring up the past wasn't such a good idea.

"Pumpkin! What a pleasant surprise!"

Sam cringed at the term of endearment her father had used since toddlerhood. She put on a forced smile. "Hi, Dad."

"Come on in. Would you like a drink?"

"No thanks. I'm fine. So…what do you think of Alex?" She followed her father into the living room and sat in a formal wingback chair.

He stopped at a small cart in the corner of the room

filled with bottles and decanters. "Such a fine young man." He poured himself a couple of fingers of scotch into a crystal tumbler. "We're going to the Omni at Barton Creek on Saturday. I'm looking forward to playing a round. It's been a while—I hope I'm not too rusty."

"Yeah, he told me you two were getting together. That's great, Dad."

He settled into the matching wingback next to her. "You should join us."

"No thanks. I'm not really into golf."

"Fair enough. During dinner the other night, Alex told me about the plans to expand the ICU. It's great to know there's another place I can send patients if I need to."

"With all the people moving here, the city definitely needs it," Sam said. They sat quietly for a moment, having run out of conversation material. Then she put on a happy face. "Congratulations on your engagement to Millie. She's seems like a wonderful woman."

"Thanks, Sam. I'm lucky she wants to keep putting up with me."

Now for the purpose of this visit. "When did you first meet?"

He tapped his chin as he looked up at the ceiling. "Goodness, I don't really remember. We've known each other a long time. You know, she was really your mom's friend before I met her. I think we first met at some function—a party or event or what have you—something related to the hospital. Her late husband used to refer patients to me."

"Huh. What a small world."

"Back in the day, before Austin started booming, all of us doctors in town knew each other. There were only three hospitals for the longest time."

Sam relaxed a little as her father became more conversational, more like he was talking to a colleague instead of his daughter. "I remember that. Things really have changed. I mean, I saw it all as I was growing up, but I guess I wasn't paying that much attention back then."

"As we get older, we become more aware, gain more perspective. Things can take on a different meaning once we start caring about them."

Sam cleared her throat. It was now or never. "So the other night, Millie mentioned that you were at that conference in Aspen together."

"Yeah, she was one of the few people from Austin there. You know how these conferences go." He shifted in his seat, appearing a little uncomfortable. Was it how he was sitting? Or was it the direction the conversation had taken? "There are always interesting colleagues to meet, to spend time with, from all over the place." He took a sip of his scotch. "But sometimes you seek out the familiar."

That word lingered in the air for a moment. He had a distant look, like an old memory had resurfaced. A flicker of sadness crossed his face.

"Is that when…" Sam scoured her mind to think of a diplomatic, non-accusatory way to ask her question. But she couldn't think of a better way, and she really wanted to know. "Is that when you first started seeing her romantically?"

Her father blinked a few times, with a brief head shake, then frowned. "No. No. That's not what happened. Millie and I talked a lot during that trip. Is that what you think?" He shook his head again. "Your mother and I were…going through some things at the time."

"That was right before she got her diagnosis."

"Yes." He brought his tumbler to his lips and tipped his head back, polishing off the last of his scotch.

"Why did she file for divorce?"

He snapped his head to glare at her. "What? How did you… Why would you say that?" His expression took on a stony appearance.

"I found papers in the box Millie brought me—the box of Mom's things."

"It's not what you think."

"And after she got sick, you seemed to change. You were much more attentive; you spent so much more time with her. You suddenly became the adoring husband you—"

"It wasn't like that. You don't understand." The hard facade began to crack.

"What happened between you? I'd like to know."

He looked at the floor. "What happened has happened. There's no point in digging up the past. I loved your mother dearly, and I know I wasn't the perfect husband." He lifted his gaze to Sam, his eyes moist. "But your mother wasn't perfect either."

"What do you mean by that?"

He hung his head as he turned the empty tumbler in his hands, the cut crystal facets catching the light. "I've said too much. Anything that happened was your mother's story to tell." He breathed in deeply, then spoke with a quavering voice. "And now she's gone."

25

Sam's father didn't say anything else, responding only with a slight nod when she stood and said she was leaving. After she got out to her car, she checked her phone. Nina had left a message saying she would talk to Sam, stating Mrs. Garza had insisted. But she wanted to do it in person, so she had given directions to her apartment.

The complex was on the south side of Austin, not far from Sam's clinic. It was an older property; the buildings had mansard roofs sloping down the sides of the topmost floors, with cutouts for windows. Nina's building had several wooden shingles missing below a couple of the windows, like a face with a gap-toothed grin.

Nina opened the door with a baby on her hip tugging on her ponytail. "This is Sofie, my brother's kid," she explained. "He's working late tonight. His girlfriend picks her up if he can't. But she's up in Dallas 'cause her dad just had surgery. Thank God she'll be back tomorrow."

The child appeared around a year old and had dark

wisps of hair, the brown eyes of a doe, and an engaging smile with two bottom teeth. Sam could see the family resemblance between her and Nina.

Sam cooed at the little one, letting her grasp her finger as she entered the apartment. The small living room had just enough space for a battered couch and a massive TV. There was a tiny kitchen off to one side, with barely enough room for a refrigerator and a stove. After Nina set the baby on the floor with a pile of colorful toys, she joined Sam on the couch, tucking her legs under her.

"Mrs. Garza said Raul may have told you more about the problems he was having at work," Sam began, "about how he kept feeling ill."

"That's right," Nina said. "He didn't want to talk to her about it much 'cause she nagged at him. She kept saying he should see someone."

Sam nodded. "She got him to drive her to clinic one day so I could take a look at him. His eyes were really irritated and red, but…" A pang of guilt hit her. She should have taken a better history and done a better exam.

"I was worried about it too," Nina said. "He kept telling me it wasn't a big deal. But one day when he came over, he had to lie down for a while. He was dizzy and said he felt like he might pass out." She hugged herself. "After a couple of hours, he was fine again."

"So his symptoms would come and go?"

"Some days he would feel okay, but other days, he'd get headaches and feel like throwing up."

"Did he tell anyone at work about it?"

"Yeah, he filed a report."

"Really?" Could there be evidence that someone—like Dale—knew about this? Maybe this is what Ernesto had been talking about when he said he could get more proof.

Nina pulled on the end of her dark ponytail. "That's what he said."

"Were they doing anything to address his concerns?"

"Not before…he died." Nina hung her head and began to weep quietly.

Sam looked around and found a box of tissues. She picked it up and offered it to Nina, who pulled one off the top. She waited patiently as Nina dabbed at her eyes and nose. On the floor, Sofie babbled and banged her toys together, blissfully ignorant of the sorrow in the room.

After a few moments, Nina continued speaking. "He said they wanted more to go on, that they couldn't do anything if they didn't know what caused it. But all he could tell them at first was about the bad smell. Like rotten eggs. And then when he started to feel bad, they just thought he was trying to get out of work."

Sofie used the edge of a cushion to pull herself up and patted her hand on Nina's leg. Nina redirected her attention back to the toys on the floor. "He said it was weird, though, when he started getting dizzy and having headaches, he couldn't smell anything bad at his workstation anymore."

Sam needed to look up the effects of the gases—the swamp gases—that Mrs. Garza mentioned. She thought it was sulfur that caused a rotten egg smell, and she knew it was possible that these gases could overcome someone and possibly kill them, like that utility worker in Richardson. What if Raul was chronically exposed to a low level of these gases—not so high that he would immediately pass out and die, but high enough to cause his headaches and other symptoms? All the research she had done earlier was getting mixed up in her mind. She would need to go back and revisit the information she had found.

"Did you know Raul's friend Ernesto?" Sam asked.

"Yes. He lived here, in these apartments. He was killed right outside his building."

Sam raised her eyebrows. "He was killed here?"

"Yeah," Nina said. She shrugged, her affect flat. "There's a lot of bad stuff that goes on."

"What do you think happened?"

Nina gave a little shake of her head. "I don't know."

It seemed to Sam that she might know more about Ernesto's demise, but she wasn't willing to share it.

"I had heard Ernesto and Raul had been in trouble before," Sam said, "but Mrs. Garza told me they'd left that life behind."

"Yes, that's all true," Nina said as she stood. "I want to show you something." She beckoned Sam to follow. She stepped around Sofie and her toys, crossing the room to a set of shelves by the front door. When Sam got close enough, Nina pointed to a collection of small trophies and plaques. "Raul was so proud of these. They were awards he got while working with the LULAC youth leadership program."

"What's LULAC?"

"It's the League of United Latin American Citizens. He wanted to make sure other kids didn't make the same mistakes he did." She picked up a framed picture and handed it to Sam. In it, Raul was surrounded by a group of boys who appeared to be around twelve or thirteen years old.

"It looks like he really cared about them."

"He did. They were devastated when they heard about him."

Sam put the photo back on the shelf and noticed another framed picture, this one with Nina and the man who had worn a bolo tie at El Morado. "Who is this?" Sam asked.

"Oh, that's my brother Nico. He used to work at CS Solar with Raul. That's how we met."

"Does he still work there?"

"No, he was…" Nina paused, then said, "He was let go recently."

Sam thought that was strange, since the company was about to go on a hiring spree. But then she remembered what Anand had said, about how the company had terminated a few employees from the work reentry program. *Was Nico one of them?*

"What does he do now?" Sam asked.

"He's working at—"

A knock at the door cut her off.

Nina peered through the peephole, then she opened the door a crack. A man's voice said, "Hello, ma'am. I'm following up because of an incident that happened here in the apartment complex early yesterday morning. Would it be okay if I ask you a few questions?"

Nina nodded as she dropped her hand down the edge of the door, allowing it to creak open a bit wider. Sam could see the man was a police officer, and once the door opened far enough, she saw that the police officer was Dylan.

"Did you see or hear any—" he said, but then he stopped and blinked a few times when he saw Sam behind Nina. "What are you doing here?"

Sam put her hand on Nina's shoulder. "This is Raul's girlfriend."

Dylan cleared his throat. "I see."

"But I was just leaving." She turned to Nina. "Thanks for speaking with me. I'm so sorry about Raul."

"Thank you," Nina said meekly.

Dylan stood aside to let Sam exit the apartment, then turned to Nina and said, "Just a moment, ma'am."

He followed Sam onto the sidewalk next to the parking lot. "What are you doing here?"

"I was visiting Nina."

"Why?"

"Because there's something still bugging me about Raul's death."

He rocked back on his heels as he hooked his thumbs in the pockets below his duty belt. "It was just an accident. He slammed into the back of a truck."

"I know. I guess I'm just here to placate Mrs. Garza." She kicked the edge of the sidewalk, then looked up at Dylan. "But before he died, Ernesto showed me cracks in the pit where Raul worked, and there was sewage backing up in the restroom right next to it. Mrs. Garza mentioned her nephew knew a coworker who died after being overcome by gases while he was working on a sewer line. What if something like that happened to Raul?"

"But that still doesn't explain why you're here."

"Raul wouldn't talk to his mom about how he was feeling very much, but she thought he might've said more to Nina. So that's why I'm here," she said with a quick nod.

"Did you learn anything?" Dylan said with some interest.

"Well, the last time I saw Ernesto, he said he could get me more proof. And just now, Nina told me Raul had filed a complaint regarding a foul smell at his workstation. But it sounds like nothing was done to address it. At least, not while he was still alive." A chill curled up her neck, lifting the hairs on end. She locked her gaze on Dylan, eyes wide. "What if Ernesto was trying to get that proof, and that's why he died?"

He waved his hand dismissively. "All the evidence

points to him going back to his old ways, getting involved with the wrong people again."

Sam squinted at him. "Are you sure?"

"Well, I can't be completely sure until the investigation is over," he said as he rocked back on his heels again. "And that's why I'm here: to continue canvassing, to find out if anyone saw or heard anything unusual."

"So you're part of the investigation?"

"Not exactly. I volunteered to help."

"Because Mrs. Garza asked you? Since Ernesto and Raul were friends?"

He squirmed a little, giving her a half shrug, then said, "Honestly? Maybe. But really," he said as he leaned toward her, like he was admitting a secret, "I've been helping out with as many investigations as I can in the department, learning the ropes. And I've been taking classes and studying for the detective exam."

"That's terrific," she said, smiling at him. "You'll make a great detective."

Dylan's chest puffed up as he stood straight, with an appreciative look on his face.

But then headlights washed over them, cutting the moment short, and Sam remembered why she was standing there, in the parking lot of an aging apartment complex with him.

"Okay," she said. "So let's say Ernesto's and Raul's deaths are unrelated. I still want to make sure I didn't miss a diagnosis that could have prevented Raul's accident."

"But, Sam, there are any number of reasons why people wreck their cars. It happens all the time."

She considered this, but she still had that nagging feeling that something wasn't right. Then she thought about the case she had read about earlier in the evening. "I don't know. If the bathroom was backing up, and there was a leak into Raul's work area, he might have been overcome with swamp gas."

"Swamp gas?" Dylan gave her an incredulous look. "Come on, Sam. You're grasping at straws here."

"Ernesto showed me where there might have been a connection—"

"I don't think you should trust anything you saw or heard from Ernesto."

Cries from Nina's niece drifted through the open door behind Dylan. Nina poked her head out. "Officer? Do you still need to talk to me? I need to change the baby's diaper."

Dylan looked over his shoulder. "Yes, I have a few questions to ask you, but go ahead. I'll be just a moment more."

Nina nodded and disappeared as she closed the door.

"Look, I don't know exactly what you're thinking, but Raul's death was just an accident." He put his hand on Sam's shoulder. "And it seems Ernesto probably backslid into some nefarious business, which got him killed." He shook his head. "You shouldn't dig around anymore."

Sam thought about the picture she had just seen in Nina's apartment. "You're probably right, but there's one thing you should know: Nina's brother was at El Morado with the guy who attacked me."

Dylan raised his eyebrows. "Really? How do you know this?"

"She was showing me a picture of Raul with a youth group he'd helped, and there was another photo of her and her brother. I swear it was the same guy."

He furrowed his brow. "You're sure?"

"Yeah. But he seemed nervous the other night at the bar," she said, "like he didn't want to be there, and he was just going along with that jerk."

"Okay. Thanks for letting me know. You should get out of here."

Sam nodded. She got in her car, started it up, and pulled away. In her rearview mirror, Dylan stood watching her.

26

Nico pulled into a parking spot, but he didn't get out of the car immediately. The cop and the woman Ramirez hounded at El Morado were standing in front of Nina's apartment. What were they doing here?

After a few minutes, the woman got into her car and drove off, then the cop went to the door of his sister's apartment and knocked. His pulse escalated, bounding at the base of his throat. Why was that cop talking to his sister?

Nico pulled out his phone and stared at it. Should he call Ramirez? Did he trust him? He wanted to get out of this situation as soon as possible.

No. Ramirez didn't need to hear about this.

As he set the phone down on the seat next to him, it buzzed. It was as if the man knew Nico was thinking about him. He answered.

"The *jefe* wants us to do something for him."

"What is it?"

Ramirez grunted. "Why so many questions? Look, it's nothing big. We just need to, you know, apply a little pressure."

Nico peered up at the entrance to Nina's apartment. The cop was standing in the open doorway, taking notes while his sister talked.

"Are you in or are you out? He'll give us *dinero* next week."

That would be just in time to cover the rent, and since his girlfriend had to take this week off, they would be short unless Ramirez was true to his word.

Nico said, reluctantly, "I'm in."

Right after Nico hung up, the cop ambled down the sidewalk, speaking into the mic on his shoulder, then scribbling in his notebook. Nico slid down in his seat, but the cop turned before he got to Nico's car and approached the door for another apartment.

Nico got out of his car, and the cop's words drifted over as he spoke to Nina's neighbor. Something about continuing to canvass the area.

When he got up to his sister's apartment, his precious *mijita* held up her arms and squealed, "Papi!"

He scooped her up off the floor and gave her a kiss on her chubby cheek.

"You were supposed to be here an hour ago," Nina said with her arms crossed.

"It looked like you were busy. I didn't want to interrupt."

"Well, the cop was here asking about Ernesto's death, if I saw or heard anything. And he asked if I knew him."

Sweet Sofie suddenly felt heavy in Nico's arms, but he didn't want to put her down, so he sat on the couch and bounced her on his lap. "What did you tell him?"

"Just what I know, which isn't much. That you and him used to work together."

Nico relaxed a little, and then Nina said, "And he asked about Ramirez." She tilted her head. "He's the one that was stealing stuff and brought you down with him, right?"

"He didn't steal anything," Nico said. "And he didn't bring me down with him."

She shook her head, wagging her finger at him, just like their mother always had. "Raul told me Ramirez was going to steal some copper wire. He said there's a black market for it. You weren't involved with that, were you?"

"No. I wasn't. They just needed an excuse to fire me."

"You aren't still talking to that guy, are you?"

Nico hesitated a second too long before he could deny it.

"You are," she said, glaring at him. "Raul said Ramirez was higher up in the *Sindicato*, that he was more than just a soldier." Now her eyes pleaded with him. "He's done some nasty things. You need to stay away from him."

"But Raul…" He stood and put Sofie back down on the floor with her toys.

The baby immediately pulled herself up by his pants leg, raised her free arm, and said, "Up, Papi, up!"

Nico ignored her as he towered over his sister. "You can't tell me who I can talk to. You hooked up with Raul, and he was in the *Sindicato* too. What makes you think you can tell me what to do?"

"He was just a peon to them," she said, shaking her head. "He never did anything more than sell a few grams. And that program got him back on the right track. Until…" She looked down for a moment, then back at Nico with fierceness in her eyes. "But you. You know better."

Sofie started crying as she grasped Nico's leg. He

picked her up and stroked her fine hair. A fat tear glistened on her dear little face. He used his thumb to wipe it away. He knew what he needed to do.

"Thanks for watching her." He pointed at his sister. "But stay out of my business."

27

I t was nearly midnight by the time Sam got home. Even though she'd wanted to work a little more on her paper—and do more research on swamp gas— she was drained.

On top of confronting her father, learning that Ernesto had lived in the same apartment complex as Raul's girl-friend had been a total surprise. Maybe Sam was entangling herself too much in this situation; she really didn't know the extent of these relationships amongst this group of people she barely even knew. All she'd wanted to do was help Mrs. Garza.

THE NEXT MORNING, Sam went about her routine, pushing aside all that had happened the night before so she could focus on her patients. But as soon as it was time to take her lunch break, she drove to CS Solar. Maybe if she talked to Anand and found out how employees report safety issues, she could learn what had become of Raul's complaint. She had to be careful, though, because she still had no solid proof, just speculation from Ernesto. Plus, she wasn't privy to the culture within the company or the working relationship between Dale and Anand.

When Sam got to the plant, she checked in with Alvera, who told her Anand would be there in a few moments. She'd hoped she could chat a bit before Anand came to meet her, maybe ask a few questions about the work environment and how well the employees were treated. But the phone rang, and Alvera answered with her cheery greeting, dashing Sam's plans.

She wandered over to the window separating the solar cell intake area from the lobby and watched the activity within as she waited. It was the same as it had been on the tour, with workers unpacking boxes and setting out solar cells for inspection while other workers took the shiny black squares and tested them at their workstations. They all went about their tasks efficiently with mechanical movements, including Miss Morales. She suddenly looked over her shoulder, directly at Sam, as if she had sensed Sam's presence.

Sam gave her a small wave, but Miss Morales didn't respond. Instead, she quickly turned back to her work. Sam noticed the crutches were no longer resting against the wall, so Miss Morales must be improving. She wondered if she'd be able to stay in this position after she fully recovered.

Anand's voice came from behind her. "Dr. Jenkins, how are you doing today?"

Sam turned to find Anand with his hand extended. She shook it and said, "I'm fine. Just watching everyone work. It's rather mesmerizing. They're so efficient."

"They are, but it's also very repetitive, so we make sure everything's ergonomic to prevent injury," he said. "Where we can, we have workers rotate through stations so they aren't always doing the same job. And of course, we built plenty of breaks into their schedules."

"That's great," she said, glancing at the conference room. The room was darkened, with several people crowded around the table, watching a presentation.

"Since that's occupied, let's head to my office." Anand motioned with his hand down the hallway next to the window. "You said you had more questions for me?"

"Yes," Sam said as she followed him. "After we went over those protocols, I just want to make sure we're prepared for any type of injury or exposure we might see in clinic. Plus, I've been reading some case studies for those MPH classes I told you about." She gave a half shrug. "I figured learning what goes on in the real world will help me understand them better."

"That makes sense," Anand said. He nodded at a couple of other employees as they traversed the labyrinth of beige cubicles, with fluorescent lights above giving everyone a washed-out hue.

When they got to what she presumed was his office, they found Dale standing next to the door.

He completely ignored Sam and said to Anand, "The subcontractor installing the cell welding machines is looking for you. He wants to go over the safeguards to prevent amputations." He gave Sam a side glance as he said the last word, as if he wanted to emphasize he knew what a real injury was.

"Tell him I'll be there as soon as I'm done speaking with Dr. Jenkins."

"He's about to leave to work on another job."

Anand nodded and said to Sam, "It should only take a few minutes. Do you mind waiting?" He motioned to a seat inside the office.

"Sure, I can do that," she said.

After Anand left with Dale, Sam looked around the small space. It was really just a large cubicle set against one of the office area walls, with the fabric cube walls high enough for a full-sized door. Anand's computer was wedged in the corner on a built-in desk, surrounded by pictures of him with his family and a few drawings from his kids. A whiteboard hung on the wall next to her, covered with lists and diagrams sketched in colorful grease marker. A table extended out below it, separating her from the desk. Shelves above the desk held binders, manuals, and textbooks, with some of the same titles Sam had in the bookshelves by her workstation in the clinic.

While she waited, she pulled out her phone, and after checking her email, she searched the web to research more about swamp gas. Even though Dylan had scoffed at her, she still wanted to know if there was even the remote possibility that Raul might have been exposed to something. The two main gases mentioned on the OSHA report Sam had read the night before were methane and hydrogen sulfide. Both could cause similar symptoms, including nausea, vomiting, headaches, and dizziness. Exactly like Raul's symptoms.

Then she found something that created a pit in her stomach. Listed on an OSHA webpage as one of the effects of hydrogen sulfide exposure was mild conjunctivitis, or "gas eye."

Could that be what Sam had seen in Raul? Could it be that the redness in his eyes was due to hydrogen sulfide exposure? And all she had done was tell him to use some eye drops. If she had only…

"Sorry to keep you waiting," Anand said as he stepped through the doorway. "Thank goodness for Dale; he's my eyes and ears out on the floor." He turned his chair away from his computer, then sat in it as he pulled it up to the table opposite Sam. "So what do you have for me?"

Sam quickly decided how she would approach this. She still didn't have any direct evidence that Raul had suffered an exposure here at CS Solar, and apparently Anand and Dale had a good working relationship, so she'd need to tread lightly. She'd start off as generally as she could, and then she would try to navigate toward finding out what had come of Raul's complaint.

"The last time I was here, we'd started talking about the differences between the semiconductor industry and what you're doing here, but there was so much for me to take in. Plus, I think we went off onto other topics. Even though you had mentioned the chemicals used in the fabrication process are much more caustic than what you use here, I was wondering: what is the risk of chemical exposure in your plant?"

"Why do you ask?"

She gave him what she hoped was a disarming smile. "Honestly, it's an area I need to brush up on because I'm more familiar with how to treat physical trauma, not exposures."

"Right," he said. "We have minimal liability in that area. The finished PV cells arrive here, and you saw how we inspect them to ensure functionality before they are assembled in various configurations depending on the requirements of our customers."

"What are PV cells? Are they the same thing as solar cells?"

"Yes. That's the technical term—photovoltaic cell. I suppose, besides the fumes from solder, that the main risk of inhalation would be the EVA—ethylene vinyl acetate—substrate we use to mount the PV cells onto the backsheet of each panel. It protects the cells and electrically insulates them from the housing so they don't short out." He swiveled his chair, reached up to the shelf over his desk, and pulled down a thick binder. "I should have the MSDS in here," he said as he swung back around, setting it on the table, and began flipping through its pages.

Sam knew from her classes that MSDS stood for material safety data sheet, the information employers are required by OSHA to have on hand for each potentially harmful substance. These documents provided details for safe handling and storage as well as potential hazards and toxic effects.

Anand stopped on a page and rotated the binder so she could read it. "It's fairly nontoxic at room temperature."

"But does it stay at room temperature during the assembly process?" she asked.

"There is a curing stage where the PV cell assemblies are placed on the EVA backsheet then fed into an oven to allow the EVA to essentially melt and encapsulate the cells. But the oven is self-contained with its own exhaust system. There's minimal chance our employees could be exposed to it." He pointed to the open page in the binder. "And as you can see, at most, the exposed individual would experience mild eye or respiratory irritation."

Sam nodded. Maybe now she could move on to what might've happened with Raul's complaint. "Could you walk me through the process, say if an employee were to identify a potentially hazardous situation? What would that employee do?"

"Uh, sure." Anand swiveled around again and pulled another thick binder down from the shelf. He turned his chair back to face her more slowly this time, then stopped with the binder against his chest, supported by his lap. He hugged it, like he was protecting it. "The procedure is outlined in our policy..." He frowned before he continued. "But as a doctor, how we handle these issues isn't relevant to your treatment of our employees, is it?"

"Right." Sam stammered, "Well, er—this doesn't really have to do with my work at the clinic. We've been learning about mitigation strategies for injury prevention in my environmental and occupational health class."

"I see." His face opened up as he slid the first binder off to the side, set the new binder down, and started turning the pages. "So this is our procedure: if any employee—and I mean anyone, even a temp or someone who is working on the custodial crew—if anyone believes there is a potentially unsafe condition here in the workplace, they should report it to their supervisor. The supervisor gives them this form." He tapped on a page in the binder. "The employee fills out the top section here and gives it back to their supervisor. The supervisor then apprises the situation and takes any steps within their ability and authority to correct the unsafe condition. If they cannot correct it immediately, then the supervisor takes a temporary precautionary measure—such as cordoning off the affected area—and escalates the issue to the next level."

"And how long does this process take?"

"As you see here on the form, the supervisor must return a copy of this with the bottom part filled out with their corrective action plan within two days. If not, then the employee can contact me directly to make sure the situation is addressed."

"That seems pretty straightforward," Sam said. "Have you had any unsafe conditions you've needed to address recently?"

Anand sat back in his chair, narrowing his eyes. "Why do you want to know that?"

"Sometimes it's easier to understand with a specific example." She shrugged. "And I'm just curious."

Anand didn't respond as he studied her, like he was trying to decide if she was friend or foe. He wasn't biting, so she tried again.

"Well, what about the bathroom in the back?" Sam said. "I saw it was taped off when we were out on the floor the other day. Would that kind of issue be handled through this process?"

He waved his hand. "Oh, no. That was just a backup in the sewage line to the septic tank. It seems the pump was damaged from all the vehicles driving around outside for the construction of the new factory floor. This structure is pretty old and was far outside the city limits when it was built. They had no choice but to put in a septic tank, and, unfortunately, it's not really rated for the increased number of workers we've had to hire."

"So what are you going to do? Put in a bigger septic tank?" Sam still didn't know if she could bring up Ernesto's suspicions about Raul, yet. But at least Anand was more talkative.

His face brightened. "Well, since there's so much growth out this way, the city has annexed the land around here and has expanded their services. They've put in sewer lines recently, so we're going to connect to those soon. Anyway, the bathroom was only closed for a few days." He shook his head. "But it turned out whoever designed this place did a horrible job, and now we're going to have to replace all the plumbing in the back half of the building."

"That's got to be expensive."

"Yeah, it's going to cut into our budget for the coming year, but we need to do it." He closed the binders, stacking them and squaring them before sliding them out of the way. He leaned forward, propping his elbows on the table and lacing his fingers together. "Is there anything else you would like to know?"

Better now than never, Sam thought. "I was wondering about someone who used to work here: Raul Garza."

Anand flattened his lips together and gave a small head shake. "What a tragic accident. How did you know him?"

"I happen to know his mother, and she told me he texted her right before the accident," she said. "He had a headache and wasn't feeling well, which is why he left work early that day."

As she spoke, a slight look of annoyance appeared on Anand's face. "Is that so? You aren't implying his death had something to do with his job, are you? I really don't see how that could be the case."

"I'm just trying to figure some things out," she said, splaying her hands on the table. "He didn't happen to work in a job where he might have been exposed to something, did he?" Even though Sam already knew the answer, she wanted to see what Anand had to say.

"I believe he worked in quality assurance—that's where we test the fully assembled panels before we package them up for shipment."

"That's what those pits are for, right?"

"That's right." He shook his head and his gaze drifted downward. "Dale's had to move some of our employees around to fill those positions, since it appears the young man who worked next to Raul has also passed away." His eyebrows lifted as if something dawned on him. "And they were part of that work reentry program I told you about. What are the chances of that?" He paused, then looked up at her. "The last time you were here, you talked to him; I believe his name was Ernesto."

"Oh, really?" Sam feigned surprise. "What happened? How did he die?"

"I don't know exactly. Dale has more information than I do, but he indicated it might have been related to Ernesto's past illegal activity." He looked disappointed. "Maybe it's good that we're not hiring through the program anymore."

He stared blankly for a moment, then took in a quick breath as he glanced at his watch. "Well, I've got a meeting I need to prepare for. Do you have anything else you want to discuss?"

Sam hesitated before answering. If what Nina had told Sam was true, Anand either didn't know Raul had filed a complaint or he hadn't done anything to address it. And now he seemed to have a different opinion of the work reentry program. She didn't know what else she could do at this point. "No, that's all. Thanks for your time and for answering my questions."

He nodded as he stood. "You're welcome. I'll escort you out."

Sam followed Anand back through the maze of cubicles, and as they walked through the hallway to the front lobby, she again noticed the restroom across from the intake area. All the coffee she drank that morning had caught up to her, so she really did need to use the facilities this time. She motioned toward the restroom. "Are these okay to use?"

"Yeah. We got the pump fixed pretty quickly; otherwise, we'd be in big trouble. All of the workers on the floor had to come up to use these restrooms while the ones in the back were out of commission. But everything's stable for the time being, until we get connected to the city sewers."

"Well, thanks again for your time," Sam said as she entered the restroom.

While she washed up after using the facilities, the door to the hallway opened, and Miss Morales came in.

"How are you doing?" Sam said. "How's your ankle?"

"It's doing much better, Doctor," Miss Morales said. Then she held her finger over her mouth and bent over to look under the stall doors. She pulled an envelope from the pocket of her lab coat and whispered, "Ernesto said I should give this to you if something happened to him."

Sam took the envelope and started to open it, but Miss Morales stopped her. "There's no time." She looked over her shoulder at the door. "You need to go."

Sam nodded and tucked the envelope into her purse. She left the building, waving to Alvera as she went through the front door. Once she was inside her car, she opened the envelope. Inside was a single sheet of paper, a copy of a hazard report form, just like the one Anand had shown her. The top of the form had been filled out and signed by Raul Garza. He'd complained of a foul odor—like rotten eggs—at his work station on October 12th. Two weeks before his death.

28

A s Sam drove back to the clinic, she pondered the implications of the report Miss Morales had given her. This must have been the proof Ernesto said he could provide, but she didn't know what had happened after Raul filed the complaint.

After she pulled into the lot behind the clinic, she parked her car and took a few minutes to read over the report a few more times, paying closer attention to the fine print on the form that she had not been able to read carefully when Anand had shown her the blank copy.

At the top, the form read: "It is usually best to discuss a safety hazard with your supervisor before using this form. Use this form if you wish to make a written notice of a hazard."

Had Raul discussed this with Dale before he resorted to filling out the form? Even though it was dated October 12th, when had he given the form to Dale? At the bottom of the section Raul had filled out, the form stated that if the employee did not hear from their supervisor within two business days, they should send a copy to the department safety coordinator. So did Raul send this to Anand too? Why didn't Anand say anything?

Sam would have to figure it all out later, because when she walked into the clinic, the board was full. She quickly put her purse away in the bottom drawer next to her computer, slipped into her white coat, then leaned forward over her chair to reach the keyboard and log in. She skimmed the queue in the system, briefly checked the record for the next patient, and made her way to that room.

Fortunately, she'd seen the patient before, and he was there for a follow-up—a wound check on a burn. Everything was going well, and Sam made a couple of quick notes on the face sheet so she could type up her note later. After dropping his folder off at checkout, she consulted the board to find out which patient was next.

She rounded the corner to the exam room and found her boss blocking the way with a dour look on his face.

"Oh! You surprised me," she said. "What brings you here, Dr. Taylor?"

"Where were you, Samantha?"

She motioned behind her with the chart in her hand. "I was just seeing a patient."

"No. Before that. Where were you?"

"I had just gotten back from my lunch break."

Dr. Taylor tipped his head to the office behind Sam, Kyle's office. "Let's step in there and have a talk."

She followed him into the small space. He sat behind the desk, and she took the seat opposite him after closing the door.

"What brings you to Austin today?" Sam said, trying to lighten up the tone.

"I had some business at the clinic in San Marcos, and I decided to stop by to check on things before I went back to

Houston." He scowled. "But you were nowhere to be found. I understand you were supposed to be back at 1:30, but it's now"—he glanced at his watch—"it's now 2:20. It shouldn't have taken you very long to see the last patient, so you were at least half an hour late getting back. Please explain yourself."

"I…I'm sorry. I was just trying to take care of some things during my lunch break, and it took a little longer than I expected."

"Take care of some things? Like stopping by CS Solar?"

Sam raised her eyebrows. "How…how did—"

"Kyle said you've gone back a couple of times since your initial visit. There's no need for that."

"But Anand, the industrial hygienist who works there, had asked me to go over some protocols with him. And I had a few of my own questions about the types of patients we see, which is why I went during lunch today."

Dr. Taylor leaned forward, placing his palm firmly on the desk. "Look, I appreciate your enthusiasm, but you've done your part. You helped move things along with renewing this contract; in fact, Kyle said there are just a couple of minor details the legal teams are hashing out, and then it should be a done deal." He leaned back in the chair. "And as far as safety protocols are concerned, Obra-Care has an in-house consultant who can assist with developing them—and bill for the work."

So that's what this is about. He thought Sam was giving away services for free. Maybe she was, but she was also benefiting from learning about the actual environment some of her patients worked in—along with trying to determine what might have caused Raul's death.

"I need you here seeing patients," he said, tapping the point of his index finger on the surface, emphasizing each word. "That's what keeps the lights on. Like I said, you've done your part as far as the CS Solar contract is concerned, and now you need to do your job."

So her earlier impression had been correct, that she really was just a sales prop during that initial visit to CS Solar with Kyle. But now that she had the report Miss Morales slipped her, she had so many questions. She still needed to go back to the site, but it would be hard if she was stuck in clinic all day.

Sam took a deep breath and looked squarely at Dr. Taylor. "There are other reasons I've been back there a few times. I'm taking environmental and occupational health for my MPH right now, and being able to see what I'm learning in practice has really improved my understanding. Plus," she said, hunching her shoulders, hoping since he was a doctor, after all, he'd at least care about this, "I think it'll help me take better care of my patients."

Dr. Taylor lifted his chin. "Fine. But make sure you do that off the clock. And if you go there during your lunch breaks, you damn well better be back on time. The way we keep these companies happy is making sure their employees are seen promptly. When the board backs up like it did today—and yes, I did see a couple of patients before you got back—employers stop sending them to us."

He said the last sentence with irritation, as if he resented having to do clinical work, back in the trenches seeing patients.

"It's not just CS Solar that is renewing their contract," Dr. Taylor continued. "We have several other companies with contracts coming up for renewal, and they look at our online ratings and NPS scores to decide whether they keep sending patients to us or go to our competition." He leaned forward, causing Sam to shrink back in her chair, then spoke with a sharpness in his tone. "If you don't do your part to keep the patients moving, you may not have any patients to see. Then we'd have to do a round of layoffs, like we did in San Marcos."

He stood up to leave, but before he opened the door, he looked down on her. "Jerry, the staff, the patients—every single person here depends on you."

29

A fter Dr. Taylor left to drive home to Houston, which was also the location of ObraCare's headquarters, the rush of patients had lulled. It figured her boss had to be there just when it was busiest.

As Sam took advantage of the downtime to work on her patient notes, Cynthia came over and leaned against the desk that ran along the back wall of the work nook Sam and Jerry shared.

"I did it," Cynthia said in an excited voice.

Sam clicked to close a chart she'd just finished, then looked up at her beaming colleague.

"What did you do?"

"For Tony's fiftieth—I booked a cruise!" Cynthia's eyes twinkled.

Tony was Cynthia's husband, and she had been talking about wanting to surprise him for the last couple of months.

"That's great, Cynthia," Sam said with a smile. "When are you going?"

"I found a great deal on a Royal Caribbean cruise out

of Galveston in February, so we can just drive there. Then we won't have to pay for plane tickets or anything. It's for four days, and it goes down to Cozumel. My sister says she'll come stay with the boys—to make sure they don't do nothing bad." Then she leaned toward Sam, grimacing as she lowered her voice. "I almost maxed out my credit cards. Thank God they let me split it up over the ones we have." She straightened up again and brightened. "But it's all-inclusive, and Tony already got the PlayStation the boys wanted for Christmas, so we're good for now."

Sam congratulated Cynthia again before returning to her computer work. In the breaks between the patients trickling through that afternoon, she contemplated what Dr. Taylor had told her. Would it really be her fault if they had to lay people off?

Jill had said the most senior medical assistant and the PA were let go at the San Marcos clinic. If the same thing happened here, that would be Cynthia and Jerry. And now Cynthia had confided to Sam that, in order to pay for her husband's surprise birthday trip, she'd overextended herself.

At the end of the day, she opened her purse to get her keys and found the envelope with the hazard report. She'd almost completely forgotten about it. As she drove home, the envelope peeked out of her purse from the passenger's seat, reminding her that there were still so many unanswered questions.

Sam didn't want to do anything to put the contract renewal with CS Solar in jeopardy. According to Dr. Taylor, the lawyers from both companies were hashing out the details. But what would happen if she started accusing CS Solar of—of what, exactly?

Just let it go. Her boss was on her back, and she had to consider how her actions affected her colleagues.

But when she got to her apartment complex, the hazard report continued to gnaw at her like a gastric ulcer. If Raul's eye irritation had been from hydrogen sulfide exposure at work, and she'd performed a more thorough clinical investigation when she'd seen him, would he still be alive?

She pulled into her parking space in front of her apartment and glanced over at the cluster of vehicles in front of James's building. She spotted his car. *Good. He's home.* Since it was Friday evening, she'd been worried he might be at his aunt's bed-and-breakfast taking photos for a wedding, but now she could talk through things with him and try to figure out what was going on.

As soon as James answered the door, Sam held out the report. "Take a look at this."

He read it as he ambled over to the couch and sat down. She perched on the chair arm next to him. When he finished, he looked up at her.

"Where did you get this?"

Sam explained how Miss Morales had given it to her surreptitiously earlier in the day and that she'd told Sam she got it from Ernesto.

"So Raul filed a report complaining about this foul odor." He flipped the sheet over. "The bottom half is empty, and there's nothing on the back. We don't know if anything was done about it."

"That's true. But what if he told Dale, and Dale didn't do anything?" Sam took the report and pointed to the bottom of the page. "It says here that if the supervisor does not respond within forty-eight hours, the employee should contact the safety coordinator. That's Anand Dhawan."

James raised his eyebrows. "I've been digging into Anand's background too."

"Why's that?"

"I met him when I interviewed Henry, so I did some research on him, like I did with the others."

"Did you find anything?"

"He got into an altercation with one of his neighbors a few years ago. It made the community weekly for his area."

"Really?" Sam said. "What kind of altercation? He seems pretty laid-back."

"According to the article I found, Anand and one of his neighbors, a guy named Nathan Hickam, had been arguing about a tree right on the property line for several months. The tree was mainly in Anand's yard, but Hickam wanted to get rid of it because the leaves would drop into his swimming pool. So one day, while Anand and his family were gone for a long weekend, Hickam cut it down with a chainsaw. When Anand came back, he went over to Hickam's house, and the two of them got into a fight in the front yard. It was bad enough that the other neighbors called the police."

"Wow," she said. "What happened? Did they get arrested?"

"Neither of them filed complaints, so no criminal charges came about. But Anand filed a lawsuit against Hickam in small claims court."

"And I take it Anand won," she said.

"He did, but not the full amount that he'd sued for. It turns out that Hickam presented evidence that Anand had swung at him during the altercation. He showed medical records that he was treated for a sprained back, which he claims he suffered when he dodged Anand's attack."

"But you said no reports were filed when the police showed up. And the judge bought that? Hickam could have hurt his back some other way."

"It might have influenced the decision," he said with a

shrug, "but it's hard to tell. Anand had asked for reasonable damages, just under $5,000. But the judge awarded him $2,500."

She shook her head. "I have no idea how much trees are worth. Is that a good judgment?"

"I didn't know, either, so I asked one of the reporters who covers real estate, and he said the value of the tree is determined by its type—an elm in this case—its height, the diameter of its trunk, etc. He said disputes like this end up in small claims all the time, and the amount awarded in this case is on par with what he's seen, since the tree was pretty mature."

"How did you find out all this information? Was there another article?"

"No," he said. "I went to the courthouse and pulled the records."

"I'm impressed," she said with a grin. "You're really getting into this. Like an investigative journalist. I thought you said this was just a puff piece."

"Well, it is. All the paper is expecting from me is a profile of CS Solar. But since you asked me to look into Dale, and since I found all that interesting stuff about Henry, I thought I'd check out Anand too."

Sam looked at the report again. "So what do I do with this? What does it mean?"

"We don't know if Raul shared it with anyone, or how Ernesto got his hands on it, do we?"

"I don't know how Ernesto got this," she said, "but Raul's girlfriend said he'd filed the report and was told it wasn't enough for them to do anything about it. The problem is, we don't know who told him that." She stood up and started pacing back and forth. "He filled this out two weeks before he died. Then, a few days before he died, I see him in clinic with his mother, and his eyes were red. I just thought he had allergies—honestly, he wasn't very forthcoming when I asked him questions, and afterward, I thought maybe he had been smoking marijuana. I thought he didn't want to talk about it in front of his mom."

"What did his autopsy show?"

"Dylan said there was nothing unusual." She stopped pacing and sat on the coffee table to face James. "This is what I'm worried about: Ernesto showed me a crack in the wall down in the pit where Raul worked. That wall is only a few feet away from a restroom that had a sewage back-up." She pointed to the report in her hands. "And Raul complained of a rotten egg smell. Do you know what causes that?"

James gave her a whimsical look. "Flatulence?"

She rolled her eyes and huffed. "I'm serious, James. I think I missed something clinical, and if I'd been more diligent, I could've saved his life."

He held up his hands. "I'm sorry. You really care about this, and I made a stupid joke." He frowned. "But why do you think you could've done something? I mean, even if Dale was a jerk—and who knows about Anand—Raul died in a car accident. You couldn't have done anything about that."

Sam sighed. "Ernesto thought the sewage backup may have led to Raul's symptoms, and when I told Mrs. Garza about it, she said her nephew knew a coworker who'd been overcome by swamp gas and died while working on a sewer line. So I looked it up, and now I think Raul was exposed to hydrogen sulfide. It smells like rotten eggs, and it can result in nausea and headaches, along with conjunctivitis. I'm pretty sure now that this caused the redness I saw in his eyes."

"How do people die?"

"If the levels are high enough, they can die immediately, not only from the toxic effects of the gas, but because there's not enough oxygen. But the gas is heavier than air and can concentrate in confined spaces."

"Like the pit Raul worked in," he said.

"Exactly. Higher concentrations lead to more toxicity, with the most significant effects in the respiratory and nervous systems. People exposed to it can feel disoriented."

"So he might have been disoriented enough to crash his car?"

"Yes. I think that could be the case."

They sat in silence for a few moments. Then James took the report and read it over again. "If Raul filed the report as it instructs the employee to do, the supervisor is supposed to respond in forty-eight hours. And that super-visor is Dale?"

"Yes."

Still looking at the page, he said, "It says here that if the supervisor doesn't respond by then, the employee should contact the safety coordinator. And that's Anand?"

"Yes."

"But he didn't tell you about this?"

"No. When I met with him—which was before I got this—I tried to find out if any hazard reports had been filed recently, and he was a little defensive. But when I mentioned that Raul hadn't felt well and left work early before he crashed his car, Anand said he didn't see how Raul could have gotten sick from anything at work."

She took the report back from James and studied it. "The woman who gave this to me seemed a bit nervous." Then Sam had an idea and stood up. "I gotta go. I need to talk to her."

30

A s soon as Sam got to her apartment, she logged into ObraCare's electronic health record to find Miss Morales's phone number in her chart. Technically, she wasn't allowed to look up patient information for something unrelated to the patient's care, but in Sam's mind, what she wanted to know was kind of related, at least tangentially. Plus, if anyone ever asked, since every interaction was logged, she could always say she was just following up to see how her patient was doing.

If she could verify that Miss Morales had used the restroom next to the inspection pits, and since Ernesto had told Sam he'd felt dizzy and had headaches after using the same restroom, then she would have evidence of three people experiencing the symptoms of possible hydrogen sulfide exposure.

Sam dialed the number, and after a few rings it went to voicemail. She left a message asking Miss Morales to call her back.

She sat there for a few moments. What else could she

do? She really hoped Miss Morales would call her back. She'd seemed a bit skittish earlier, but maybe she would talk to Sam if she was away from work—and away from Dale.

While Sam waited, she decided to make some progress on her term paper. She found a chart she could include in her report summarizing work fatalities due to chemical inhalations from the Bureau of Labor Statistics. From 2011 to 2017, the two most common chemicals leading to fatalities were carbon monoxide and hydrogen sulfide, causing 162 deaths. The number of fatalities from other substances dropped off significantly after that, with the next groups of chemicals—coal, natural gas, and petroleum fuels and products—causing eleven deaths during that same time period. Plus, the majority of deaths caused by hydrogen sulfide were in confined spaces.

Sam paused a moment to think how awful this was. She was looking at hard statistics, stark numbers and bar charts on a web page, but these represented real people, people who had gone to work one day, never to come home. How horrible it must be for their families.

She took a deep breath and went back to the OSHA website to review the information on hydrogen sulfide again. Colorless, usually smelled like rotten eggs at low concentrations, extremely flammable, highly toxic. Produced or used in a number of industries. Sometimes called sewer gas or swamp gas, just like Mrs. Garza had said. On one page under the heading "Why is hydrogen sulfide so deadly?" the website stated: "After a while at low or more quickly at high concentrations, you can no longer smell it to warn you it's there."

That's exactly what Nina had said about Raul, that after a while he'd told her he couldn't smell the bad odor anymore. Sam was now more convinced than ever that Raul had been exposed to hydrogen sulfide.

Her phone buzzed. Miss Morales was returning her call.

"Thanks so much for calling me back. How is your ankle doing?"

"It's almost completely better, Doctor."

"That's good. And are you doing okay otherwise? How is your job?"

"It's good. It's much better working intake than assembly." She let out a small laugh. "Spraining my ankle was probably the best thing that could've happened. Everyone wants to work in the front."

"I'm glad you're better and everything worked out."

"But that's not why you called, is it, Doctor?"

"No, it isn't." Sam switched her phone to her left ear so she could take notes. "Do you know why Ernesto told you to give me the report?"

"He just said things were looking bad. He didn't want to tell me too much. He said he didn't want me to be in danger."

This rankled Sam's nerves. "What kind of danger?"

"I don't know," Miss Morales said. "I thought he was making it up, but then...well, you know what happened, right?"

"Yes," Sam replied. "Did you look at the report?"

"Yeah."

"What did you think?"

"About what?"

"That Raul had filed the report," Sam said, "that he was feeling bad."

"I don't know," Miss Morales said slowly. "I didn't really know Raul. But I knew Ernesto, since we grew up in the same neighborhood. He was always getting into trouble."

Sam didn't expect her patient to know, but she asked anyway, "Do you know who might have killed Ernesto?"

The young woman hesitated on the other end of the line, then said, "I'm sure it had to do with the stuff that sent him to jail."

"So you don't think it had anything to do with the report he gave you?"

"Not really. Why would it?"

Maybe Dylan was right, Sam thought. *Maybe Ernesto really was murdered because of his gang involvement, as Miss Morales has just alluded to.*

Sam's anxiety began to dissipate. She needed to rein in her active imagination.

She scrolled through Miss Morales's record on the computer. "When I saw you in clinic, you told me you tripped and sprained your ankle right after you'd used the restroom. Was it the one on the factory floor that had to be shut down?"

"Yeah, that's it. I was feeling a little dizzy when I came out, and there was a pallet that had fallen over, so I tripped." She paused, and then said, "Wait, that was right next to the pits where Raul and Ernesto worked."

"Did you notice an odor in the restroom?"

"Now that you say it, it reeked. But I didn't pay no attention, 'cause, you know, some bathrooms just have a funk."

"Did you complain about the smell?"

"Why would I? They wouldn't do anything. They'd just tell us that's how bathrooms are." Miss Morales let out a little laugh. "But then one of the toilets backed up, and it really stank up the place."

"So that's when they closed the restroom?"

"There was gross water all over the floor. They had to do something."

This confirmed Sam's thinking about the restroom. If Miss Morales was feeling light-headed, she might have been exposed to low levels of hydrogen sulfide in the bathroom. The question now was, who did Raul file his complaint with?

"The report says Raul should have discussed things with his supervisor before filling it out," Sam said. "Was Dale his supervisor?"

"That's right. Dale thinks everyone's just lookin' for excuses not to work."

"Do you know if Raul gave this report to Dale?"

"No idea."

"What about Anand?"

"Who?"

"Anand, the safety coordinator."

"Oh, that guy. He's one of the new bosses."

"It says here on the report that if Dale hadn't responded within forty-eight hours, Raul should've contacted the safety coordinator."

"Dale would get real pissed if you went around him."

"So what would you do if you couldn't get Dale to listen?"

"Well, he had to listen to me," Miss Morales said. "He kinda couldn't ignore me limping. But I don't know what Raul did."

"What do you think about Anand and Henry?"

"The new bosses?"

"Yes, the new managers who came in after CS Solar bought the company."

"They're okay. The ladies I work with now, they said

they didn't get their breaks, and now that guy with the funny name comes in to check."

"You mean Anand?"

"That's him. He comes a couple times a week. He asks us how we're doing."

"Is Dale still your supervisor?"

"It's Marcie now. She's good. The ladies said she got the job after they made a fuss about the breaks."

Sam thanked Miss Morales again for returning her call and hung up. She hadn't learned what she wanted about the hazard report—if Raul had done anything other than filling out the form. But she had to assume he'd at least given it to Dale. And if Dale didn't do anything, she didn't know if Raul had taken the next step and contacted Anand.

The fact that Miss Morales was experiencing dizziness after using the restroom next to Raul's workstation further pushed Sam into thinking he'd suffered from hydrogen sulfide exposure, which meant she'd likely missed it when she'd seen him. And if that was truly the case, she felt awful.

While she couldn't do anything about his death, she could find out if Dale had blocked Raul's attempts to have the problem addressed before it turned deadly.

Despite Anand's defensiveness around Sam's probing to learn more about safety complaints, she genuinely thought he wanted to do the right thing. Based on what Miss Morales had said—that he was checking to make sure the workers were getting their breaks—she was even more convinced that he could be trusted.

She snapped an image of the hazard report and attached it to an email. She added a quick note outlining her hypothesis about hydrogen sulfide exposure, including that she strongly suspected the restroom might be the origin, since she knew of at least three employees who had experienced symptoms. She purposefully left the source of the hazard report vague, not wanting to get Miss Morales in trouble. Then she decided to copy Henry on it. Surely he would want to know that he had a supervisor working for him who did not take safety seriously.

31

The next morning, Sam and James hiked the greenbelt behind their apartment complex, enjoying the fresh air and absorbing the changing colors of fall, with some trees turning yellow and rusty, while the evergreens held on to their darker tones. She filled him in on her conversation with Miss Morales; then she told him about the email she'd sent to Anand and Henry with her hypothesis.

"Are you sure you trust them?" James asked. "What if they're part of the problem?"

"You've met them." Sam shrugged. "They seem like they really care about improving things at this Austin facility."

"Sure, that's what they told you, because you're a doctor," he said. "So of course they'd focus on health and safety. They know their audience."

They'd come to the end of the path, at the edge of a shallow stream feeding into the larger creek running alongside them. James sprang across easily in long strides, using a couple of small boulders nestled in the rocky bed as steppingstones. As Sam followed him, her foot slipped when she launched off the last stone to reach the other side, but James put out his arms to catch her and kept her from stumbling to the ground.

"When I interviewed Henry," James said as they continued along the trail, "he spent a lot of time touting the cash infusion they would be getting. He carried on about how that would increase their operations, along with the amount of capital the site would bring to the local economy."

"And that's what he would talk about with you, because he knows his audience," she retorted lightheartedly. "Aren't those profiles aimed at promoting businesses?"

James grinned. "Fair enough."

When they finished their hike, James asked if Sam wanted to grab some lunch. "Sorry, but I've got a date with Alex and my dad. They're playing golf right now, and they want me to meet them at the country club when their round is over."

He raised his eyebrows. "So they're getting along pretty well, huh?"

"Yeah, I guess they are," Sam said.

"You don't seem very happy about it."

So much had happened in the past few days, since she and James had gone shopping for his sister's birthday gift. Normally, she would've shared more with him, giving him all the details of the argument she'd had with Alex and her suspicions that Millie and her father might've had an affair before her mother died. But for some reason, she didn't want to dump it all on him. He certainly had dealt with his share of family drama.

"Are you okay?" James asked, breaking Sam's rumination.

She gave him a weak smile. "I'm fine."

ALEX HAD TEXTED Sam saying he and her father would finish their round soon so she could meet them for a late lunch. She still felt bad about her argument with him, as mild as it was. But his attitude made her wonder if she could trust him, if his restless instincts would return if she ever were to settle down with him.

During residency, he'd brag about how late he'd stayed out going to clubs, even when he knew he would be on call the next day. The couple of times she ventured out with his group of friends, he was always hitting on the local coeds.

When they reconnected recently, it seemed like he had changed. In the few months they'd been dating, she hadn't sensed that he would revert to his previous philandering behavior, but she would always wonder.

Then there was her father. Would he forgive her for practically accusing him of having an affair with Millie before her mother had passed away? Did he even know she would be joining them for lunch? She supposed Alex would have told him.

The trip out to the Omni in Barton Creek was scenic and winding. The brisk fall day, with only a few wispy clouds in the brilliant blue sky, brightened her mood. Sam drove westward into the hills outside Austin, then turned onto the road leading into the posh neighborhood with well-manicured landscaping surrounding the resort. She followed the signs to the clubhouse and pulled into the tree-covered parking lot.

Once inside, Sam gave her father's name to the host. He welcomed her and led her through the clubhouse bar, named after a famous local golfer, to a terrace overlooking the luxurious property. Sam's father and Alex were already seated, both with pints of beer in hand. When they saw her approach, they set down their drinks and stood. She was a little apprehensive—it was the first time she'd seen or spoken to her father since she probed into the past. How would he act?

Her unease melted away when she saw broad smiles on their faces. They were happy to see her, and they were relaxed, their faces radiant and pink from the sun. Her father kissed her on the cheek, then she gave Alex a quick peck on the lips.

"Will Millie be joining us?" Sam asked tentatively as she took a chair.

"She's spending the weekend with her sister in New Orleans," her father said.

She unwound a touch more, glad that she wouldn't have to put on pretenses for Millie. "How was your round?"

"Not bad," Alex said. "I have a penchant for finding the water and the brush, but Steven was generous and usually let me replay from the drop zones with only a one-stroke penalty, even if I kept ending up in the hazards."

"You did pretty well, considering you said you've only played a handful of times before." Her father signaled the waiter.

After they placed their orders, her father excused himself to use the restroom.

Alex leaned closer to Sam, his demeanor more serious. "What did that cop friend of yours want the other night?"

She'd almost forgotten that Dylan showed up right as Alex was leaving. "He wanted to check on me," she said.

"Right." Darkness began to cloud his fine features. "He wanted to check on you."

"No. It's nothing like that." Heat prickled her neck. "He wanted to make sure I was okay because someone we knew had died."

He frowned as his head jerked in confusion. "What do you mean?"

"I was trying to tell you before you had to leave—how is that patient by the way?"

"He's fine. I bronch'd him, removed a mucus plug, and his sats improved. His pneumonia is clearing—his lung fields looked good on chest X-ray yesterday, so we stepped him down to the floor." He pursed his lips. "But don't change the subject. What's going on between you two?"

"There's nothing going on," she said. She explained to him how she'd been pulled into looking into Raul's death at Mrs. Garza's request, how it led to her going with James to El Morado to speak with Ernesto, and how Dylan was there because of an incident. She left out the part about the incident being her pepper-spraying a man who'd attacked her.

"Anyway, Dylan wanted to let me know that something had happened to that guy I'd spoken with, which is why he showed up at my apartment."

Alex looked at her skeptically. "So you're investigating a death that was probably an accident? What was so important that Dylan had to tell you?"

"That the person I talked to had been killed."

"What?" He looked alarmed. "What are you getting into?"

Sam didn't need another person telling her what she could and couldn't do. "Look, I'm just trying to…" Her voice trailed off as her frustration escalated. This wasn't going well. Why was she having to defend herself?

"To what? Are you trying to be an investigator? Just like you did with your friend's brother?"

She sat back in her chair and crossed her arms.

Her father returned to the table, glancing back and

forth between Sam and Alex as he sat down. "I'm not interrupting anything, am I?"

"No," Sam said. She put on a smile, hoping they could move on. "Alex and I were just discussing something."

"Sam was telling me why a police officer visited her the other night. Someone she knew in high school."

Apparently, Alex wasn't ready to let this go just yet.

"Oh, really?" her father said. "It wasn't Dylan, that guy you dated for a while, was it?"

Sam glared at her father as Alex shot her a look. She could feel his eyes burning into her.

The tension broke when a couple of servers arrived with their food. They set out the dishes along with condiments, and then they replenished everyone's water, with ice clanking into the glasses as they poured, filling the awkward silence.

After the servers left, the men dug in to their sandwiches, and Sam picked up her fork and pushed a tomato around her salad. A mockingbird in an oak branch above them cycled through its repertoire. She watched it as it chirped cheerfully for a few moments, then flew away. She wished she could join it.

Her father took a bite of his sandwich and washed it down with a gulp of beer. "So, Alex," he said, "it doesn't happen often, but if I need to fast-track a patient into the ICU, who should my office contact? Millie told me that, since Peggy retired, it's hard to figure out who pulls the strings around there."

"Unfortunately, it's been a bit of a revolving door," Alex said, shrugging. "Peggy was awesome, but no one has really stepped up to make sure things run as smoothly as she did."

And so the conversation went, with the men discussing hospital politics and interesting cases. For the most part, they ignored Sam, even though she understood everything. In fact, at one point, when she tried to interject to offer a possible solution to a situation her father was dealing with, he looked at her like she was being a nuisance.

She couldn't tell if Alex was just going along because he was still trying to impress her father, or if he had the same sentiment. By the time the men had finished their meals, Sam had only eaten half a tomato.

After her father closed out the tab, everyone stood up to leave, with Sam and her father exchanging a perfunctory goodbye. That was par for the course. She smiled as she laughed inwardly at the pun, despite her unease with everything.

Alex walked her to her car and stopped next to the trunk. "If we're going to continue this thing we have, we need to be honest with each other," he said. "You've already got enough on your plate right now, especially with your classes." He placed his hand on her arm and squeezed. "You want to get into that residency program, right?"

She nodded.

"Then why are you snooping around?"

Sam took in a deep breath, then said, "You're right."

She'd already sent the email with her theory to Anand and Henry. It was out of her hands now.

"So you're not going to talk to that cop anymore?"

"Why would I?" she said. "There's no reason to."

Alex's shoulders dropped, and he smiled. It seemed like he'd expected her to put up a fight, and when she didn't, he turned back into Prince Charming. He caressed her face, then brought her into his arms, and kissed her. When he pulled back, he said, "That's my girl."

32

After lunch at the country club, Alex and Sam decided to see a movie that evening, so they went their separate ways—Alex to his condo to get cleaned up, and Sam to her apartment so she could work on her class assignments. With all the research she'd already done into hydrogen sulfide and the other chemical exposures that led to workplace fatalities, she felt she'd made enough progress for the time being on her term paper. So she decided to work on a biostatistics problem set she'd been assigned and get ready for an upcoming test. However, she couldn't contain her curiosity, so before she dove into her homework, she checked to see if either Anand or Henry had responded to her email.

No response. It was the weekend, though, so they probably just hadn't seen it yet. She needed to be patient.

Sam worked through the problems and came up with a study plan for the test. She finished just in time to head over to Alex's condo, conveniently located in the new mixed-use space right next to the Alamo Drafthouse on South Lamar.

The Austin-based chain was perfect for dinner-movie combos, and they placed their orders in the theater as funky vintage film clips ran on the screen before the feature started. She loved how the Drafthouse always tied preshow snippets and menu items to the themes of the movies they played. Their food arrived just as the lights dimmed for the previews.

After they watched the latest star-packed thriller—with a somewhat implausible storyline—and escaped from the worries of the world for a few hours, Sam stayed over at Alex's condo.

When she awoke the next morning, nestled in Alex's arms, she felt a sense of calm. She didn't know if she was in love with him, but they were certainly compatible, and her father was already treating him like he was part of the family.

Can I spend the rest of my life with him?

She didn't know what his goals were—or what he wanted long term—since they'd only been dating a short time. Did he want to spend his career in Austin, or would he want to move on at some point?

Heck, she didn't even know what *she* wanted. So how could she know if their lives would align?

Alex grabbed coffee and breakfast from the gourmet grocer and deli on the first floor of his building, and they ate at his dinette table next to a window overlooking Lamar Boulevard. As Sam perused the Sunday paper, he said, "Let's go out to Fredericksburg for the day, like you wanted to do."

She looked up from the article she'd been reading about the opioid crisis. "Sorry, I can't. I really need to study. I've got a biostats exam coming up."

He frowned. "When is it?"

"I've got to complete it by Wednesday. I'd like to study

as much as I can today, and possibly take it tonight so I can get it out of the way." Just like she'd done with her occupational health exam the week before. It was how she made sure her courses didn't interfere with her job.

He stood and put his hands on her shoulders. He began to massage them, releasing the tightness she didn't even realize she had accumulated. *God, his hands feel good.*

"Why don't you forget about the exam today?" he said as he continued to work on the knots in her traps with just the right amount of pressure, melting away the tension.

"I can't. What if something comes up during the week and I have to stay late in clinic?"

"How often does that happen?"

"Not often, but…"

"But what? You only see strains and sprains, not true emergencies."

Sam pulled away from him, turning around in her chair so she could face him. "I don't typically see emergencies, but not all patients know where to go when they're having problems." She stood so she could be on level with him. "I've had to deal with MIs a few times, and those patients always seem to come in at the end of the day."

It was true. She didn't normally see heart attack patients, but when someone had severe, crushing chest pain, they just wanted a doctor, any kind of doctor.

"So what are you gonna do," he snarked, "take them to the cath lab?"

"No. We call 911."

Alex scoffed. "That's something they could do on their own."

Sam clenched her fists as she glared at him. "When they come to my clinic, I do the same thing I did in the ER. I assess them. Get an EKG. Start them on oxygen. Give them nitroglycerin."

She grabbed her purse and stomped to the door. "You don't respect me, do you?"

"Of course I do," he spluttered. But he'd hesitated just a fraction of a second too long before answering.

"You're an awful liar."

SAM'S BODY buzzed with anger as she drove home. She should have known; Alex would never change.

Sure, she'd always been at least a little attracted to him, despite having seen him banter and trash talk with the other male residents. She'd not engaged in that behavior, but she'd viewed it as a way for them to blow off steam and cope with the stress of medicine.

Over the last few months, she'd thought he'd outgrown it.

Until now.

Her phone vibrated as she drove, but she ignored it. Once she stopped at a light, she couldn't help peeking at it. Alex had left a voice message.

When she got home, she didn't even want to listen to what he had to say. She jumped in the shower and let the warm water cascade over her, washing away all her frustrations.

Focus on the goal. Finish classes so she could get her MPH.

She needed to take that biostats test today. Just get it out of the way before the workweek started.

She checked her phone again. Nothing more from Alex.

Fine with her.

After she calmed down a little more, she was grateful to have the logic of biostatistics to keep her mind occupied.

She immersed herself in Kaplan-Meier curves and survival functions, only taking breaks to eat a snack at lunch, then to heat up a frozen dinner in the evening. She studied for another hour and took her exam.

With that finally out of the way, she checked her phone. Alex had texted several times with various apologies, admitting that he was a jerk and asking if they could talk.

Sam texted back: Let's take a break.

THE NEXT DAY, Sam saw Mrs. Garza on the clinic schedule, so she'd planned on updating the grieving mother with what she'd learned. She hoped she could also let her know that someone at CS Solar was looking into it, but when she checked her email midmorning, there was still no response from either Henry or Anand. She figured her email was probably buried in the deluge of Monday morning messages.

Sam worked through the queue of patients, trading off with Jerry on seeing the new injuries that came in. When she got to Mrs. Garza's appointment, she was ready to share the report, her theory about what happened to Raul, and that she had let management at CS Solar know about it.

However, as soon as she entered, she found Mrs. Garza sitting on the exam table with her legs hanging over the edge, looking more like a child than a grown woman. She kept her head down, focusing on her hands in her lap, and said, "I'm all better and I'm ready to go."

"That's good. Are you having any pain at all?"

Mrs. Garza shook her head with tiny pivots.

"Okay," Sam said slowly. Something was off. "Let's take a quick look at you."

On exam, Sam found Mrs. Garza still had a mildly decreased range of motion with some continued sensitivity on palpation of her lower back muscles. Even though she cooperated fully during the exam, Mrs. Garza maintained a flat affect. She'd improved slightly from the last visit, but Sam couldn't tell if her patient's change in mood was part of the ups and downs of her continued grieving process or if something else was going on.

Sam glanced at the chart. "We removed all your restrictions the last time you were here, but you still have one more PT session left. How are you doing at work?"

"I'm doing fine. I can go."

Sam hesitated. "Are you sure everything is okay, Mrs. Garza?"

"Yes. Just let me go."

"But I also want to talk to you about Raul. I think I've figured out what might have happened to him," Sam said as she pulled the hazard report from her coat pocket.

Mrs. Garza closed her eyes, her breathing slowing, and for a moment, it looked like she might cry. Then her eyes popped open. She sniffed in deeply and said, "That doesn't matter anymore."

"But let me show you what I found." Sam held the report out for her to see. "I think you were right, that something happened to him at work."

"There's no point now. Raul is gone," Mrs. Garza said with a blank gaze, ignoring the paper in front of her. "I'm ready to go, Doctor."

And with that, she slid off the table and left the room.

Sam rushed after the older woman, but Cynthia stopped her in the hallway. "Dr. Jenkins, Jerry needs your help with the lac in Room Two."

"Uh, okay," Sam said. She watched her patient hurry away. "Mrs. Garza just left, and I wanted to talk to her about Raul. But she said it doesn't matter anymore. Do you know what's going on?"

"No," Cynthia said. "She hasn't said anything to me."

33

J erry's patient was lying in the flattened procedure chair of Room Two, with his head turned to the side. The upper part of his body was covered with paper drapes, exposing only his injured ear.

Jerry's concern was that the patient's laceration included the cartilage, and he wanted Sam's opinion on what to do. She donned gloves and assessed the damage, but the injury to the cartilage was minor, with only a tiny bit nicked. She thought Jerry could sew up the skin around it just fine. Plus, the patient didn't really care about the cosmesis of the repair—he already had cauliflower ears from his wrestling days in high school. But she was glad that Jerry wanted to double-check with her anyway.

As she moved on to see the next patient, she avoided thinking about Mrs. Garza, but questions bubbled to the surface of her conscience. What had changed? Why was she acting that way?

She stood for a second outside an exam room, took a deep breath, then flipped a mental switch to focus on the next visit as she entered. It was a follow-up for an urgent care patient who had developed De Quervain's tenosynovitis from lifting her infant. The strain and inflammation from the repetitive motion had resulted in pain in her wrist and the base of her thumb.

Sam had treated the new mom with a steroid injection in the tendon sheath the week before, and her symptoms had resolved almost immediately. The patient reported she'd been able to do her usual activities—including taking care of her baby—without any issues, and the pain had not returned. She was so grateful, she asked Sam if she could be her regular doctor, but Sam had to explain to her that she didn't practice primary care. Maybe someday, once she completed residency and could have more independence.

As Sam entered the clinic work area after leaving the patient's room, she saw Dale standing outside the drug-testing bays, looking at some paperwork. When he raised his head and spotted Sam, he gave her a dismissive look.

Sam strode over to him. "Hello, Dale. What brings you here?"

"I've got two new hires getting tested."

"Are they replacing Raul and Ernesto?"

"That's none of your business," he said, turning away from her. "And I only want to deal with that other doc, Jerry. He's the only reasonable one around here."

"Well, that's tough," she said, "because he's a Physician Assistant, and I'm his supervising doctor, so you're still going to have to deal with me."

She reached in her coat pocket, pulled out the hazard report, and held it out in front of him.

"Why didn't you escalate this?"

As Dale skimmed the document, a scowl formed on his face, and then he snatched it away from her. "How did you get this?"

"That's none of your business," Sam retorted as she shoved her balled fists into her pockets.

His face was florid with anger, but it was also laced with something else. *Is he worried?*

She squinted at him. "You knew about this, didn't you? Why didn't you escalate it?"

"This is an internal company document. We'll have to deal with whoever gave this to you." He glared at her. "How did you get it?"

"Why didn't you do anything about it? Raul filed the complaint two weeks before he died."

"Raul died in a car accident outside of work."

"But he wasn't feeling well when he left. This may have something to do with his death."

Dale shook his head. "There's no proof."

"Is that what you want to believe? Because you feel guilty that you didn't do anything and could have saved his life?"

He glowered at her. "Look, missy. You think you know it all, with these ideas in your little head. But you don't know anything." He poked the paper. "This isn't the whole picture. For your information, I *did* escalate it, and the rest is none of your business."

Sam drew back as she felt the eyes of the staff on her, along with the stares of several patients.

Jerry appeared at her side, like an apparition, and gently tugged on her sleeve. "C'mon, Doc. Let's not make a scene."

She followed him, numbly, back to their work nook and plopped down in her seat. He pulled up his chair to join her.

"What was that all about?" he asked with concern in his eyes.

Should I tell him? No. She didn't want to get him

involved. Plus, after the way he'd handled Miss Morales's case, he would just tell her to leave it alone.

She sighed, just wanting it all to go away.

Perhaps Jerry had the right approach. Don't stir up anything. Don't rock the boat. Go along to get along.

She closed her eyes and shook her head. "It was nothing. He just knows how to push my buttons."

"I have to admit, he's not the most agreeable person."

"You can say that again."

34

That evening, after Sam got home, she replayed the events of the day in her mind. The blowup with Dale in the clinic was definitely not a good thing. It wasn't like her, and it wasn't very professional.

Plus, what if she'd just screwed up the deal with CS Solar? Dale probably went back and told Henry what had happened, and now she was sure he was reconsidering renewing the contract.

It would be her fault if Cynthia and Jerry lost their jobs.

Dr. Taylor would end up hearing about this, one way or another.

Who told him she was spending time away from the clinic anyway? Was it Jerry?

Maybe he wasn't as easygoing as he appeared to be.

After ruminating for a few minutes, she decided to work on her term paper to get out of the fruitless cycle. There was nothing better to clear the mind than dry government regulations.

Even though she still had a couple of weeks to finish it,

the paper would hang over her head until it was done. She'd gathered plenty of information during her research, but she needed to synthesize everything, to make a cohesive narrative, and to actually start writing the damn thing.

She went over to her small desk with full intent to start her work, but as she scooted her chair forward so she could reach her computer, her feet kicked the box of her mother's items that she'd slid into the foot space underneath.

What had her father told her?

That what had happened was her mother's story to tell.

He kept denying that anything had gone on with Millie before her mother died. And he'd said Millie was a friend of her mother's.

Why hadn't Millie told her that?

Sam still hadn't finished going through her mother's things. She was too shocked after finding the divorce paperwork, avoiding painful memories that might resurface.

Would she find anything in that box that would let her know what had really happened?

Maybe her father was lying. Maybe he was trying to push the blame onto her mother when he was the one who was at fault.

Why had her mother wanted a divorce?

Sam pushed her chair to the side, sat on the floor between the dinette table and her desk, and pulled the box toward her.

She straightened her back, psyching herself up for the task. *Just go through it quickly. There's probably not anything else of significance. And then get back to work on that assignment.*

As she shuffled through the contents, she found various papers, random bills, a few magazines. Near the bottom she found an envelope filled with pictures.

In some of the pictures, her mother was with a man who was not her father.

He had dark, shaggy hair with a five o'clock shadow framing a broad, handsome smile. He appeared slightly younger than her mom. They were clinging to each other in one of the photos, as if they had just kissed.

Sam sucked in a breath, as if she had plunged into an icy pond.

It couldn't be, could it?

Her hands trembled as she picked up the photograph to study it more closely. They seemed so happy.

Did Mom have an affair?

Did Sam have it all wrong? Was it her mother who had cheated on her father, not the other way around?

If her father wouldn't tell her, maybe Millie would. She dialed her number.

"Sam, what an unexpected surprise!" Millie said.

"I found pictures in the box you brought over."

"What pictures, dear?"

"Pictures of Mom with another man."

"Oh," Millie said. "I'll be right over."

35

Millie showed up at Sam's doorstep twenty minutes later. She sat at the dinette table with Sam next to her and leafed through the photographs, a wistful smile adorning her face when she saw her old friend alive and well again. She stopped on the image of Sam's mother and the unknown man embracing each other.

"My father told me you and my mother were friends," Sam said.

"That's true."

"Then why weren't you at the funeral?"

"I was, darling, but you didn't know me then," Millie said.

Sam blinked a few times as she tried to remember the event. It had been so painful, and she was so distressed. There were waves of people she didn't know who had come to pay their respects. It was entirely possible that Millie was just another person in the sea of faces.

"I have to admit...I suspected that you and my father had an affair before Mom died."

Millie gasped, raising her eyebrows. "Oh, goodness. No, dear. That certainly wasn't the case. Sure, we've known each other for some time, and dear Chuck, my late husband, used to refer patients to your father when we lived out in Marble Falls, and he continued after we moved closer to Austin."

"Why did you move?"

"So Chuck could get better care after his heart attack." She paused. "He kept practicing until he was too sick to see patients anymore. A year later, he passed away."

Millie stared straight ahead, absently, as if she was watching a stream of old memories. Sam put her hand on the older woman's and gave her a gentle squeeze. She wasn't the only one suffering.

A few moments later, Millie drew in a breath and continued speaking. "Chuck and I would see your parents at social events, and then your mother and I struck up a friendship. We had a lot in common and liked a lot of the same things. We'd usually have lunch or coffee together once or twice a month. We'd talk about the books we were reading." She smiled. "And she talked about you. She was so proud of you."

Hearing her mom had shared her pride in Sam created a glow, like a hug from within from her mother's spirit. She wished she could relish that feeling forever.

But there was more she needed to know, so she asked, "What happened in Aspen, at that conference?"

Millie turned to Sam. "Oh, is that why you thought your dad and I…"

"You mentioned something that happened in Aspen when we all went to dinner. I know Dad went to that conference before Mom died, so I just thought—"

"Oh, no, no," Millie said as she squeezed Sam's hand. "I can see why you thought that, but no. It just happened that we both attended the same conference. But while we were there, your father wanted to know...he knew I was fairly close to your mother, so he wanted to know why she wanted to leave him."

"So you knew about the divorce?"

Millie raised her eyebrows. "What divorce?"

"I found divorce papers in here." Sam tapped the box on the floor with the side of her foot.

"I didn't realize she had taken it that far, but I knew she wasn't happy. She never overtly stated she wanted to leave your father," Millie said. "She would talk about how absent he was, how he was always in the hospital or staying late to see patients. How even at home, he wasn't present—if you know what I mean."

"Yes, I know exactly what you mean," Sam said, folding her arms in front of her. "He's been that way with me too. Unless I'm talking about something that matters to him, it's like I'm not even there. He's always reading a journal article or reviewing charts."

Millie nodded. "So he kept asking me—every chance he could get during that conference—if I knew why she wanted to leave him."

"What did you do?"

"Well, I kept putting him off as much as I could, but he was persistent. I really didn't feel it was my place to intervene. I tried to be diplomatic about it." She shifted in her seat. "But one night in the bar of the hotel, after we'd both had a couple of drinks, I finally told him, from my perspective, he was married to his work, not to your mother. I said she felt neglected."

Sam waited for Millie to continue, and when she didn't, she pointed to the picture of her mother with the other man. "Did you know about this?"

Millie shook her head. "No, but I suspected. There was

a time when she seemed happier. She kept rescheduling our get-togethers, but she would be vague about why. She never had been that way before—she would usually be pretty transparent."

Sam breathed in deeply. It all made sense now. "So when my mother was diagnosed with ovarian cancer…"

"Your father finally became the man your mother had married again. He became attentive and did everything he could for her. Until…"

"Until she died," Sam finished.

Millie turned her chair so she could face Sam directly, and took both of Sam's hands in hers. "He truly loved her. We both did."

Sam broke down, with small whimpers at first, which eventually stretched and grew into sobs that engulfed her. Millie opened her arms, crying along with Sam and embracing her, letting Sam rest her head on her shoulder.

After a few minutes of shared grief, Sam pulled back and said, "Why did it have to take my mother's cancer to get my father to change?"

"I don't know, darling. Sometimes the only way someone will change is to face imminent death."

36

S am felt as if she had been put through an emotional wringer, but now it all made sense. Her anger toward her father had diminished, not entirely, but it had ratcheted down a notch, and had been replaced with pity.

Not because she thought he was a victim, but that he couldn't see past his own faults, that he didn't have the insight to see how his behavior affected those he loved most. It wasn't as if her mother's illness and death awakened him in all respects, for he still seemed to view her, his only child, with disappointment and, sometimes, disdain.

She would not allow his assessment of her to cloud her perception of herself.

∼

THE NEXT DAY IN CLINIC, Cynthia came to Sam as soon as she got there.

"Elma's acting weird," Cynthia said.

Sam blinked for a moment in confusion, her ruminations on the revelations of the previous evening receding. "I'm sorry? Elma?"

Cynthia frowned. "Elma Garza. You were worried about her, so I checked on her last night."

"Right. Mrs. Garza. What happened?"

"She didn't want to talk. She only said since Raul is dead, there is no point to anything."

Now Sam started to worry that maybe Mrs. Garza was slipping into depression, that it wasn't just grief. She would check on her and maybe help her find some counseling.

But Cynthia continued, leaning closer to Sam and lowering her voice. "The thing is, Dr. Jenkins, her front window was busted. She told me it was just some kids, that they accidentally knocked a ball through it. But I'm not so sure."

"Thanks for letting me know. I'll check on her as soon as I leave work today."

After Cynthia walked off, the voices of a couple of men carried over from the drug-testing bays, reminding Sam of the confrontation with Dale the day before.

Was he telling the truth? Had he really escalated Raul's complaint?

Then a conspiratorial thought struck her. *Maybe he had something to do with the change in Mrs. Garza's behavior.*

And what was the deal between Dale and Jerry?

She glanced over at Jerry sitting beside her, typing on his keyboard, seemingly unaware of the turmoil in Sam's brain. The thought dawned on her again: *Would Jerry call Dr. Taylor to complain about me?*

"Hey, Jer," she said, trying to act casually. "Thanks for seeing those patients the other day when I was late getting back from lunch."

Jerry waved his hand. "Not a problem, Doc. It's what I'm here for."

"But Dr. Taylor seemed concerned enough to stop by. You didn't happen to mention it to him?"

"Mention what to him?"

"That I had gone to CS Solar?"

Jerry tugged at the hairs on his goatee. "Naw, why would I do that? I know you've got other things you need to do to keep this clinic running. And wasn't Dr. Taylor the one who told you to go there in the first place?"

"Yeah, he was, but—" Sam stopped because Jerry didn't know Dr. Taylor had now told her to stop visiting the company, at least during work hours.

"But what?"

Sam did a slight shake of her head. "Nothing. You don't think Jill would have said something to him, do you?"

"I don't think so. Jill likes you, so if she had any concerns, she'd come directly to you about it." He turned his chair toward her, a concerned look on his face. "Are you doing okay? It seems like you've been stressed out lately."

"Do I really look stressed out?"

"Well, you know, you snapped at that supervisor yesterday."

"Like I said, he just knows how to push my buttons." She paused, then drew in a deep breath. "And, actually, I'm worried I might have missed a diagnosis on someone."

"Oh, I think you got it right, but honestly," he lowered his voice, "we don't need to throw everything at someone with a sprained ankle. It's a balancing act—ObraCare wants us to refer to physical therapy, but the companies don't want us to put their patients on restrictions." Then he frowned. "You aren't still mad at me for changing the restrictions on that patient, are you?"

Sam shook her head, confused for a moment. Then she realized—he thought she'd been talking about Miss

Morales. "No. That's okay. I understand, and it seems like Miss Morales is doing fine—I saw her at CS Solar, and she's been moved to another job, one that she had been requesting anyway. But I just wonder..." She looked directly at Jerry. "It just seems like Dale, that supervisor, is a little bigoted. In the way he treated her and the way he may have treated others..."

"Well, there certainly are those types around," he said, waving his hand. "You've just got to deal with them and not let them bring you down."

"But I can't shake the idea...I was asked to check out someone, and they had conjunctivitis, but I didn't do a really thorough history, and I think it led to..." She paused. She shouldn't have brought this up with Jerry. He didn't need to get involved in this.

"You were asked to check out someone—so this wasn't a patient?"

"No, it was a family member of a...a friend who asked for some medical advice."

"Oh, one of *those* situations." He smiled knowingly. "All you can do is tell them what you think and that they should follow up. They're not your patient, so you don't have any more responsibility than that."

"I suppose you're right," she said. "Thanks, Jer."

Sam meant what she'd said. She knew she couldn't be responsible for everyone, but now that she'd gone down this path, it was hard for her to completely give up her pursuit of the truth.

She turned back to her computer and checked her email. Still nothing from Henry or Anand, and it was now Tuesday, so surely they would have seen her message by now.

Maybe the incident with Dale had caused them to think she was a bit looney and disregarded what she'd sent them. Some men were always looking for excuses to discount women's ideas.

Kyle shuffled by on his way to his office.

His office.

He was the one who had escalated things when Sam said he couldn't have it, that it was hers, since she was the clinic's medical director. But then Dr. Taylor had called and told her Kyle should have it, because she didn't really need it—because she was supposed to be in the exam rooms seeing patients or out in the work area watching the board to make sure patients weren't waiting too long.

He told her this, even though there were plenty of times between patient visits when she needed to speak on the phone with adjusters, peer reviewers, specialists, and, yes, the patients themselves. Times when she had to discuss private matters and protected health information, topics that should not be revealed out in the open where her workstation currently was, where others, anyone walking by, could hear. But sure, the sales guy needed the office. The sales guy who only spent a few hours a week at the clinic.

She couldn't help but think the situation would've ended up differently if she'd been a man, that this was just another microaggression, and if she made too big a deal out of it, she'd be labeled as emotional and petty.

Sam stood and marched into Kyle's office. She closed the door, in case she couldn't control her temper; she didn't want a repeat incident, like she'd had with Dale.

"Did you call Dr. Taylor to complain about my visits to CS Solar?"

Kyle looked stunned. "What? No. Why would I?"

"I don't know. You didn't seem to have a problem calling him before."

"I didn't even know you'd gone over there again. Why would you need to?"

"Anand wanted me to review a few safety protocols with him."

Kyle leaned back in his chair and grinned. "That's great. Putting more face time in with the customer. That's what gets these deals done."

The tension in Sam's shoulders loosened a bit, but then Kyle sat up and logged into his computer. "However, I just got a text from big Kahuna Carl to ask Henry about the contract negotiations. It said more details were in an email chain. Let's see…" He clicked and scrolled. "Apparently our legal team hasn't heard back from their legal team for a week." He shrugged. "Really, that's not too unusual—these negotiations can drag out for months sometimes. But Carl likes to ride my ass."

As Sam left the office, a pit formed in her stomach. Even though Kyle seemed to think the delay wasn't anything, maybe her actions really had put the contract in jeopardy.

37

B y the end of the day, Sam still had not received a reply from Henry or Anand, and despite her apprehension about the delay in the contract negotiations, she had to believe Kyle. She had little experience with these types of business dealings, and Kyle didn't seem worried. Maybe she was drawing too many conclusions about things she didn't have insight into and didn't fully understand.

But she was concerned about Mrs. Garza, especially after what Cynthia had told her. Why had her demeanor changed suddenly?

Sam drove to Mrs. Garza's house, but unlike the last time she was there, the street was quiet. It was the week before Thanksgiving, so a few houses had fall decorations, with wreathes of colorful leaves and cutouts of cornucopias and turkeys dressed in Pilgrim costumes. Many houses had cars tucked away under carports, and there were only a few parked on the street, so she had no problem finding a spot in front of her patient's home.

As Sam walked up to the house, she noticed a piece of

cardboard taped over one of the panes in the front window. Just like Cynthia had mentioned.

She knocked on the front door, and after a few moments, the door opened an inch, restricted by a chain. "Hi, Mrs. Garza. Do you mind if we talk?"

Sam made out what appeared to be a nod through the narrow gap. The door shut, followed by the sliding of metal; then Mrs. Garza opened the door fully. A folded dish towel was over her shoulder and reading glasses hung around her neck. Her eyes quickly darted back and forth down the street before she extended her arm to welcome Sam inside.

"I'm not disturbing you, am I? Were you making dinner?" Sam said. "I can come back."

"No, no. I was just getting a bite to eat."

After showing Sam to a seat at the kitchen table, Mrs. Garza remained standing, hovering over her like a bee. "Do you want something to drink, Doctor?"

"No, ma'am. I'm fine, I just wanted to talk to you about—"

"How about something to eat? I'm sure you're hungry after a busy day in the clinic."

"No, really, Mrs. Garza, I'm not hungry."

"Well, it's almost dinnertime. Surely, you need to eat dinner." She went to the stove, lifted the lid on a pot, and peered in. "I have plenty—I keep forgetting that I don't need to make so much since Raul is…" She slowly lowered the lid back onto the pot.

Sam paused for a moment, then said softly, "Thank you, but I'll eat a little later." She patted the table in front of the seat next to her. "Please, Mrs. Garza, sit down with me."

The older woman worried the edge of the dish towel for a moment before she finally joined Sam.

"I want to show you something," Sam said as she took out her phone. She brought up the image of the hazard report from the email she had sent to Anand and Henry.

Mrs. Garza put on her reading glasses and scanned the document. She suddenly burst into tears and dabbed her eyes with the dish towel.

Sam put her hand on her shoulder, giving her a moment for the grief to pour out of her. Once the flood of sorrow receded, Sam said, "I'm so sorry to bring this up. It's just that...right after Raul died, you asked me to look into this. But then yesterday, you didn't want to discuss it."

Mrs. Garza took a couple of deep breaths and seemed to calm down a bit. She looked up at Sam and said, "Do you think this is why Raul wasn't feeling well? This smell?"

"Possibly," Sam said. "But I was wondering: why didn't he say anything when I saw him in the clinic?"

Mrs. Garza wagged her head. "I don't know. At that point, he hadn't told me how bad it was. I just saw his eyes were red and bothering him. If I had known, I would have told you."

Sam nodded. She didn't feel completely off the hook for missing Raul's diagnosis, but she clearly hadn't had all the information to make it. Still, she should have asked more questions while he was there in front of her.

Mrs. Garza continued, "It was a few days later that he was really starting to feel bad. Headaches and nausea. I asked him if something was going on, but he wouldn't talk."

"Do you know if anyone at work knew about his symptoms?"

"I told him he needed to let them know, but he said to stop nagging him, and he...he finally said he was going to tell someone, but he died before I could ask him if he did."

Mrs. Garza began to sob once more, tears anew streaming down her face.

Sam thought through what must have happened with Raul. Dale told her he'd escalated things, but he didn't say how or with whom. Of course, that's if Sam believed him. The form stated that Dale should've responded to Raul's request, filled out the bottom section, and returned it to Raul within two business days. Otherwise, Raul should contact the safety coordinator for the site.

Anand.

Why hadn't he gotten back to her? Even if her spat with Dale had disrupted the contract negotiations, or if her theory had made the men think she was just a crazy person, she had the feeling Anand would at least have responded to her. She would call him.

Mrs. Garza sucked in a deep, stuttering breath, then said, "Raul told me they just gave safety lip service around there. They would do safety meetings like they're supposed to, but then everyone was pressured not to report things. The supervisors didn't want to look bad." She dabbed her eyes again. "But he only told me this the day before he died. He wouldn't complain unless he really felt bad. These men…they try to be macho all the time. If you complain, you are weak."

Sam nodded. She knew plenty of men who fell into this category.

"Mrs. Garza, yesterday you told me this doesn't matter anymore, but I think I might know what made him sick. I just don't have proof of it yet. Do you want me to keep looking into this?"

A nervous look came over the older woman's face. "No. You need to stop." She glanced at the front window covered in cardboard. "You should go now."

Sam blinked, surprised by her sudden change in behavior. "Are you sure? What if someone else gets hurt?"

"You just need to go." Mrs. Garza stood and walked to the front door.

Sam grabbed her purse and followed her. When she got to the door, Sam said, "Is someone threatening you?"

The older woman didn't answer. Instead, she just opened the door.

Sam stepped outside. She turned to persuade Mrs. Garza to tell her what was going on, but Mrs. Garza's eyes were wide with fear. "Just go," she said as she quickly shut the door.

NICO WAS SITTING in Ramirez's car with him when they saw the woman leave Mrs. Garza's house.

"Hey, that's the bitch from the club," Ramirez said.

Nico grunted in the affirmative, not wanting to say anything that might reveal he had seen her with the cop at his sister's place.

"And look at that old lady, all freaked out." Ramirez laughed. "Didn't take much to scare her."

A brick through the window tends to do that, Nico thought. He was just glad that Mrs. Garza didn't know he was involved. She probably wouldn't recognize him, since they had only met a couple of times before—once before Raul died, and once when he came to her house to pay respects. He had actually liked Raul. Thought he was good for his sister.

A devious look came over Ramirez's face as he watched the woman get in her car. "Let's follow that bitch. Teach her a lesson." He made an obscene gesture with his hands. "We can have some fun."

S am got in her car outside of Mrs. Garza's house,
and as she started the engine, a flicker of light
caught her eye. It was the flare of a match, inside a
car parked about a block away. The flame highlighted the
face of the man who had attacked her at El Morado, the
one who had worn the cowboy hat. She saw the silhouette
of another man in the passenger's seat. After a moment,
the car pulled away from the curb, turned down a side
street, and disappeared. As the vehicle rounded the corner,
she thought she saw Nina's brother watching her through
the side window.

Sam's heart pounded in her ears. She picked up her
phone with shaky hands, fumbling to bring up Dylan's
number. Seconds felt like minutes once she dialed. He
answered after the third ring.

"I just saw them," she blurted.

"What? Saw who?"

"The men from the club."

"Where?"

"Just now, in front of Mrs. Garza's house. I think

they've intimidated her. She told me to stop looking into Raul's death."

"Are they still there?"

"No. They drove off."

"Do you see anything else suspicious right now?"

Sam peered out her windows at the surrounding neighborhood. Lights were on in most homes, but the street was still. The scattered cars parked along the curb were empty.

"No," she said. "I don't see anything."

He paused for a moment, then said, "All right. I'm in the middle of something right now, but I'll come by and talk to Mrs. Garza as soon as I can. You should go home. I'll check on you after I see her."

"Okay," she said. Then she remembered. "Wait—I won't be there. I'll be at James's. He wanted me to read over a piece he wrote for the paper."

"That sounds better. At least you'll be with someone until I can look into this."

She gave him James's apartment number, and he promised he'd see her soon. Before she could put her car in gear, her phone buzzed. It was Anand.

"Hi, Dr. Jenkins. I apologize for not getting back to you sooner—I was out of town this weekend and got back in the office today. I saw your email late this afternoon. Where did you get this report?"

"Uh, I'd rather not say."

"I see," he said. "Well, the document you sent is not complete, and I haven't had a chance to speak with Dale to see how he addressed this."

Sam began to say Dale told her he'd escalated the issue, but then she thought better of it.

"Anyway," Anand continued, "even though the restroom has been repaired, for the most part—we're still not connected to the city sewer—I want to take some measurements. Your theory seems plausible."

"Really?"

"Yes, I think it's plausible. I'd like to discuss it with you further. Would you be able to come by this evening?"

"Right now?" Sam glanced at the clock on her dashboard. It was just after 6:00 p.m., and James was expecting her to show up around now.

"I know it's a little late," he said, "but I'll probably be here a few more hours; I've got to catch up on everything after taking a day off. A friend who has access to an analyzer just brought it over, and I'd like to take some measurements as soon as I can, since—if there actually was a hydrogen sulfide accumulation—the levels might have decreased after they repaired the septic pump."

She really wanted to see what those measurements showed, to see if there was any validity to her theory. James would understand if she was late meeting with him. "Okay. I'm on my way."

SAM CALLED James as she drove to CS Solar and explained why she'd be late meeting with him.

"If Dale said he escalated Raul's complaint, but Anand says he didn't know about it, doesn't that mean someone is lying?" James asked.

"Well, obviously Dale is lying," Sam said. "Based on the way I've seen him act and how he pushed the Physician Assistant I work with to change my orders, I'm sure he ignored Raul's complaints."

"That does sound pretty dubious."

"Plus, a lot of the workers at the factory are Hispanic, and I think he's prejudiced against them," she said, "especially based on the stuff you found about him, after his daughter died."

"Right," he said. "I'd forgotten—she was killed in a hit-and-run by an undocumented immigrant."

"And he was a vocal advocate for the bill allowing police officers to ask for immigration status during traffic stops," Sam said. "What if he neglected to escalate Raul's complaint because he's a bigot?"

"You do have a point."

"Anyway, Anand thinks there is some merit to my theory on what happened to Raul, and he's going to take some measurements for hydrogen sulfide in the pit where Raul used to work. I want to see what they look like."

"Are you sure it's a good idea to go over there right now?" James asked. "It's pretty late."

Sam had exited the freeway and had just turned onto the old farm road leading to the solar factory. With no traffic around, darkness swallowed the beams of her headlights between the sparsely placed street lamps. She glanced at the clock on her dashboard. "It's not even 6:30; that's not late."

"Ugh, you're right," James said. "It just feels late. I hate how early the sun sets this time of year." He paused, then said, "Okay, what if Anand is upset that you've uncovered a safety issue he should've known about? You said he got defensive when you asked him about Raul before."

"He did, but I was trying to be too sneaky. I'd asked about how employees report hazards, in general, and if there had been any recent reports before I finally just asked him about Raul. He probably thought I was questioning their practices, so he got defensive."

"But there's also that info I dug up on him," James said. "He punched his neighbor over a landscaping issue.

Seems like he's got a temper, so if he is upset about your probing around—"

"What? You think he might get violent?" Sam let out a short laugh. "I really don't think so. I've spent a bit of time with him, and he's a pretty upright guy, very technical. I just think he wants to get to the truth."

"I hope you're right," he said. "How long do you think you'll be there? I'd love for you to read this profile I wrote, to make sure I didn't miss anything. My editor wants it by tomorrow."

"It shouldn't take very long—maybe only an hour—so I should get back in plenty of time."

Then she remembered what she'd seen before Anand had called. How quickly she'd gone from being terrified to being overcome with curiosity.

"Oh," she said, "and Dylan will probably stop by."

"What? Are things not going well with Alex?"

"Why are you always trying to assume there's something going on between me and Dylan?" she said. Then she added, "Actually, things aren't going well with Alex, but that's beside the point."

"Did something happen?"

She let out a breath. "I'll tell you about it later."

"Okay, fine," he said in a pouty tone. "So why is Dylan coming over?"

She explained what happened after she left Mrs. Garza's house—how she saw the man who attacked her and that she called Dylan.

"What? You think they're intimidating her? Why would that be?"

She thought for a moment. "That's a good question. Because it doesn't seem related to Raul's death at all."

"Huh. Maybe there's more to this than we know. Raul

had been involved with a gang, right? And so had Ernesto?"

"That's right. Dylan said the evidence pointed to a bad drug deal causing Ernesto's death, and that the guy who attacked me was a suspect. Maybe they're harassing Mrs. Garza because of something related to Raul's past, in which case, it should all be handled by the police."

Sam could see the entrance to the parking lot on the road up ahead.

"I'm almost there, so I need to go," she said. "Anyway, Dylan's going to talk to Mrs. Garza, and then he'll stop by afterward. So he probably won't get there until after I'm back."

"Okay, I'll see you soon," James said. "Just be careful."

39

As Sam turned in to the parking lot, she saw a figure walking to a pickup truck next to the pole supporting a light fixture. The sodium vapor lamp cast an eerie glow over the man next to the vehicle. It was Dale.

She parked next to the entrance of the building and glanced in his direction when she got out of her car. He shook his head with contempt before getting in his truck and driving off.

Anand must have talked to him. She was glad she wasn't there when that conversation took place. She watched as his truck drove down the street, and his headlights washed over a car going the opposite direction. It slowed down, as if it was about to turn in to the parking lot, but then it kept going until she couldn't see it anymore, with her view of it blocked by the building.

The car looked like the one that had been outside Mrs. Garza's house, the one with the men from the club. Her pulse picked up.

She couldn't be sure though. It was a generic import.

There were lots of those around. Plus, she wasn't sure about the car's color, not in the dimness of the streetlights.

Stop. You're just being paranoid.

She scanned the parking lot. There were a few cars scattered about. She approached the lobby and could see Alvera standing behind the reception desk, packing up her things for the day. The door was locked, so Sam tapped on it.

Alvera looked up, smiled, and reached under the desk. A buzzing sound came from the door, and Sam pulled it open.

"You're here late," Sam said as she walked up to the reception desk.

"Actually, this is pretty normal for me. Even though we have a new parent company, in many ways we still act like a startup. I've had to wear a lot of hats." Alvera's face brightened. "But we have a new hire starting after Thanksgiving to take over receptionist duties so I can focus on my main job."

"Oh, really? What's that?"

"HR," Alvera said. "With this acquisition, it's been crazy dealing with all the changes in benefits." She shrugged. "I mean it's worth it—we'll have a much better health plan. It's just hard getting everything done up here, especially since I often need to speak with people confidentially."

Sam nodded as she mentally chastised herself for assuming Alvera was just a receptionist. Not that she saw anyone as "just" a receptionist. She felt most receptionists and administrative assistants were underappreciated. They were the glue keeping organizations together and the grease to help everything run smoothly.

"How did you get roped into this?" Sam asked.

"When the last receptionist quit, Henry asked me to

man the front desk until we found a replacement." Alvera rolled her eyes. "I should've never agreed to it, but I just wanted to help out."

Sam smirked. "Yeah, us girls tend to get taken advantage of, don't we?"

"You can say that again." Alvera resumed packing up her things, squaring up a stack of folders to take with her. "So what brings you here this evening?" she asked.

"Did you know Raul Garza?"

"Yes. Quite tragic how he died in that car accident." Alvera shook her head. "His mother has been calling almost every day, wanting answers. I don't know what to tell her. It was horrible what happened to him, but when I ask, everyone here tells me it had nothing to do with his work here." She paused. "He was one of the success stories from our work reentry program. He got a fresh start and was helping out in the community. But now..." She pursed her lips together, then continued, "Unfortunately, our new owners don't want to continue with the program."

"Did you have problems?" Sam asked.

Alvera waved her hand. "There were some individuals who took advantage of the situation, so we had to let them go." She sighed. "In one case, it was probably for the best. In the other case...I'm not so sure."

"That's too bad," Sam said.

"Yes, but it doesn't negate the value of the program." Alvera smiled ironically. "Of course, I'm a little biased, since I was the one who recommended it, back when we were just a small company. You see, I had a cousin who turned his life around because someone gave him a chance when they hired him through a reentry program." She laughed. "I had to sell it to the higher-ups as a way to find talent in a tight labor market with the added benefit of tax breaks."

Anand appeared through the hallway just then, and when he saw Sam, he said, "Oh, good, you're here already."

"It's been nice talking to you, Dr. Jenkins," Alvera said as she glanced at her phone. "I've got to get to my kids' school. They're in a play, and I'm meeting my husband—thank goodness he's picked up the slack lately." Then she looked at Sam and frowned. "But you mentioned Raul Garza? Is there something I should know?"

Sam began to speak, but Anand cut her off.

"No," he said. "I'm about to take some measurements with a piece of equipment I borrowed from another industrial hygienist. I've got to get it back to him as soon as possible, and Dr. Jenkins was interested in how the process worked, so that's why she's here."

"Oh, okay. Well, I'll see you tomorrow then," Alvera said, then she smiled warmly at Sam. "It's so great that you're interested in how we do things around here. I'm sure I'll see you again."

Sam followed Anand to his office, through the room full of cubicles, now empty and dark, except for a handful of overhead fluorescent panels creating sparse cones of light. As they traversed the corridors between the cubicles, Sam asked, "Why didn't you want to talk about Raul to Alvera? He is the reason I'm here."

"She can be…let's just say, she can be a little overly dramatic at times," Anand said. "Raul's mother has been calling and has convinced her that something here was connected to his death." He tilted his head and looked at her. "Of course, now you've provided a convincing argument that this may be the case, but I don't want to discuss this with her until I have more definitive data."

They entered Anand's office, under one of the lit fluorescent panels. An orange shoebox-sized piece of equipment sat on the table, with a display and a keypad embedded in its metal enclosure and a handle mounted in front. It looked just like the Geiger counters from old disaster movies.

"This is the hydrogen sulfide analyzer that my buddy brought over this afternoon." Anand leaned over the device, squinting at the display. "And it just finished the regeneration cycle, so now I need to calibrate it."

He picked up a small white cylinder with connectors on both ends and inserted it into the top of the instrument; then he pushed the sample button on the end of the handle, like on a video game joystick.

"This filter keeps hydrogen sulfide from entering the analyzer so I can zero out the reading for calibration," he explained. "I need to take several samples while it's attached to make sure it's operating correctly."

Sam nodded, then said, "Even though the problem with the septic line's been fixed, do you think you'll be able to get a reading?"

Anand shrugged. "I'm not sure, but I want to find out."

After a moment the device beeped, and he pushed the sample button again.

Then, without warning, he grunted and kicked the trash can under his whiteboard. "Damn it," he muttered.

His outburst startled her, and she backed away, closer to the office door. Maybe James was right. The man did have a temper.

The analyzer beeped again. He pushed the button, then looked up at Sam, noticing her wary expression. He held up his hands with a concerned look.

"I'm sorry. I didn't mean to alarm you." He closed his eyes as he took in a deep breath. When he opened them again, he said, "I'm just mad at myself for not even considering this. I've been so focused on this expansion and all the new equipment. I've been thinking about the potential safety issues and how we need to train everyone." He shook his head. "I didn't even see this as a possibility, that the infrastructure in this old building could cause harm to anyone. I can't believe I let this slip by."

Sam didn't know what to say, if she should reassure him or not, but she understood his frustration. So she just nodded slowly.

The analyzer beeped.

"Okay," Anand said with a nod. "We're all set."

He picked up the device and pulled the filter out of the port.

"Let's see if we can detect anything."

They went to the manufacturing floor. As it had been in the office area, it was eerily quiet and dim, with just a few of the overhead sodium vapor lights lit.

Anand threw an industrial switch next to the door, and the back half of the space became a little brighter when more lights clicked on, casting an unnatural pink tinge as the lamps began to warm up.

They walked to the back of the manufacturing floor, with a stop by a storage area so Anand could grab a respirator.

"Just in case the levels are still high," he said.

When they got to the pit, Anand shook his head.

"I'm so stupid," he said.

"Why do you say that?" Sam asked.

"This railing. When we had to install it, that should have clued me in that there were more issues we needed to address around here." He handed her the analyzer and a black plastic wand, like a conductor's baton. "Hold on to these while I put on this respirator."

Even though the analyzer looked like a bulky metal brick, it was lighter than she expected. He donned the air-purifying respirator, with the gray facepiece covering his nose and mouth, and two white filters jutting out on either side. He descended into the pit as Sam watched from the railing.

Once he was at the bottom, with only his head above the lip of the pit, he reached up. "Hand those to me," he said, his voice muffled through the mask.

As Sam bent over to give him the analyzer, she caught the whiff of rotten eggs. He went to the back corner of the pit, where the cracks in the wall were largest, and pushed the button on the handle of the device with his thumb. After a moment, he said, "It's elevated at three ppm."

She knew that ppm meant parts per million, so the analyzer had detected three parts hydrogen sulfide per one million parts of atmospheric air.

"That's not too high," he said, "but really, there shouldn't be any hydrogen sulfide here at all."

While Anand repeated the measurements a couple more times, Sam pulled out her phone and searched for the OSHA page with information on the gas. "At this level, it says, 'Prolonged exposure may cause nausea, tearing of the eyes, headaches or loss of sleep. Airway problems—bronchial constriction—in some asthma patients.' That could explain some of the symptoms Raul was having."

Anand nodded as he attached the black baton-like piece of plastic to the port on the top of the analyzer. "Let's see if there's a higher concentration inside these cracks. Hopefully this probe will let me get a sample."

He inserted the tip of the probe a couple of inches into the wall, then pushed the button. After a moment, he said. "I've got seventy-two ppm. Man, that's high."

He poked around the crack and took a few more measurements.

"Yeah. These are all elevated."

More evidence for Sam's hypothesis. When the septic system had backed up, the levels were probably even higher in the space behind those cracks, so the air in the pit could've been toxic.

After Anand climbed out and doffed the respirator, he cursored through the readings on the analyzer. "These are all between sixty-five and eighty-five ppm. What does it say for those concentrations?"

Sam checked her phone again. "It says, 'Slight conjunctivitis—gas eye—and respiratory tract irritation after one hour. May cause digestive upset and loss of appetite.'" She looked up at Anand. "Raul had conjunctivitis when I saw him, but I thought he was just suffering from allergies."

He cocked his head. "You didn't tell me you'd seen Raul. When was that?"

"A few days before he died. His mom's one of my patients, and she made him come with her to my office." Now it was Sam's turn to be frustrated with herself. "I missed his diagnosis."

Anand put his hand on her elbow. "Hey, you didn't know about this exposure, just like I didn't know."

They were silent for a moment, both contemplating how things might have turned out differently had they known this information.

"You told me the report I sent wasn't complete," Sam said. "Did you talk to Dale?"

Anand nodded. "Just before you arrived, I finally got the chance to ask him, and he said after Raul gave him the form—"

He stopped as something behind Sam caught his attention. She turned to follow his gaze.

40

When Ramirez turned onto the dark farm road, Nico finally realized where they were going. He'd asked a few times and Ramirez responded with increased irritation, telling Nico to shut it, that he just needed to do what he was told and he'd get paid.

The first time Nico asked was while they were sitting in front of the old lady's house. After that woman got in her car, and Ramirez decided to follow her, his phone buzzed. All he'd said was, "The *jefe* needs us. *Vamanos.*"

Nico had been slightly relieved, because he didn't know how he could stop Ramirez if he went after that woman. He didn't approve of rape, but since he was pretty sure that Ramirez had killed Ernesto, he didn't want to die either.

They'd stopped at a gas station, and Ramirez talked to someone on his phone while he pumped gas. Nico wanted to get out of the car, to get out of this situation—whatever it was—but Ramirez was right there next to his door

After Ramirez hung up and put the gas nozzle away, he

walked around the front of the car, staring at Nico, then pointed his finger like a gun at him and winked.

A shiver slinked down Nico's spine as Ramirez got in the car. "We're good to go. I know what we need to do."

"And what is that?" Nico asked.

"You, with all the questions. Just follow me." Ramirez started the car. "He'll pay us tonight."

"For what? What does he want us to do?"

"Shut it," Ramirez barked and pulled out of the gas station.

TEN MINUTES later they were on the road to CS Solar. The car's headlights lit up a truck pulling out to turn across the road up ahead. It was Dale's.

"There's that asshole," Ramirez said. He scowled at the rearview mirror. "We could go fuck him up."

Nico looked over his shoulder, watching the taillights shrinking into the darkness.

"He's lucky the *jefe's* gonna pay us," Ramirez said. He slowed the car, passed up the main parking lot for their old jobs, and turned in to the service entrance behind the building.

Nico was a little relieved. The *jefe* wasn't in the *Sindicato*.

Ramirez was a total fraud. He wanted everyone to think he was a tough guy. But, as far as Nico knew, he didn't even speak Spanish.

One time, when he and Raul had been in the break room, Raul had asked Ramirez a question in Spanish, and Ramirez looked confused. He'd only answered after Raul repeated it in English.

Now it made sense that Ramirez kept calling the guy

they were working for "the" *jefe* instead of "*el*" *jefe*. Because he was probably a *gringo*.

Ramirez drove to the loading dock farthest away from the street and parked. He got out of the car and motioned for Nico to come with him. They went to the man-sized door next to one of the overheads for loading and unloading big rigs.

Nico relaxed a bit more. Ramirez was so full of shit. He didn't kill Ernesto. They were probably here for the same reason Ramirez got fired in the first place—stealing.

Nico wasn't involved in that scam, but he got canned anyway. Dale was just looking for an excuse to get rid of him, because of those pits. There hadn't been a railing or nothing, and Nico had almost fallen one time. Dale had laughed at him. It wasn't a big drop—just a few feet—but still.

Dale wouldn't listen when Nico kept telling him they needed to do something, and then he used the copper-wire scam as a way to fire him. Then, a few weeks later, he'd heard Dale's brother-in-law had fallen and broken his leg. Really bad.

Karma's a bitch.

The more Nico thought about it, the more it made sense. They were just going to rip off the company, and this didn't have anything to do with the *Sindicato*.

Why'd he been so worried?

Ramirez punched a code on the keypad next to the door, but before he opened it, he gave Nico a menacing look. "Don't ask questions. Just do what I say."

If Nico could get through this—and get paid—he'd be set for the next month. There'd be a nice Christmas for his baby girl, and he'd have enough in the bank to take a few days to look for a better job in January.

Nico nodded and followed Ramirez inside.

41

S am followed Anand's gaze to look over her shoulder and turned to find Henry approaching.

"I wasn't expecting you back until tomorrow," Anand said.

"We wrapped up everything this morning, and I caught an early flight back. They were impressed with how we turned things around last quarter, so the next tranche has been released." A big grin came across Henry's face. "And they've approved our bonuses."

"That's great," Anand said.

"So what are you and Dr. Jenkins up to this evening?"

"We're measuring levels of hydrogen sulfide down in the pit," Anand said, holding up the analyzer.

"Huh." Henry wrinkled his brow. "Why's that?"

Anand motioned to Sam. "Did you happen to see the email she sent?"

"I might have, but I didn't get a chance to read it," Henry said, with an aw-shucks smile. "I was kind of preoccupied, putting together all the data for my slide deck."

"Of course," Anand said with a nod, looking a little embarrassed. "That definitely was a higher priority."

"So what did your email say?" Henry asked Sam.

She went on to explain her theory about how Raul might have been exposed to hydrogen sulfide. Then Anand added how he got the analyzer and invited Sam to be there when he took the measurements.

"And what did you find?"

"Even though the levels in the pit aren't very high right now," Anand said, "there's an opening in the cracks where they're elevated quite a bit—enough to be toxic." He paused, as if convincing himself how the pieces fit, then continued, "If the levels in that space were significantly higher during the period where the septic pump was out, I think Dr. Jenkins's theory about what may have happened to Raul Garza is plausible."

"Is that so?" Henry said. "Well, I suppose we'll have to figure out what to do about it. Thanks for bringing this to our attention, Dr. Jenkins."

"Yes, and thanks for coming by tonight," Anand added. "I'll show you out."

As they started walking toward the front of the building, Henry stopped and said, "I heard some of the new automated soldering and welding machines are up and running. Could you show me the progress we've made?"

"Uh, sure," Anand said.

"Dr. Jenkins, you might be interested in seeing this too," Henry said. "With your interest in robotic surgery, you'll appreciate what we're doing. These machines are amazing."

"Thanks, but I should go," Sam said. "I don't want to impose." She checked her watch.

"Really, you're not imposing," Henry implored. "I

insist. You should see this, since you're here already. It won't take very long."

She had told James she'd be an hour or so, and she'd only been there about thirty minutes. Plus, she really wanted to see these robotic machines in action. She could spare a few minutes. "Okay, I can stay for a little bit."

"Wonderful!" Henry beamed. "You won't be disappointed."

He turned and walked toward the double doors leading to the new manufacturing floor. Sam looked at Anand, and he shrugged as they followed Henry.

The space had changed quite a bit since Sam and Kyle had received their tour. While many pallets remained stacked with equipment still wrapped in gauzy plastic, much of the open area had been filled with fully constructed machines laid out in rows, like boxy metal beasts.

Henry stopped by one of them. It was a large rectangular apparatus with one end enclosed in plexiglass. "This baby will improve our quality and efficiency," he said as he patted the side of it, a gleam in his eye.

"You may remember seeing our employees laying out individual PV cells into rows and having to hand solder them together," Anand said.

Sam nodded.

"This unit does the same thing—it automatically and precisely places the cells in line here." He pointed to the enclosed area. "Then it solders the whole row and conveys it down there." He motioned to the opposite side of the machine. "The completed rows are neatly stacked for retrieval to use in the next assembly step."

"Are those blanks in the hopper?" Henry asked. "Can we see this puppy in action?"

"Sure, we can run a demo."

Anand set the analyzer and respirator on top of a nearby box and moved to a display panel on the side of the machine. It was mounted at eye-level above a keyed switch and several colored lights, like a traffic signal—red, yellow, and green—along with a big red emergency stop button.

He turned the key, which lit up the display, and a humming sound came from the unit. He tapped on the screen a few times, and the green light came on; then the mechanism behind the plexiglass started moving.

A metal arm picked a cell off a stack and placed it on a track. A blocky device came down and emitted a bright glow for less than a second before it raised up, allowing the cell to slide down the rails. The process was repeated several times until an entire row of cells was completely assembled and transferred to the other end of the machine.

The group watched the tightly coordinated maneuvers for a few minutes, then they walked alongside the machine as they followed one of the completed rows gliding down the track. A metal bar lined with suction cups lifted the row of cells and moved it to a growing stack. As soon as the row they'd followed was out of the way, another slid down the track to replace it.

The choreographed movements captivated Sam. However, as she thought about it from an occupational safety point of view, there was a risk of amputation, like Dale had mentioned. The plexiglass should prevent this, but there were hinges on the edges of the frames holding the panes in place.

"What happens if someone tries to open this while it's running?" Sam asked.

Anand did exactly that, unlatching one of the panels and swinging it open. The whole machine shut down, and an alarm blared from the panel on the end while the red light flashed. "As you can see, the unit is outfitted with sensors to prevent injuries." Anand closed the plexiglass door and shut down the machine. "These should only be opened for maintenance and repairs, but I'm pretty satisfied with this vendor's mitigation approach."

"And each unit has the throughput of five workers," Henry said. "Plus, these babies can run around the clock."

"You know, Henry," Anand said as he scratched his chin, "now that I think about it, we really should talk more about the measurements I took tonight. I'm really concerned we may have overlooked an issue we should've addressed, and it might've caused harm to one of our employees."

Henry looked back and forth between Anand and Sam. "So you've bought in to this theory? This idea that someone *may* have been exposed to something that *may* have caused him to wreck his car?" He huffed. "Really? That seems like an absurd string of assumptions."

"I certainly believe it's worth investigating further," Anand said.

A disappointed look descended on Henry's face, and he slowly shook his head. "I was afraid of that." Then his gaze traveled past Anand and Sam, and he made a short, quick lift of his head, signaling to someone behind them.

Sam felt someone grab her arms and pull them back behind her. She struggled, but she couldn't break free from the firm grip. A voice whispered in her ear, "Stay calm. I won't let anything happen to you."

She strained to see who it was and caught a glimpse of Nina's brother. She glanced at Anand. He'd been restrained by the man who had attacked her.

"Get rid of their phones," Henry said. "And those watches. We don't want them calling for help."

Ramirez did as he was told, but Sam's assailant hesitated.

"C'mon, Nico," Ramirez said. "Do as the man says. Don't let her grab that damn pepper spray."

Nico hesitated a moment more, then followed orders, tossing Sam's things aside. They clattered on the concrete floor.

"What's going on, Henry?" Betrayal marred Anand's face. "Why are you doing this?"

"You knew how tight our budget was, and if we didn't hit those milestones last quarter, the investment—and our bonuses—were in jeopardy. We just needed to keep everything ship-shape, no accidents, no unexpected expenditures, for just a few more weeks." Henry blew out a long breath. "Then that car crash happened, and that woman kept calling, saying something had happened to her boy. The accident didn't have anything to do with us."

"But it might have," Anand said. "I didn't think so before, but now I'm not so sure."

"It has nothing to do with us!" Henry thundered. "It's just a bunch of suppositions from a crazy old crone."

"But I just took measurements. The hydrogen sulfide levels tonight were high enough to cause toxicity, and that's after we had the septic pump repaired. This place was not built to support the number of workers we have. We need to connect to the city sewer lines as soon as—"

"No!" Henry boomed, wagging his head vigorously. "You don't know if those levels were high at the time of the car crash. There's no way to prove it."

"You tried to cover it up though. You told Dale not to bring any complaints to me, to only report them directly to you, which goes completely against our safety protocols," Anand said as he struggled against Ramirez, who held his grip tight.

"Everyone complains, for stupid reasons, all the time." Henry looked at Sam. "And then you had to get involved. You came up with this quack theory—"

"Why, Henry? Why did you do this?" Anand pleaded. "When you brought me on board to work here, you said safety was your number one priority. But it sounds like you did it for the money." He hung his head, shaking it. "All anyone in this country ever cares about is money."

Sam's mind raced through everything that all happened over the last few weeks, and she suddenly saw how it all fit together. "You need to pay off your medical debt," she said. "You had half a million in medical bills after your son was born, from all that time in the NICU and his surgeries. It still isn't paid off, is it?"

"Bingo!" Henry said. "You found that article on me, didn't you?" He ran his hands through his hair. "I needed this bonus so we could finally pay off the last of it. It was hanging over us, tearing our marriage apart. My wife was going to leave me. The collection companies call incessantly, even though we'd already agreed to a payment plan. They call and call and call, and they treat you like shit, like you're a criminal!"

The last word echoed as he slammed his fist against the wooden crate beside him, his face contorted, nostrils flaring.

He began pacing back and forth, as if he were delivering the final argument in a trial. "They act like it's your fault for getting in debt, when it's the damn insurance companies' fault. They used some obscure clause in their contract based on our birthdays to get out of paying. It's so arbitrary. The media ate up the story. Friends and family chipped in, but it still wasn't enough. We've been paying off what we can, but the collectors keep hounding us."

He shook his fist as he spat out each word. "This bonus will finally clear the slate, and I will win back my wife."

Henry stopped and scanned the faces around him. "Too bad things got out of hand."

He slammed his fist into the crate again. "That's it. I'm done talking about this." He looked at Anand. "I'm sorry, friend, but you're about to have an unfortunate forklift accident." He nodded to Ramirez. "You know what to do. Then you can take the girl."

Ramirez pulled Anand backward, toward the aisle behind them.

Anand reached out and grabbed the gas analyzer off the box where he'd left it. He swung the metal device, trying to hit his captor, but he couldn't get a full arc.

Ramirez continued to drag him, and Anand tried again. He connected this time, but the analyzer wasn't very heavy, so it only struck a glancing blow.

Ramirez crashed Anand against a crate, dropping him to the floor, just a few feet away from Sam.

Anand lay motionless.

Sam gasped and tried to pull away from Nico. She met some resistance, but not much, and she broke free. She scurried over to Anand and knelt beside him, assessing him. His breathing was shallow, but regular.

Suddenly, a deafening crack rang out.

Sam jumped and looked up at the source of the sound.

It was the gun in Henry's hand. She followed the barrel's aim.

Nico lay on the floor with a small black hole through his shirt in the right lower quadrant of his abdomen. He yelled out expletives as he writhed in pain.

Ramirez stood over Sam, laughing. "You suck, man," he said. "Can't aim worth shit."

"You told me he was on board with you," Henry snapped. "That he'd do whatever you told him."

Ramirez shrugged. "Thought so, but guess not."

"And you told me he killed Ernesto," Henry said with skepticism, "but it was you, wasn't it? You only needed to get him to stop asking questions, but you let things get out of hand, like you did with Anand just now."

"Hey, you said to make it look like an accident." Ramirez looked down at Anand's limp body. "He's going to be smashed up anyway."

Henry lowered the gun and said, "Get to work. We need to clean this all up."

"You gotta help me move these guys," Ramirez said.

Sam glanced around, trying to come up with a plan.

Anand was still breathing shallowly beside her, but he couldn't be her concern anymore. She needed to save herself.

A groan leaked out of Nico. He'd stopped crying out, his movement less frantic. He'd survive, as long as he got help soon.

No vital structures where he was shot. Maybe a bowel perf. Needs a stat ex-lap.

Sam blinked. *Jeez. Why am I even thinking this way?*

Because the most stressful situations she'd been in were the shock rooms in the emergency department. So her mind defaulted to the comfortable realm of treatment options for the result of violence, not how to combat it.

Snap out of it. If you don't save yourself first, you can't help them.

"Okay, okay. We can make this work." Henry nodded. "We can say Nico came here tonight because he was still upset about losing his job. He and Anand got into an altercation. Anand shot him just before Nico ran over him with a forklift."

He looked down at Sam. "Tie her up so we can take care of these two."

Ramirez tried to grab Sam's arm, but she used all her weight to pull away, to stay on the floor next to Anand. They were nestled between two massive crates. She was boxed in with Ramirez on one side of her, Henry on the other; the injured bodies of Anand and Nico flanked her, impeding her escape. "What's going to happen to me?" she asked.

Henry shrugged. "It's up to Ramirez. I'm sorry it had to come to this, Doctor, but everything would have been fine if you had just minded your own business."

Ramirez grabbed her arm again as Henry closed in, but she fought as hard as she could.

Then Henry said, "Screw it. She's too much of a pain in the ass."

Something hard hit her on the head.

She crumpled onto the floor, between the bodies, feeling her consciousness slipping away.

42

W hen Sam came to, she didn't know how long she'd been out.

It couldn't have been more than a minute. Her head hurt, but she didn't move, not wanting to let on that she was awake.

She heard voices, Henry and Ramirez, as they stood over her, talking about how they were going to stage the accident. She squinted, opening her eyelids just enough so she could see through the slits.

Ramirez bent over Anand, still lying next to her, and grabbed him under the arms, while Henry lifted his feet.

"We'll put Nico in the forklift and prop Anand up against a crate," Henry said. "Anand will fire the fatal shot at Nico as the forklift slams—"

Without warning, a figure came from behind Ramirez, smashing a piece of wood over his back, knocking him to his knees. He turned toward his attacker, who finished the job by slamming the board into Ramirez's face.

Sam peered up at the figure towering over her, but due

to the bright sodium lights above, she couldn't make out the shadowy face without fully opening her eyes."

Then she heard Dale's voice. "You lied to me!"

"Now, Dale," Henry said, "you did a great job keeping everything under wraps. You did exactly what you should——"

"Anand said there's swamp gas in those pits from that bathroom. You said it wasn't anything, that people were just trying to get out of workin'."

"That's right, Dale. You said it yourself. People complain so they don't have to work."

"You used me, you lyin' son of a bitch! You said nobody'd get hurt." Dale stepped over Sam, as he loomed closer to Henry. "But Anand said——"

"Oh, so you believe Anand now, do you?" Henry backed up a step to keep Dale at arm's length. "You called him a towel-head who should go back where he came from. But now you're best buddies with him?" He tutted. "It doesn't matter. You're the one who neglected your workers."

Dale closed the space between him and Henry in a split second and snatched his boss's collar.

Sam saw her chance and scrambled over Ramirez's body to get away.

"You're not gonna blame me! I'm not gonna be your fall guy."

Once she was safely behind a crate, Sam peeked at the men.

Even though Dale had pulled him up by his collar, Henry still had a sinister grin. "It was so easy to manipulate you, you intolerant fool!"

Henry reached in his pocket.

Sam yelled, "Watch out! He's got a gun!"

She ran as the shot clapped loudly, echoing around her.

"Don't run away, Doctor! You'll only prolong the inevitable," Henry called over Dale's moans.

Sam zigged and zagged between the crates and machines, jumping over construction debris here and there. The exit was getting closer.

She passed the table where Anand had pulled out the expansion plans when she'd first come to the factory. *Just run straight down the corridor between the rows of crates, then hang a left.*

She could do it. She remembered seeing a phone mounted on the post next to the storage area. She could call for help, then either find a place to hide or get to her car out front.

As she made her way down the aisle, a shot rang out, and the wood next to her head splintered.

She ducked to the side between two crates and was going to keep running, but her way was blocked by a forklift. She snuck back toward the corridor and peered out.

There was Henry, stalking after her.

Her hand brushed something loose hanging over the side of the crate. It was the control box for the hoist mounted on the ceiling, the one with the hook that almost hit her during the tour.

She peered around the crate again.

Henry was getting closer, but she could see the huge hook hanging above him.

She grabbed the yellow control box. *Here goes nothing.* She pushed the button marked "down."

The clank of chains rattling through the pulley filled the air, followed by the thud of blunt force trauma—metal impacting flesh—followed by a loud grunt from Henry.

Then silence.

Sam froze. She slowly crept toward the main corridor.

Henry lay on the ground, gasping for breath.

She approached him, and as she got closer, she saw fear in his eyes.

He continued to gasp, his mouth opening and closing like a goldfish.

The gun lay on the floor next to him, so she kicked it away. It skidded across the concrete, stopping next to a pallet with a clunk.

She knelt next to him, immediately noticing the jugular veins in his neck were beginning to bulge, his trachea deviating to the right.

She ripped open his shirt, and saw an injury to his upper left chest, burst capillaries surrounding a small gash with a trickle of blood. She palpated the area and felt movement where there shouldn't be. There were at least a couple of broken ribs.

The injury didn't look very bad, but she could hear air being sucked into the wound every time Henry took a breath.

The sound of approaching footsteps took her attention away from the injury, triggering another adrenaline surge, prickling her skin.

She scrambled to her feet and ran. She could make it to the door in just a few steps.

Then a voice yelled out. "Wait, Doctor! I won't hurt you."

She looked over her shoulder and saw Dale, holding onto his right arm with his left hand, blood seeping between his fingers.

"I've called 911," he said. "Are you okay?"

Sam nodded. "But you aren't," she said. "And Henry isn't."

She came back to Henry's collapsed form on the floor, his breaths now shallow and ragged. "I need to help him, or he's going to die." She looked around, seeing the gauzy plastic wrapped around the equipment on the pallets around her. "Do you have a knife?"

Dale let his injured arm hang as he dug into his jeans pocket with his good hand. He extracted a folding knife and tossed it to her.

She caught it. It was slippery with blood, so she wiped it off with her shirt, then cut through the plastic wrapping on the crate next to her, creating a square big enough to cover Henry's chest wound. "I need some tape."

"What kind?"

"Any kind will do."

Dale nodded and scanned the area around them, while she held the plastic square over the wound to stop more air from entering Henry's chest the wrong way.

A moment later, Dale held up a roll of duct tape. "Will this work?"

"It will have to do."

He tossed the roll to her, and she tore off four pieces, applying each to a side of the improvised dressing, leaving a small open gap in one corner. Thank goodness he didn't have much chest hair, or this wouldn't work.

Henry's skin now had a bluish tinge, and he was floating in and out of consciousness.

Sam patted him hard on the cheek. "Henry! I need you to stay with me. I need you to take deep breaths right now, as deep as you can."

His eyelids fluttered, and she smacked his face, harder this time, repeating the instructions. His eyelids popped open, and he complied, struggling at first.

But with each inhalation, the plastic clung tightly against the wound, blocking more air from entering his chest. And with each breath out, the plastic bubbled up, the duct tape holding around the sides, and the untaped free corner flitted, allowing air to escape.

"What's going on with him?" Dale asked.

"He has a tension pneumothorax from a sucking chest wound," Sam said. "Before I put the dressing on, every breath he took pulled air into his chest around his collapsed lung. His wound acted like a one-way valve, increasing the pressure inside his chest and squeezing his heart." She pressed on the edges of the dressing, making sure they stayed secure. "Now the plastic is acting like a one-way valve the other direction, allowing the air to escape out of his chest."

Dale nodded with an appraising look. "So that will bring his lung back up?"

"Not completely, but it will decrease the pressure so his heart can fill with blood again and pump it to the rest of his body."

Sam studied her unintended patient. Henry's color had improved; he no longer gasped for each breath, and the veins in his neck were no longer bulging. His eyes were closed as if he were asleep.

She could hear the faint sounds of sirens as she looked up at Dale and said, "Let's take a look at your arm."

Before she got a chance to examine him, Ramirez suddenly appeared behind Dale. He wrapped his arm around the bigger man's neck, putting him in a chokehold.

Dale resisted, flailing his arms and kicking his legs. His boots pounded the floor as he tried to get Ramirez off him. But his efforts were impaired by his wounded arm, which began to seep more blood, the red drops plopping on the concrete.

Sam scurried backward on the cold floor, distancing herself from Ramirez as Dale began to lose consciousness. She looked around for something to defend herself with, and she spotted Henry's gun a few feet away from her.

Ramirez dropped the unresponsive Dale and stalked toward her. "I'm gonna make you pay, bitch!"

The sirens were louder, but they still seemed too far away. Ramirez would kill her before they got there.

The gun was just out of her reach.

She had to go for it.

She scrambled toward it, but just before she could grab it, a hand appeared and picked it up. She looked up as Nico, his left arm clamped over his wounded abdomen, his face pale and sweaty, aimed the gun and shot at Ramirez.

Ramirez laughed with bravado, and said, "Ha! You missed!"

But a small hint of fear flickered on his face as he backed up a few steps.

His body was tense, his eyes glancing back and forth, as if he were running through his options.

The pitch and volume of the sirens crescendoed to a peak before stopping abruptly, heralding the arrival of help.

At first, Ramirez took a small step, a turn, like he was about to dash away from them. Instead, he stutter-stepped and suddenly rushed toward them.

Nico fired again.

Ramirez fell forward, crumpling to the ground.

A crashing sound came from the rear of the building.

Nico dropped the gun, and it clattered on the floor.

A voice yelled, "Police! Come out of the building with your hands up!"

43

Nico collapsed on the floor. He was shivering, his lips white.

Sam found a thready pulse in his wrist, then she gently lifted his hand off the wound on his belly. The stench of fecal matter nipped her nose as she examined the area around the wound. Not much blood, but his shirt was wet with brown fluid. *Definitely perforated bowel. He'll need an ostomy.*

"You're going to be okay, but you'll need surgery as soon as possible," she said over the distant voice yelling the instructions to exit again. "But help is here."

She stood and shouted, "I'm coming out!"

Sam exited the building with her hands raised, but she couldn't see anything as blazing floodlights blinded her. She could hear more sirens, and as she turned her head toward the road to relieve her eyes from the painful brightness, she could make out a couple of ambulances mixed with the seared afterimages on her retinas.

They cut their sirens as they turned in to the lot, but she could still hear the continuing cascade from the horns of more emergency vehicles approaching in the distance.

A voice that seemed to come from the lights said, "Is anyone inside?"

"There are four men," Sam replied. "All need medical attention." She started to turn toward the door. "I can show you—"

"Stop right there! Do not move!"

Sam froze and a pair of police officers emerged from the light on either side of her. One patted her down, and then the other handcuffed her.

"We'll assess the situation, ma'am," said the officer who'd handcuffed her. He led her to a squad car.

"Am I under arrest?" She tried to look back at his face, but all she could see was the name tag on his chest that read "Gardner."

"Not at this time, but we heard gunshots, and we need to make sure everything is secure."

"But I can tell you what happened."

"We'll get your story in a moment." He opened the rear door and assisted her into the SUV, placing his hand on her head as she entered. "I'm leaving you here for now, for your safety."

Sam started to object, but he shut the door, then walked over to the other police officers. She was now trapped; plexiglass panels blocked her from the front seats, and a cage barrier separated her from the back cargo space. She watched helplessly through the windows with her arms pinned unpleasantly behind her back.

Several officers, with their guns at the ready, disappeared into the building through the pedestrian door Sam had just exited. Officer Gardner stood right outside, waiting, slowly sweeping his head back and forth as he scanned the area around the building. On the other side of the vehicle, EMTs pulled gear and equipment out of the ambulances.

Moments later a couple of officers spilled out the door, yelling and motioning for the EMTs, who quickly ran over and scampered inside. Seconds passed before the motor for the adjacent overhead door activated, and a pair of EMTs rushed out to fetch stretchers.

Officer Gardner came back to the cruiser, opened the front passenger door, and leaned in to grab the handset. He stood with the door ajar, just outside the vehicle, and Sam could hear clips of his words as he spoke on the radio. One word stood out: homicide.

A sinking sensation washed over her. *Who died?*

The officer leaned in again, replaced the handset, and popped the rear hatch of the SUV. As he grabbed some supplies from the cargo area, Sam pressed up against the cage barrier and tried to ask him questions, but he ignored her.

He walked back to the building, setting up a couple of folding stands along the way, and as he tied the end of the caution tape to a post near the door, Dylan, still in his uniform, and James came running around the corner of the building. Dylan stopped cold and grabbed James's arm to keep him from advancing.

Gardner paused his task of stringing out tape, and Sam could hear him say Dylan's name through the open rear hatch. Both Dylan and James had concerned looks on their faces, and she could hear James say, "Where's Sam?"

Sam yelled through the grate behind her, "Dylan! James! I'm in here!"

They both looked over at the vehicle; then Dylan and Officer Gardner spoke for a few moments before the officer led Dylan over to Sam. James began to follow, but

Gardner held his arm out to stop him. Dylan spoke to Gardner again, and the three came over to the vehicle.

Gardner opened the rear passenger door, and Sam started to scramble out. But Dylan said, "Stay there, Sam." He tipped his head toward the officer. "I was Ray's training officer when he first joined the force, so he's doing me a favor by letting us check on you, but they need to interview you."

James squeezed between the officers so he could hug her. "Are you okay?"

Her hands were still restrained, so she awkwardly fell into him. "I'm fine," she said. The words were muffled against his shirt.

James looked at Officer Gardner. "Is this necessary? Can you uncuff her?"

The young officer glanced back at the building with a look of uncertainty.

"It's okay, Ray," Dylan said. "If anyone gets upset, I'll take the blame."

Officer Gardner hesitated, then nodded. "Turn around," he said to Sam, and she complied. She rubbed her wrists once the cuffs had been removed.

More emergency vehicles had shown up, and Officer Gardner made his way over to let them know what was going on.

Once they were alone, James and Dylan said in unison, "What happened?"

"When I got here," Sam said, "Anand and I found elevated hydrogen sulfide levels where Raul worked, most likely from a leak in the septic line. But this was after they repaired the pump, so it seems the levels might have been even higher when he crashed his car. High enough to cause impairment."

"Might have been higher?" Dylan said. "So it's still not definite."

"That's true," Sam replied. "But the problem is: there was a cover-up. Henry told Dale not to report hazard complaints to Anand, who is the safety officer. Then Ernesto was killed because he kept looking for answers."

"But why?" Dylan asked.

"Apparently, Henry had to keep everything under budget until the end of the quarter so the company would receive the last block of funds from their investors. Plus, he was counting on a big bonus when the deal was complete."

"So that's what this was all about? Money?" Dylan shook his head in disgust.

"It was," she said, "but he needed the money to—"

"Pay off medical debt," James said, completing her sentence. He explained to Dylan, "His son was born prematurely and had a prolonged stay in the ICU with a couple of surgeries, racking up over half a million in medical bills."

"If he needed the money, then I take it insurance didn't cover it all," Dylan said.

"No," Sam replied. "In fact, Henry said the insurance companies used some obscure clause in their contracts to get out of paying the hospital. He saw this bonus as his way to get out from under the bill collectors."

Commotion from the large doorway drew their attention as EMTs rushed a stretcher out to an ambulance. They were shortly followed by a second stretcher. Sam couldn't tell who was on the stretchers as the EMTs loaded them up and took off.

The noise died down and Sam asked, "How did you know to come here?"

"After you called, I went to Mrs. Garza's house," Dylan said. "She told me that someone had been threatening her with phone calls and threw a brick through her window. They said she must stop looking into Raul's death." He looked at Sam. "When I spoke with Raul's girlfriend, Nina, she told me that her brother Nico—the one you saw at El Morado—used to work here, along with that guy Ramirez."

"Yes, I know." Sam tipped her head toward the building. "They were here."

Dylan nodded knowingly. "So my suspicions were correct."

"And get this," James said, giving Dylan a light punch on the shoulder, "when he showed up at my apartment, and I told him you'd come here, he got nervous."

Dylan flushed and muttered under his breath, "Did not."

"We tried calling you, but when we didn't get an answer, we knew we had to check on you."

The men then peppered Sam with questions about exactly what had happened before they'd arrived. She recounted all the details, ending with what she thought she'd overheard Officer Gardner say on the radio.

"So homicide is on the way," Dylan said. "Makes sense based on what you've told us. Who died?"

Sam shook her head as she thought through the events one more time. "I don't know."

44

Vehicles from the crime scene unit and medical examiner's office arrived, along with more police, and eventually Sam, Dylan, and James were separated and each interviewed. Officer Gardner received an admonishment from one of the more senior officers for uncuffing Sam and allowing Dylan and James access to her. But in the end, after Sam had been thoroughly questioned and her purse was given back to her, she was finally released.

She asked repeatedly about what had happened to the others involved in the ordeal, but she continued to get this same response: "We can't discuss an ongoing investigation."

When she got back to her apartment, she found a bouquet of flowers waiting on her doorstep from Alex with an apology.

Even though it was almost midnight, she knew Alex would be up, since he had a shift at the hospital that night.

"Thank you for the flowers," Sam said with minimal sincerity. Sure, the arrangement was lovely, but did he really think she could be bought off with something so trite?

"I'm sorry. I was a complete and total ass," Alex said. "Please forgive me?"

"Hmm...I think you might have shown your true colors the other day."

"But I didn't mean it. I think I..." Alex paused. "Look, I was stupid. And I fell back into my asinine ways. You know how us guys like to razz each other. It was just trash talk, and I shouldn't do that with you."

Damn right you shouldn't.

"What can I do to make it up to you?"

"I told you," she said. "We need to take some time away from each other."

"How long?"

"I don't know. Maybe a few weeks."

He was silent, but she could hear the familiar beeping and dinging of ventilators and telemetry monitors from the ICU in the background.

Finally, he said, "Okay. But your father has invited me to come over for Thanksgiving. What should I tell him?"

Ugh. Her father. He and Alex got along so well together. They certainly seemed to have a much better relationship in the short time they'd known each other than Sam had ever had with her father.

Alex was exactly everything that her father had wanted Sam to be.

Thanksgiving was a little over a week away. Would she be ready to see him again at that point?

Maybe.

Plus, if Alex was there, he would garner her father's attention and perhaps she could have a little peace.

"Fine," she said. "You can go."

"Want to get together beforehand, so it's not so…awkward?"

"No. We're grown-ups," she said. "We can handle this. I'll see you there."

～

SAM CALLED in sick to work the next day. Dr. Taylor would just have to deal with finding another physician to fill in on short notice. It wasn't her concern.

James came by periodically to check on her throughout the day, filling her in with more details on what had happened the night before.

The profile assignment on CS Solar was no longer his and had turned into a larger news story to be handled by more seasoned journalists; however, because of his extensive research, James would receive credit as a contributor, and he was rewarded by being kept in the loop on new developments in the case.

It turned out the homicide team had been called to the scene because Nico's second shot had struck Ramirez in the upper abdomen, nicking his aorta. He'd bled out and died within seconds from internal hemorrhaging.

Fortunately, Anand had only suffered a mild concussion and seemed to be recovering without any issues. He had been discharged from the observation area of the ER after they monitored him for twenty-four hours.

James had other juicy info about him. He'd learned more about Anand's altercation with his neighbor—apparently the reason why Anand had lost his temper is because his neighbor had told him to go back where he'd come from, that European descendants were the true heirs of America.

"And do you know what Anand said right before he

punched him? 'I'm more European than you are!'" James said with a chuckle.

Dale had regained consciousness when the police and EMTs first entered the building. The EMTs had checked him out after they took care of the more critical patients, and as far as James knew, he went home after the police questioned him.

As for Nico, he'd gone into the OR immediately upon arrival to the hospital and was now in stable condition.

Whatever that meant. Sam had always heard those terms in news reports about patients, that they were in "stable" or "critical" condition, but those were never the words doctors used to describe patients.

James had learned from his colleagues at the paper that Nico was cooperating fully with the police. They would need his help to prove Henry was the culprit behind the events that led to Ernesto's and Ramirez's deaths.

Thanks to Sam's quick thinking, Henry would survive to face the consequences of his actions. He happened to be in the ICU at Alex's hospital, which was reporting that he was also in stable condition. Maybe she could learn more about what happened to Henry from a clinical perspective when she spoke to Alex.

It actually gave her a reason to look forward to seeing him.

WHEN SHE RETURNED to clinic the next day, exactly one week before Thanksgiving, she continued to work like nothing had ever happened. She'd hoped Kyle would be around so she could find out what the repercussions of her ordeal would be for the CS Solar contract, but she kept missing him because he showed up only a couple of times at the clinic between his sales calls.

Frankly, she wouldn't be surprised if the whole deal was off.

She spent the weekend before Thanksgiving focusing solely on her term paper for her environmental health class. It was a way for her to block out the rest of the world. She used her experience at CS Solar as a "hypothetical" example—leaving out the attempted murder, of course. Since the paper wasn't due until the week after Thanksgiving, she put it to the back of her mind, deciding to give it one more read-through before she turned it in.

The three days in clinic leading up to the holiday were quiet, allowing Sam and the rest of the staff to catch up on administrative tasks, taking inventory of supplies and medications and making lists of workers' comp patients who never showed up for their follow-up appointments to determine how to close out their cases.

When Sam pulled up to her father's house for Thanksgiving dinner, Alex's car was already in the driveway. She took a deep breath before she rang the doorbell. *I can do this.*

Millie greeted her at the door, with the warm scents of holiday spices wafting out and welcoming her in.

As Sam entered the foyer, Millie said, "Alex told us he has a shift tonight, so that's why you took separate cars."

Sam nodded, going along. "Yes, that's right."

Millie focused on her for a moment, a glint of understanding in her eye, then said, "Well, come on in. The men are watching the game, and I'm doing some last-minute prep for dinner."

Sam went into the living room and said hello to her father and Alex, who then followed her into the kitchen.

Millie excused herself to leave the couple alone.

"Can we talk?" Alex asked.

"Not now," she whispered as she glanced toward the living room. Over the back of the couch, she could see Millie's head leaning on her father's shoulder. A commercial flashed on the TV.

She inched farther away from the living room, not wanting to draw their attention. "Let's just pretend things are normal, and we can talk later."

But then her father got up off the couch and came into the kitchen. "What are you two lovebirds up to?"

Alex straightened up, put on a huge smile, and said, "We were just discussing our plans for the weekend."

Sam blinked and looked over at him. "Our plans?"

"Really?" her father said. "What are they?"

"I booked a room at the Valencia on the Riverwalk." Alex beamed at Sam. "I figured a nice, romantic weekend away from everything would do us some good."

Her father smiled and slapped Alex on the back. "Yes, my boy. A trip to San Antonio is a great way to reset."

Alex kissed Sam on the cheek and whispered, "Surprise!"

Sam was taken aback. How did she feel about this? Sure, it was flattering to be pursued by this handsome man, but she felt cornered.

Millie, seeming to read Sam's feelings, raised an eyebrow and said, "Why don't you two get back to your game, and Sam can help me with a couple of things so we can eat."

The men wandered back into the living room, accompanied by her father's blurting out, "Damn. The Cowboys missed that chip shot of a field goal."

Millie gave Sam instructions for setting up the platters and plates while she drained the drippings from the roaster into a sauce pan. Once Sam completed her tasks, she stood next to the stove while Millie whisked a slurry of flour and a few tablespoons of stock in a measuring cup before pouring them into the pan of drippings for the gravy.

"Thanks for going through all the trouble to make dinner," Sam said.

"Oh, it's my pleasure, dear," the older woman said as she continued to whisk away. "Thank goodness they sell just the breast now. There's no way I would have done this if I had to buy a whole turkey!"

She poured stock into the pan, adjusted the flame below it, then continued to stir more slowly as the gravy transformed into its final creamy state. The smell of roasted meat made Sam's stomach grumble.

Millie glanced toward the living room, where the men were distracted by the football game, then leaned closer to Sam and lowered her voice. "Is everything okay between you two?"

Sam hesitated, trying to figure out how to put things. She'd discussed at length how she felt with James, who told her, in his colorful way, to drop Alex if he didn't respect her.

She was planning on doing just that, but then Alex had sprung this trip to San Antonio on her.

"We had a fight, and…it's complicated," she said. "But I suppose it's just the usual relationship stuff."

"No relationship is ever without its ups and downs," Millie said. "But if you ever need to talk, I'm here for you." She turned off the flame and motioned behind Sam. "Could you hand me that gravy boat, dear?"

As Millie ladled the gravy into the boat, Sam almost felt like telling Millie everything, not just about her issues with Alex, but also what had happened at CS Solar.

Millie had that quality about her. Perhaps that's why

she and her mother had become friends. Maybe after dinner they could talk.

They got everything else ready and placed on the dining room table; then the foursome sat down to eat.

Her father seemed to be in good spirits since the Cowboys pulled off a game-winning touchdown drive right before the clock ran out. He and Alex recounted some of the critical plays as they passed around the dishes and everyone filled their plates.

While they ate, there was a pause in the conversation, and Sam thought she might find out more about what had happened to Henry. "So, Alex, have you had any interesting cases lately?"

He perked up, and said, "You wouldn't believe this, but we had a patient with a tension pneumothorax from a sucking chest wound that had been successfully treated in the field."

Sam's father looked up from his plate. "By the EMTs?"

"No, by someone else who was there when the injury occurred. Saved the guy's life—but it sounds like he'll go to jail once he gets discharged. They've got a police officer posted to his bedside." Alex shook his head. "Anyway, whoever treated him made use of what they had available. They made an improvised occlusive dressing with a plastic sheet and duct tape."

"Wow," Sam's father said. "That's pretty impressive."

"Yes it is," Millie said. "Sam knows what she's doing."

45

T he men snapped their heads to stare at Sam. Her cheeks flushed, but inside, she felt a touch of pride.

"What are you talking about?" Sam's father asked.

"Sam treated that patient in the field," Millie replied.

"Is this true?" Alex said.

Sam nodded slowly, then squinted at Millie. "How did you find out?"

The older woman shrugged. "I have my ways."

Alex furrowed his brow. "What happened?"

"I can't discuss an ongoing investigation," Sam said, just like the police officers. It was true; she was told not to talk about the case with anyone—although she'd already broken that rule with James. They'd said she may need to do another interview and could possibly be called as a witness during prosecution.

"Oh, come on, Sam," Alex said. "What's going on?"

"I told you." She crossed her arms. "I'm not going to talk about it."

"What happened?" her father prodded Millie.

"If Sam doesn't want to talk about it, I won't, either."

"But there was a homicide and several other injuries," Alex said. Alarm swelled in his eyes. "Were you in danger?"

Her father, normally stoic, joined in Alex's concern. "What? There was a homicide?"

"Look," Sam said, "I'll tell you later. You know the most important parts—I'm fine, and I still know my stuff." She scooped up a forkful of mashed potatoes and ate it.

"But—" Alex said.

She held up her hand. "Not gonna talk about it," she said, enjoying how she now commanded the table, the place where her father had always shown dominance. She ate another bite of potatoes.

The men stared at her, watching her eat as if they weren't there.

After a few moments, they all continued eating the delicious food Millie had prepared. Like a good motherly figure, she got the conversation going again by asking Alex about his family. They carried on for a few minutes about where he grew up and how he hoped to see his parents around the Christmas holidays since he'd missed them for Thanksgiving.

Then her father put his fork down and studied Sam. "Your skills really are underutilized," he said. "You should go back and finish residency."

"I am, Dad. I've found that program—the one I think I can get into after I finish my MPH."

"I mean a real residency program." The words slipped out. He blanched when he realized his blunder.

Alex raised his eyebrows, looking like a kid who'd just gotten away with something.

Sam fumed. *Figures*. Her father would never change.

Silence enveloped the room for what seemed like hours.

Then Millie cleared her throat. "Who wants pie?"

Glancing at his watch, Alex said, "Thanks, but I really need to go. My shift starts soon." He stood and pushed in his chair. "Steven, Millie, thank you for having me over."

Sam's father took in a quick breath, then put on a smile as he stood and shook Alex's hand. "Always a pleasure, my boy."

Millie nudged Sam. "Why don't you walk Alex out?"

She reluctantly trailed him to the front door.

"That case...that was pretty amazing what you did." He smiled at her weakly. "Now I know why it was so late when you called that night—I'd just finished admitting that patient." He looked down. "Even though I'd sent those flowers, I didn't think I'd hear from you."

She ignored his pining for sympathy. "So he's doing okay?"

"Thanks to you," he said. "We stepped him down to the floor over the weekend, and they pulled the chest tube earlier this week. He'll probably be discharged tomorrow."

He stepped closer to her, taking her hands in his, caressing them. "I'm sorry I was such an ass to you. Will you forgive me?"

Sam inhaled deeply, hesitating, a whirl of thoughts clouding her mind. Was she ready to move on?

When she didn't say anything, Alex pushed on, stammering, "And...I'm sorry...about springing the trip to San Antonio on you...like that. I really wanted to talk to you about it...before your dad asked." He released her hands and took a step back, staring at the floor. "It's okay if you don't want to go. I understand."

Sam studied him, exposed and vulnerable. He really cared for her, but was it in the right way?

After a moment, she thought, *Why not?* There was no way to tell how this relationship would work out unless they moved forward.

Plus, she needed a break, and San Antonio wasn't that far—just an hour-and-a-half drive.

Worst case, if things didn't work out, she could just come home.

"Okay," she said.

He pulled his gaze from the floor to lock on her eyes. "Really?"

"Yes. It will be nice to get away."

AFTER ALEX LEFT, her father was quiet, hanging his head like he'd received a scolding, as he gathered plates and took them into the kitchen. Based on how Millie was ordering him around, Sam guessed that's exactly what had happened.

Once the table had been cleared, they each had a slice of pecan pie with a scoop of vanilla ice cream and a cup of coffee. The warm pie melted the ice cream, which dribbled down the sides, swirling into puddles around the crust. The gooey brown sugar filling with crunchy nuts brought a respite from the tension in the room. No wonder people find so much pleasure in eating.

Little was said while they ate, just a few superficial attempts at small talk. But when they had all finished, Millie gathered the empty plates and said, "I'll leave you two to talk," before disappearing into the kitchen.

Sam ran her finger around the edge of her saucer while her father took a sip of his coffee.

Finally he said, "I'm sorry."

She looked at his face, trying to determine if he really meant it, or if he was only saying this because Millie had told him to.

"Look," he said, "I know we've had our issues. And when I've been tough on you, it's only because I want the best for you. I know you're capable."

As he spoke, his voice transformed into that of the father she remembered from childhood, the one who had encouraged her, helping her back on to her bike when she'd fallen, instead of the professional perfectionist she now endured. A wistful smile formed on his face, with moisture sparkling in the corners of his eyes.

He extended his hand across the table, opening his palm.

She placed her hand in his, and he gently squeezed.

"You're my baby girl. You always will be." His gaze became distant. "And I'll never forget the first time I laid eyes on you, on your mother's chest, so tiny, so helpless."

After a moment, he focused on her again. "Please forgive me if I sometimes have a hard time seeing you as the strong young woman you've become."

Sam nodded as tears welled in her eyes, clouding her vision.

Her father smiled and glanced at her neck. "You're wearing your mother's necklace. The one you gave her."

"I found it in the box Millie brought over." She used the back of her free hand to swipe away the tears. "And I need to apologize to you too. I'm sorry I accused you and Millie of...of having—"

He raised his hand to stop her. "No. There's no need to apologize."

He looked at the doorway leading to the kitchen, where

the sounds of Millie's cleaning up, plates and dishes clinking, trickled toward them.

"She's amazing, isn't she?" He let out a small chuckle as he squeezed Sam's hand again. "Once more, she shows me what matters most in my life."

46

Overall, the weekend with Alex was better than Sam had expected. The Riverwalk was magical, with a slight chill in the air and clear skies that Saturday evening. Alex was the perfect gentleman, not only tending to Sam's every need, but listening—intently listening—to everything she had to say. She wondered how long this would last.

After dinner, they strolled hand in hand along the water, lights twinkling in the trees above, music and laughter swirling around them. They passed groups of families and other couples enjoying the extended holiday weekend, and they eventually meandered to a branch of the Riverwalk leading to the convention center. It was away from the main artery of water crowded with restaurants, and here, they found solitude.

They sat under a towering willow tree hugging the edge of the river, on a bench surrounded by its knotty roots, watching the occasional boat filled with tourists passing by.

"I have something for you," Alex said as he dug into his coat pocket.

He pulled out a slim black box, flocked and velvety smooth. He opened it, revealing a delicate diamond tennis choker, the single row of stones catching the sparkle of moonlight above. It was a modest piece, but Sam knew he still must have spent quite a bit on it.

"It's lovely," she said. "Thank you." And she kissed him.

"I'll help you put it on." He lifted it up out of the box.

She shifted to face away from him and scooped her hair up.

He strung the necklace around the front and latched it over the nape of her neck. Then she felt him fumbling with the clasp on her other necklace, the silver chain holding the tiny hummingbird.

Sam dropped her hair and turned around to face him. "What are you doing?"

"I just thought…"

She reached up behind her neck, feeling to make sure the clasp on the silver chain was secure.

"You thought what?"

"Now that you have this, I just thought you wouldn't want to wear that pendant anymore."

Sam picked up the little silver bird, its reassuring form pressing against her fingertips. "I'm never taking this off. I gave this to my mother when I was in high school, and she wore it until the day she died."

When she looked up at him in the dim light reflecting off the water, his face registered surprise.

"Wait—" Sam squinted at him. "Did you think—" She sat up straighter and moved away from him. "You didn't think someone else gave this to me, did you?"

"No, no. I didn't," Alex said, shaking his head. "I just thought you wouldn't want to wear two necklaces. You said you didn't like to wear a lot of bling."

He chuckled at his poor attempt at levity, but he stopped when she didn't join in.

She stared at him for a moment. She didn't entirely believe him, and his apparent jealousy toward Dylan in the golf club parking lot had left a trace of doubt.

"I'm sorry," he finally said. "I should have asked."

He gazed out at the water as another boat passed by, but this one wasn't packed with tourists. Instead it carried a young couple dining by candlelight, with a mariachi trio serenading them.

As the boat drifted farther away, he hung his head. "I just keep screwing things up with you, don't I?"

During the drive from Austin to San Antonio, Alex had told her Henry had been released from the hospital the day before, and he would spend the weekend in jail since his court appearance wasn't until Monday. After telling Sam this information, he waited, as if he expected her to share more about the events that had led up to Henry's hospital-ization, but she remained silent.

Alex didn't press any further after that, and in fact, now that she thought about it, they had only spoken of superfi-cial things, as if he'd been tiptoeing around, trying not to trip on a topic that would upset her.

He lifted his head, locking his eyes with hers. "I under-estimated you. Please forgive me."

Should I let this go?

Sam took in a breath, the crisp air filling her lungs and refreshing her perspective. It wasn't like they were commit-ting to something more serious, like moving in together or getting married. Not yet, anyway.

For the most part, she enjoyed Alex's company, just not when he acted like he had something to prove.

And he was beginning to recognize this. At least he was trying—for now.

She nestled up against him, placing her head on his shoulder. "Yes, I forgive you."

∽

AFTER THAT SUBLIME moment on the bench under the willow tree, Sam relished the remainder of the weekend. But an underlying tension persisted, as if there was an unspoken agreement that some areas of her life were off-limits to Alex. It seemed he was beginning to understand she would not conform to his idealized view of her, but he had not completely accepted this reality yet.

He dropped Sam off at her apartment late in the afternoon on Sunday, and no sooner had she set her bag down, James showed up.

"So how was your—" James stopped when he saw Sam's choker. "Wow! Must have been great! That's some sweet bling!"

She touched the choker with her fingertips, and a short laugh escaped her lips. "That's funny. That's what he called it, trying to lighten things up because I was upset."

He frowned. "Alex gave you that, and you were upset?"

"Because he tried to remove this," she said, rubbing her fingers over the silver hummingbird.

"Your mom's necklace."

"I got the feeling he thought Dylan had given it to me. He tried to make light of it, saying he noticed I didn't wear much jewelry."

She reached around behind her neck to unfasten the

choker. The stones caught the light in the room as she studied it.

"It's quite nice, but it's a little too fancy for me. I'll just wear it on special occasions." She dug in her bag for the box to put it away. "Plus, I think it would be in bad taste to wear a diamond necklace like this in the clinic."

"You're probably right," James said as he plopped down on her couch. "And, in a kinda creepy way, it's almost like he's trying to brand you, like you're his possession."

His shrewdness gave Sam pause. She really didn't think that was Alex's intention. He wasn't that overt, was he?

Wanting to move the conversation away from her romantic life, she said, "I heard Henry got discharged from the hospital. You have any other updates?"

"Yeah, the guy spent the weekend in lockup, and his arraignment is tomorrow morning."

Sam winced. "I can't imagine what it would be like—having to deal with broken ribs in jail."

"He tried to kill you, and you feel sorry for him?" James looked at her with incredulity. "Anyway, it seems likely they'll need you and the others as witnesses, since the person who could provide the most damning evidence is dead."

"Great," she said sarcastically. "Something to look forward to."

"I don't know." James smirked. "I think it would be interesting, something that could be used for a story."

"You're a witness too."

"Not a useful one—I was outside the building when it all happened, so I doubt they'll need anything more from me. Anyway, I heard the police found the burner phones Henry and Ramirez used, so that will help the prosecution's case."

"I just wonder about Henry's family," she said, thinking about the reasons for his actions. "This will make their situation worse."

"They are in a tough position," James said, "but it doesn't justify murder."

47

When Sam arrived at the clinic the next morning, the schedule was filled with the usual post-holiday rush. She went about her routine, and in between helping her and Jerry with patients, Cynthia and the other medical assistants changed out the festive decorations, from Thanksgiving to Christmas and Hanukkah. Sam didn't mind; it made the place a little more cheery. Plus, she knew she and Jerry were the main bottlenecks in patient flow, not the staff.

She continued darting from room to room throughout the morning, and just before lunch, Kyle surprised her with a basket of treats.

"What's this for?" she asked.

"For helping me close the deal with CS Solar."

She raised her eyebrows. After the events of that night and Henry's arrest, she thought she had screwed up any possibility of a deal.

"Ah, I see your confusion," he said with a smile. "Anand is now the interim site manager, and he definitely wants to have ObraCare—and you, of course—helping them bring the new expansion online."

"Wow. I wasn't expecting that."

"Well, the parent company in California views what happened as the actions of a single person. And there's too much at stake for any delay, so they want to keep moving forward and build up their new capacity as soon as possible."

Sam thanked Kyle and took the basket to the break room to share with the staff. She marveled how, at the end of the day, business was business, and the world would keep moving on. At least she could worry a little less about being responsible if Jerry and Cynthia had lost their jobs.

By early afternoon, even though she and Jerry had been working hard to keep the patients flowing through the clinic, the rooms were full. The computer showed several patients parked in the lobby, with their wait times getting longer than ObraCare deemed optimal.

After she dropped off a patient chart at checkout, she turned, hurrying to the next patient in the queue, and ran into Dale. He stood right outside a drug-testing bay. She hadn't seen him since that fateful night.

"Dr. Jenkins," he said with a curt nod.

"Dale."

They stood uncomfortably for a moment; then Sam asked, "Are you here with more new hires?"

"No. I'm getting tested so I can work with a temp agency." He looked down and muttered, "Got fired."

Next to Sam, Mrs. Garza and Cynthia appeared, chattering as they came through the door from the lobby.

"Dr. Jenkins! I couldn't wait to see you, to thank you for finding out what happened to Raul."

Dale blanched, and his bulky frame seemed to deflate.

His eyes darted around, like he was looking for a place to hide.

"I have so much to tell you," Mrs. Garza continued, "and I'm feeling so much better!"

"That's wonderful!" Sam said. "You'll have to fill me in when I come see you in a bit."

As they spoke, Dale had rested his arms in front of him, one hand over the other, and closed his eyes as if in silent prayer. When he opened his eyes again, he said, "Ma'am, I'm so sorry about Raul."

Mrs. Garza blinked in confusion. "Thank you, but… who are you?"

He grimaced and said, "I was Raul's supervisor."

Wrath filled her eyes as she realized what this meant.

Dale put his palms out and stepped back, bumping into the wall behind him. "I know now I–I should have listened to him," he stammered, "and I know how you feel—"

"You can never know how I feel," she said, her voice escalating, "how it is to lose a child, how much I'm suffering."

"But I do, ma'am. I lost my daughter, and my rage caused me to misjudge others, and now I will forever be repentant."

Dale's words pierced through Mrs. Garza's fury, but only briefly. She continued to glower at him, her body tensing as she revved up to lay into him again.

"Cynthia," Sam said, touching her patient's shoulder, "let's get Mrs. Garza to her room."

As they walked away, Dale mumbled, "I truly am sorry."

They led the grieving mother to an exam room, and Sam left for a moment to give Jerry a heads-up that she would be awhile.

After she explained the situation, he nodded in his

nonchalant way. "Not a problem, Doc. I'll hold down the fort for you."

When she got back to the room, the two women were sitting in the chairs next to the exam table, and Mrs. Garza had calmed down significantly.

"I can't believe I lost my temper," she said as she clutched her rosary.

Cynthia squeezed her arm. "Oh, Elma, you have every right to be upset at him."

"I know, but still—I shouldn't have yelled at him." She rolled the rosary beads in her fingers. "I must forgive him. I must."

Cynthia stood and said, "I'll come by this evening to check on you."

"That's okay. Remember, I have those plans?"

"Oh, that's right." Her friend smiled, glancing quickly in Sam's direction. "Well, call me if you need me."

Sam took her place in the chair next to Mrs. Garza, the seat still radiating Cynthia's warmth. Her patient was much more talkative than the last time she'd seen her, the night of the incident. She felt a little guilty that she hadn't checked on her since then.

"Officer Myers came over last week and told me everything," Mrs. Garza said.

Sam was relieved that at least Dylan had been by to see her.

"And now that nice safety manager—what's his name? Andy? He's helping with the cost of Raul's funeral."

"Anand convinced the company that Raul's death was their fault?" Sam asked.

"No, but he thinks the company should've listened to my son, so he wants to do the right thing. He's giving us money out of his own pocket!"

"That's terrific," Sam said. "And how are you feeling? Is everything going well at work?"

"I'm doing good, Doctor. But I have something else to tell you—the best news of all—Nina is pregnant!"

"Oh, that's wonderful!" Sam hugged her and was glad there was joy in her life again.

"My Raul will live on in my grandbaby!" Jubilant tears glistened in Mrs. Garza's eyes. "Nina gave me the news when she came over last week. They were all there—her brother and his girlfriend and their little baby Sofie!" She grasped Sam's arm. "Oh, how it filled *mi corazon!* To cook for them in *mi casa.*"

Sam was a bit surprised to hear Nico had come to her house for Thanksgiving.

Mrs. Garza must have registered Sam's reaction, because she went on to say, "And that Nico. He really is a good boy. He fixed my window and said he was sorry for everything." She paused. "I didn't believe him at first, but Nina told me he had nothing to do with Raul's death, and that those awful men had used him." She'd wrinkled her nose as she spoke of those responsible for such tragedy. Then she continued, "But I understand. My Raul was used by bad men too."

"Nina showed me pictures of him with the kids in that youth group," Sam said. "It looked like he was really turning things around and giving back to the community."

Mrs. Garza smiled at the memory of her son. "Yes. He was a good man."

They shared a quiet reflection for a moment, and then Mrs. Garza's face brightened, and she grabbed Sam's arm again. "But there's more. Alvera—your ears must have been burning with how much she talked about you! Alvera is trying to get—what's his name again?"

"Anand," Sam said with a smile.

"Yes. Alvera is working on Anand to give Nico his job back, since he was fired for no reason."

"Really?" *The surprises keep coming*, Sam thought. At least this was more good news.

"Alvera said Nico should never have been fired, that his boss got mad that he kept fussing about stuff that wasn't safe. Anyway, Nico still needs to heal more—he couldn't eat very much when he came over—and he needs another surgery."

Sam nodded. Based on what she'd seen of Nico's injury with the perforated bowel, he probably got an ostomy. She was sure they'd needed to remove the damaged section of bowel during his emergency surgery. And then, after he received antibiotics and his body healed a little, the surgeons would take him back to the operating room a few weeks later to hook everything up again in a controlled situation. He was young, so he should do well.

Mrs. Garza continued, "The doctors said he'll be good by New Year's. And hopefully, Alvera can get him that second chance. He deserves one, just like my Raul."

A knock on the door interrupted their conversation. Cynthia poked her head in and said, "There's a new injury, and Jerry's stuck on hold with an insurance company, so he told me I should let you know."

"What is it?"

"Looks like a fractured toe. She's in a lot of pain."

"Okay," Sam said. "Ask her about medication allergies so we can line up something to relieve that pain, and have X-ray set up for a toe series. I'll be there in a sec to take a look."

"Got it."

Sam turned to Mrs. Garza after the door closed. "Sorry, but we need to finish up."

Mrs. Garza told Sam she'd finished her last PT session

right before Thanksgiving, but she was continuing to do her exercises at home. On exam, she was no longer tender and had full range of motion—at least as full as one could expect for a woman her age.

"Great, I can release you from care, so there's no need to come back to see me. But if you have any problems at all, we can always reopen your case."

"Thank you, Doctor—for everything," Mrs. Garza said.

They walked out of the room toward the checkout desk.

"To show my gratitude, I'd like you to come over for dinner tonight."

"Oh, I couldn't impose on you," Sam said.

"It's no trouble, Doctor. I made *pupusas* this weekend. All I have to do is heat them up."

Homemade pupusas sounded delicious, and since her term paper was finished, she didn't have any plans that evening. "That sounds wonderful. Then I accept," Sam said. "What time should I come over?"

"Six o'clock."

"Perfect. I'll see you then," Sam said.

She handed the chart to the clerk and turned to go see the woman with the injured toe.

"Oh, and Officer Myers will be there too," Mrs. Garza said with a whimsical smile. "Did I tell you what a wonderful job his mother did raising her boys?"

ABOUT THE AUTHOR

Stephanie Kreml is an emerging author of mysteries and thrillers after working as an engineer, a physician, and a life science consultant. *Neglected Truth* is her second novel.

Sign up for her newsletter and receive a FREE copy of *Accidental Truth: A Dr. Samantha Jenkins Novella.*

Go to
www.stephaniekreml.com
and sign up today!

ALSO BY STEPHANIE KREML

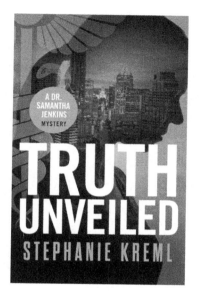

Book 1 of the Dr. Samantha Jenkins Mystery Series

COMING SOON

Book 3 of the Dr. Samantha Jenkins Mystery Series

Made in the USA
Las Vegas, NV
24 April 2022

47937022R00167